The Miles That Move You Forward

The Miles That Move You Forward

***

by Melanie Lageschulte

Also by Melanie Lageschulte

MAILBOX MYSTERIES SERIES
The Route That Takes You Home
The Road to Golden Days
The Lane That Leads to Christmas
The Path That Turns Toward Spring
The Miles That Move You Forward
The Trail That Leads to Trouble (late 2026)
Tales from Eagle River (short stories)

GROWING SEASON SERIES
Growing Season
Harvest Season
The Peaceful Season
Waiting Season
Songbird Season
The Bright Season
Turning Season
The Blessed Season
Daffodil Season
Firefly Season
A Tin Train Christmas (short story)

✳ **1** ✳

She was sweating before she made it across the post office's back lot. It was only the first week of June, but it felt like the dog days of August.

"I'm glad I left Hazel at home today. That poor dog would be panting every time I rolled down my window."

Kate Duncan had been a member of the Eagle River postal crew for just over a year now, but was still its shortest-tenured employee. And with a roster packed with seasoned veterans showing no interest in retirement, that post was hers for the foreseeable future.

But she loved it, because it meant she didn't have an assigned route. Floating from one delivery zone to the next gave Kate a carrier's-eye view of her hometown, and the rural Iowa gravel roads that surrounded it.

Jack O'Brien was on vacation, so she had his rural northeast route for most of this week. That meant she could steal a few minutes to check on Hazel, her German Shepherd mix, and the cats after she stopped at her own mailbox one mile out of town.

"Here's another one for the 'shorts' column," Marge Koenig sang out as Kate came into the post office's spacious back room. The senior carrier turned to Mae Fisher. "Are you sure you can last out there today in those pants?"

"Maybe not; I might have to run home at lunch and change." Mae shrugged. "Claire's only seven, but she's already critiquing my fashion choices. This morning, between bites of cereal, she gave my look two thumbs down for that very reason."

Randy VanBuren showed off his bare knees and hairy shins while the ladies hooted. "I'm going to get my vitamin D today," Randy declared as he sorted his delivery stacks. "Mae, that's a smart girl you have there; it's way too hot for pants. As long as she's not being a smart mouth about it, I'd suggest you take Claire's advice."

"Telling me what to do is Andy's job," Mae informed the group. "He's twelve, so he's an expert on life in general." Then she grinned. "But there are always dishes that need washing, or a toilet to scrub. He's learning about that, too."

Marge shook her head. "My nest has been empty for some time, but I remember it well. I don't envy you, having two boys in the house!"

"Well, I have three ... if you count my husband."

The ladies laughed while Randy groaned in good-natured protest; he was clearly outnumbered.

Bev Stewart soon arrived, her forehead shiny even though it was only seven in the morning. "Goodness, it's humid out there!"

"It'll make the corn grow." Aaron Thatcher, one of the younger carriers, followed Bev in the back door. "My dad loves this weather."

"It'll make the corn *sweat*." Bev settled her purse in her locker, and ran one hand through her short white hair. "And that means the rest of us will, too. I'm lucky to be on inside duty today."

Bev, a retired teacher, was the post office's lone part-timer. While she sometimes covered a route during her three days each week, she could often be found sorting deliveries and helping Postmaster Roberta Schupp at the front counter.

Roberta soon arrived, along with Jared Larsen and Allison Carmichael. The two carriers were deep in debate over the high school softball team's seasonal prospects, but the postmaster didn't partake in their chatter.

Come to think of it, Kate decided as she set up her mail tray to tackle Jack's route, Roberta seemed unusually quiet as she ferried her lunch to the break room and powered on her computer. She was also late this morning; Roberta was often the first carrier in the door.

Mae had noticed, too. "Is something wrong?" she asked the boss.

"Well, I don't know." Roberta put her head in her hands for a moment. "I can't even believe it! What is this world coming to?"

Mail stacks were set aside; busy hands became still. Bev, whose past profession had made her an expert in emotional strategies, was the first to speak. "Do you want to talk about it? Whatever it is, maybe we can help."

"Well, yes." Roberta rolled her chair away from her desk. "We have to, I guess."

As she quickly covered the few steps to the end of the closest sorting counter, the postmaster seemed to be grappling with what to say next.

"Spill it," Randy suggested. "What's the deal?"

Roberta studied her crew, her usual smile nowhere to be found. Was that a bit of fear in her eyes? Kate was suddenly worried.

"Something happened last night. Not at home," Roberta quickly added as gasps of concern echoed among the carriers. "It was here, in town. I had a call from Chief Calcott this morning. It had me running late, but I'm glad he reached out."

She shook her head. "I never thought I would hear of something like this in Eagle River. But there was a burglary last night; a home was broken into on the east side."

"What?" Marge gasped. "That's terrible. What did they take?"

Randy couldn't believe what he was hearing. "You're not talking about a package theft, or a swiped yard ornament. That's bad enough," he added, "stealing is stealing. But to go into someone's home, and ..."

"That's not the worst of it." Roberta sighed. "The police chief didn't say what was stolen, but that doesn't really matter now. The woman who lives there, alone? She was injured during the burglary. Attacked! Marie Lindgren's in bad shape; she's still in the hospital."

"Marie?" Bev clasped her hands together. "Oh, that poor woman!"

Kate was as surprised as the rest of the carriers. Eagle River had fewer than twelve hundred residents; it was the sort of place where people knew their neighbors, felt safe, and didn't always bother to lock their doors. Thefts occurred in the area from time to time; but Kate couldn't recall an incident where someone had broken into a home while it was occupied and assaulted someone in the process.

She remembered Marie Lindgren, who had to be eighty by now, from all the years the older woman had volunteered at the Eagle River Public Library. Marie's husband, Floyd, had worked as a realtor until he'd passed away about three years ago. The Lindgrens were well known for their many contributions, of both time and money, to causes within the Eagle River community.

Mae was the first to fully process this shocking news. "How badly is Marie hurt? When will she be able to come home?"

"The chief didn't say." Roberta shrugged. "I'm sure he can't give out details; you know, health privacy laws and all. But Marie's hurting, for sure; I was able to glean that from what little Ray told me and his tone of voice."

Jared was a member of Eagle River's fire and paramedic

crew. "Before anyone asks, I knew about this already. But I wasn't on call last night, so I wasn't there."

Roberta nodded in understanding. "And you can't talk about it, anyway."

"Nope. But I'll say this: Marie needs everyone to offer up whatever good vibes they can."

"I just stopped there two days ago with a package," Randy told his co-workers. "Marie looked good; she told me she's been getting a walk in every day since the weather turned warm. Between that, and her gardening, you could just about see the spring in her step."

Jared tried for a smile. "I'm glad to hear that. If she's been getting her exercise, she might have her strength up, at least a little. It could help her bounce back faster."

Had Marie put up a brave front when the burglar entered her home, Kate wondered, and pushed back against the criminal's demands? Or had she simply been in the way as he'd barged through the door? Kate needed to be careful when making assumptions about the case. But the intruder had likely been male; it was also possible that more than one person had forced their way into the Lindgren home.

Marge had reluctantly turned back to her sorting. "It's not just Marie's physical injuries that worry me. There's going to be an emotional toll, as well. How will that poor woman ever feel safe returning to her home, especially at her age, even once she heals?"

Bev had to agree. "Normally, I'd say getting home is the thing that helps people recover. Being in your comfortable space, sleeping in your own bed. But after something like that? I don't know how she's going to cope."

The consensus was that Marie and Floyd had purchased their white ranch house on Vine Street over thirty years ago, after their youngest child left home. The family had previously lived in a grand Victorian house on the northwest side of town, a structure they had painstakingly restored to its former glory. Marge recalled that even though Floyd worked as a realtor, it had taken the couple several years to find the right home when they decided to downsize.

"It's not every day that a house goes on the market here," Randy added from across the table. "And we haven't had any new construction in this town since all that land was annexed around the new secondary school campus. All the other lots in town are full. Have been for decades."

While Kate was as stunned as everyone else to hear about Marie's unfortunate incident, her mind kept going back to the person who'd shared this news with Roberta.

"Did Ray Calcott say anything else? I mean, he must have had a reason for calling you, especially first thing this morning."

The postal carriers' chatter stalled again as everyone awaited an answer to Kate's question.

"He certainly did." Roberta seemed to have regained some of her usual unflappable demeanor. "While he wasn't able to tell me any more details than what I just shared, he's asking us to be vigilant as we make our rounds."

She looked at Randy, and then Aaron. "Especially the two of you with regular in-town routes. But we all need to stay alert. If you notice anything or anyone unusual, please let me know and I'll pass it on to the police chief. I don't know how many residents are aware of what happened last night, given the early hour; but that's going to change, and soon."

"Something like this will generate gossip as well as fear," Allison observed. "I'm sure everyone is going to have a theory about what happened. It'll be interesting to see if any of those hold water."

"I am all for helping the police get to the bottom of this situation," Roberta told her team. "But please, be careful. Do not, under any circumstances, attempt to intervene if you see suspicious activity. Retreat to your vehicle, or at least a safe distance down the street, and call in whatever's going on."

Kate recalled the rumors she'd heard last winter about a burglary and theft ring operating in the area. Could that be related to last night's incident? Kate looked at Bev, and suspected her friend was thinking the same: Was this home invasion part of a larger web of crime?

The cheerful chatter that had filled the back of the post office minutes ago was long gone. Most of the carriers returned to their sorting duties with shakes of their heads, while Roberta, Marge, and Allison huddled around one corner of their metal-topped cabinet.

"Marie will need meals brought in, once she can come home," Marge was saying. "They don't keep people in the hospital for long these days. She goes to my church; I'll see if a food rotation is being set up."

Roberta reached for a nearby notepad. "Seems like her daughter lives out in Colorado; I think Scott and his family are down in Cedar Rapids. I wonder who has his number? I'm sure they're too worried about Marie right now to think about mowing the lawn, and whatever else needs to be kept up at the house."

Allison guessed Marie might have someone on retainer for yard maintenance, but there was likely a real mess inside the house given what happened last night. "Maybe a cleaning crew needs to mobilize, make sure everything is back in place before she gets out of the hospital."

"Put me on that list," Bev called over to the others. Roberta gave her a nod.

Bev turned to Kate. "No one's going to be allowed to touch anything in that house until Calcott finishes his investigation. It'll probably be a few days before anyone can go over and clean."

"You're right. This is going to take time to sort out."

Kate's mind was already searching for theories, but a sense of dread arrived so swiftly that it threatened to push those ideas aside.

The terrifying memories of her on-the-job attack in Chicago had faded during the past year. She rarely visited them these days, kept them locked away in a far corner of her mind. But it was frightening how swiftly they'd reappeared in the span of a moment or two. While the assault wasn't the main reason she'd moved back to Eagle River, its emotional toll had certainly followed her home.

Being in her early thirties, Kate was far from elderly. And she was usually confident in her ability to fend for herself. But she did live alone out in the country, far from the streetlights and across-the-fence neighbors town residents so often took for granted.

When she'd moved to her little acreage last fall, it had taken Kate a while to get used to the solitude of her new place, especially at night. Too many times, she'd had to remind herself not to be afraid, not to overreact to every odd noise outside her brick farmhouse.

After a few weeks, her fears had eased and she'd found herself enjoying the slower, quieter pace of rural life. Her porch lights stayed on all night, and the doors remained locked until morning; but Kate had nearly forgotten how nervous and vulnerable she'd felt when she left her Main Street apartment behind.

But now ... was this a reminder that sometimes, it paid to be afraid? Should she install motion-sensor lights on the machine shed and the garage? Resume her nightly security walks along the fences that bordered her yard? Until this home-invasion case was resolved, Kate decided she'd be smart to stay inside at night. The thought of some stranger creeping onto her porch, forcing their way in ...

Bev's hand on her arm made Kate jump.

"Hey," Bev said gently. "I don't want you to worry, OK? It's likely this is an isolated incident. The Lindgrens have always been known to be well off; I could see why someone would think Marie had valuables in her home."

"I completely agree," Randy put in from across the counter. "But why in the world would someone want to harm Marie? I mean, steal whatever you came for, but leave the poor woman alone. She was probably just in the wrong place at the wrong time."

"In her own home." Kate stared at the counter. "The one place we should all feel safe."

Bev glared at Randy as she put her arm around Kate. "You are not helping, sir."

"Oh." Randy got the hint. "Yeah. Sorry, Kate." And then, he had an idea.

"Tell you what: Maybe you'd feel better if you started looking for clues? Because I know that you're going to," he added with a wry smile. "You too, Bev."

Randy reached down and rubbed his right leg. "Maybe my knee's acting up on me this morning. Maybe this isn't the best day for an old geezer like me to be walking a route."

Kate and Bev just stared at him. Randy was pushing sixty, but he was as spry as many of the post office's younger carriers. He'd always been on the go, had farmed for decades before he and his wife took an early retirement from that career and moved closer to town. He reliably walked a town route in all kinds of weather, logging miles of daily exercise with only short breaks to move the Beast, the older of the post office's two mail trucks.

But Randy's regular territory was the east side of Eagle River. The one that included Marie Lindgren's house.

"Oh, that's a shame about your knee," Bev said with a dramatic burst of sympathy as she reached for her clipboard. She was sorting parcels this morning. "You don't want to overdo it. Best to give it a rest, if just for one day. I wonder who might be willing to trade with you? It's last-minute, sure, but ..."

Despite her concerns, Kate had to laugh. "OK, you two; twist my arm and I'll say yes."

"You're always willing to help out." Randy gave Kate a high-five across the table. "Here at the post office, and all over town. Of course," he added sarcastically, "I'm sure Calcott has everything under control."

"Ha!" Bev said. "You mean he's lounging around over at city hall, his feet propped up on his desk with a cup of coffee in his hand."

The Eagle River police chief sometimes seemed more invested in the prominent community role that came with his job, rather than the effort it required. If last night's home invasion had happened out in the county, under the watchful eye of Sheriff Jeff Preston, Kate would have felt more confident the situation was in good hands.

But ... was she up to walking a town route today? When someone could be lurking about, trying to decide which house, or which person, to attack next?

Kate decided she had to be. She couldn't let a past incident, or her current fears, stop her from doing what she could to get justice for Marie Lindgren.

And make it easier for everyone, including herself, to breathe easier once the suspect was apprehended.

"It's been some time since the Beast has been out on the gravel," Randy was telling Bev. "He needs to stretch his legs, I think. The best thing for that old engine is to give it a good run once in a while."

It was settled. Bertha, Kate's mail car, would help her cover the east side of town, and Randy would pick up Jack's route for the day. There was just one problem.

"Do you think Roberta will go for it?" Bev wondered. "The schedule was made up weeks ago."

"Hey!" Randy called over to where the postmaster was still huddled with Allison and Marge. "Do you mind if Kate and I switch today?"

Roberta only shrugged and made a dismissive hand gesture, then went back to her conversation. Kate knew that by noon, several networks of volunteers would be mobilized to give Marie all the help she needed, while she remained in the hospital and once she got home.

Kate now had her own opportunity to pitch in.

"You've got yourself a deal," she told Randy as they switched route lists. "Jack emailed me a rundown of who is on vacation this week in his neck of the woods. I'll send it to you."

✳ 2 ✳

There were more houses east of Main Street than west, which meant Aaron handled the business district as well as the west-side homes. Taking Randy's route wouldn't give Kate a reason to pause at the commercial properties, and perhaps pick up gossip while handing off letters and packages, but that was fine.

Because she would have a chance to interact with Marie Lindgren's neighbors, and would get a closer look at the scene of last night's crime.

It was a Wednesday, which meant many residents were at work. But school had let out on Friday; and, since it was summer, a few more people might be at home. If someone was enjoying the fresh-if-humid air on their porch, or pulling weeds in their flower beds before the day's heat became unbearable, Kate could strike up a conversation or two.

Before the carriers left the post office, they huddled with Roberta to figure out how to best help their community through what was going to be a trying day.

In rural areas, dropped-off parcels were rather difficult to spot from the road. But what if a box left on an in-town stoop or porch tempted the burglar to make that home a target?

This person wasn't simply a porch pirate, the carriers decided, as the criminal had taken the extra step of forcing their way into Marie's house. Even so, Randy contended, an unattended package indicated no one was home, which might entice the burglar to attempt entry. But Allison thought no one would risk committing two crimes at once in broad daylight.

Until the burglar was apprehended, Aaron suggested that the in-town carriers could knock and announce they were leaving a package. If someone happened to be home, they could quickly retrieve the box. It would take more time, but ...

Roberta decided to let the carriers make case-by-case decisions. "You know your customers," she told them with pride. "If you think someone might be a target and you have a minute to spare, try to make that extra effort until this gets resolved."

With Bertha loaded down for the first half of the day, Kate took a left on Main Street and started toward the southeast side of town.

"I can understand why Calcott asked for our help with this," she decided as she waited for Eagle River's lone stoplight at the south end of the main bridge. "With seven mail carriers out and about today, we're more than three times the size of his whole department."

Calcott's crew consisted of only himself and Zach Bevins, Eagle River's *other* police officer.

"People move here, and continue to live here, because of our small and safe community. But something like this? Everyone is going to be on edge. And there's going to be a great deal of pressure on Calcott to find them answers."

Kate eased Bertha to the curb along South Fifth Street, whose right-side homes were backed by the cornfield on the far edge of town. She could cover about two square blocks in one walk, if there were no large packages to carry.

Kate pushed some stray strands of strawberry-blonde hair back under her navy cap, then filled her mailbag.

"You're getting a break today." She patted Bertha's dash.

"Enjoy it; we'll be putting on the miles again tomorrow. Unless Randy's knee continues to suffer from its mysterious malady, and we get another chance to check in with the people in Marie's neighborhood."

The homes in the southeast quadrant of Eagle River were mostly ranches built in the 1960s and 1970s. Farther north, and closer to the back side of Main Street, there was a cluster of century-old houses surrounding the historic elementary school and its adjacent city park.

Most of the yards were neatly mowed, and their sidewalk edges carefully trimmed. Porches and front stoops were swept clear, many of them decked out with bloom-filled flowerpots. The air was filled with birdsong, and the excited chatter of squirrels checking under bird feeders for dropped seeds and field corn.

It was an idyllic scene, the last place anyone would expect to come across trouble. Even so, Kate felt uneasy. She was being watched.

Not by the burglar; or at least, she hoped she wasn't. But by the neighborhood residents who happened to be home this morning. Blinds and curtains shifted in several windows as Kate hiked down the sidewalk, her mailbag clutched to her side as she kept a close eye on her surroundings.

There were some packages today, but all of them were for later in the route and still locked in Bertha's backseat. With no reason to knock on anyone's door, Kate covered these early stops as quickly as the sweltering air would allow.

A cluster of evergreens sat at the corner of South Fourth and Sycamore; as soon as Kate popped around them, she came face-to-face with a woman walking a Chihuahua. The other lady's shoulders quickly dropped with relief, and they both allowed themselves a small chuckle.

"I'm glad it's just you," the woman said as the dog sniffed Kate's work boots. "I mean, I don't know who I expected to run into this morning, other than Randy. Is he off?"

"Nope. But Jack is, and Randy has his route."

"I'm sort of surprised Roberta let you walk this route today, since you all work alone." The woman lowered her voice. "Samson insisted we go for our usual stroll, not just hang out in the yard while he did his thing. My husband's at work, the kids are at camp until Friday … I wasn't sure if this was a good idea."

Kate understood. "It's a beautiful day. It's too bad we feel like we can't enjoy it."

She was eager to ask the woman what she'd heard about Marie's situation, but the lady seemed so anxious that Kate decided to let that opportunity pass.

After a few more stops, it was time to retrieve Bertha and deliver some of the packages. Those would be her best bet to uncover more details, if any of those residents happened to be home. The morning was ticking by; but Kate was willing to burn a few minutes on someone's front porch if she could collect something useful.

At the first two houses, no one seemed to be around. Kate knocked anyway, left the packages on the porches, and moved on. The next parcel delivery, however, seemed to hold promise.

Once she was under the shade of the small entry's roof, Kate noticed a television screen glowing through the front window. This small house was still about two blocks from Marie's home, but word had likely traveled fast since last night's incident.

"Post office!" Kate pushed the button on an ancient electric doorbell, but didn't hear an answering chime inside. There was no sign of a security camera at this home. She opened the screen door, and knocked on the front door.

"I have a package! I can leave it on the stoop, but I'd like to hand it to someone."

Just as Kate was about to move on, she heard footsteps. Next came the click of a lock being undone, and then another.

A young man in a faded tee shirt and cargo shorts smiled when he saw Kate on his front step.

"Oh, hey. You are who you said you were. Cool."

It was only then that Kate noticed the tire iron gripped in the guy's fist. "Well, I guess I don't need this," he said as he set it aside.

"Sorry if I startled you. We don't normally knock when there's a package, but ..."

"Oh, I appreciate it." He accepted the stack of letters and the parcel Kate held out to him, then hugged it all to his chest. "The last thing anyone wants is something sitting on their porch that might draw the attention of ... well, the jerk who's responsible for what happened to that old lady."

Kate was fairly certain the eyes she felt on her back were only those of an anxious neighbor across the street. "Yeah, I heard Marie Lindgren's house was broken into last night. I also heard she was sent to the hospital."

"The dude knocked her in the head." The young man's blue eyes scanned the street behind Kate as he matched her quiet tone of voice. "Damn near put her out cold, is what I heard. She's got bruises all over, too; maybe a few broken bones, even."

Kate inhaled sharply. Chief Calcott hadn't been at liberty to divulge such details, but this young man had no privacy laws holding him back.

It was still possible the situation wasn't quite that dire; the degree of danger may have ratcheted up as the story passed from neighbor to neighbor, from text to phone call. But given the worry and fury on this resident's face, Kate knew he believed the severity of what he'd heard.

"I just can't believe it," he said with a shake of his head. "This is a safe town, a quiet place. Who'd attack a nice old woman like her? Or anyone, for that matter? Makes you wonder what he was after, there in the house."

Kate had the same question. "I wondered if she might've

had a safe." The way she'd just mentioned poor Marie in the past tense made Kate shiver. "Or maybe jewelry? Older folks do, sometimes."

Some elderly people were raised to be distrustful of banks, given how their parents and grandparents had suffered during the Great Depression. Money that younger generations would keep in an online-accessible bank account, or valuables that were best locked in a fireproof safe-deposit box at a secure location, were sometimes stashed inside their homes.

"But then," Kate said, "I don't recall seeing Marie wearing any more jewelry than just her wedding ring and some small earrings."

"I've never met her. We just moved in, my wife and I, two weeks ago. Came up from Waterloo." He glanced up at the little house's roofline with a look of pride.

"My wife found a job in Swanton. I work remotely, and we wanted to live in a small town. There was hardly anything on the market there," he said of the county seat, which was about twenty miles away. "We were lucky to grab this place when we did. She wrote a letter to the sellers. I swear that's the reason they picked us."

"Well, welcome to Eagle River." The note of sarcasm in Kate's voice made the young man laugh as she gestured at the tire iron waiting just inside the door. "I'm sorry you feel the need to arm yourself."

He sighed. "Yeah. I never thought I'd need something like that in a place like this."

"If you see anything, or hear anything, please call the police. Don't try to handle it yourself, OK?"

"That's what George said." The tip of the young man's head indicated the house next door. "I'm anxious for that video doorbell to get here." He gave Kate a wry grin. "Yeah, I ordered one first thing this morning! It's coming tomorrow from, oh, you know, one of your competitors."

Kate laughed as she adjusted her packed-full mailbag and

another parcel still tucked under her other arm. "No, that's fine. There are more than enough packages to go around."

* * *

She moved Bertha again, walked a few more blocks, and soon passed Eagle River's water tower. The green space around it wasn't a park, in the official sense; but evergreen trees, rose bushes, and blooming shrubs had been planted along its margins years ago. Kate couldn't be sure, but she thought a garden group had once been active in her hometown.

"Marie would have been a member," Kate decided as she swatted away a bug. "It seems like she's known for her roses and tiger lilies."

As she neared the scene of last night's crime, she pondered how someone might slip into this part of Eagle River and make their way to the Lindgren residence without drawing attention to themselves.

While many people were less connected to their communities these days, most in this town would recognize a neighbor by sight, if not by name.

Unless everyone had already been inside, and possibly asleep, when the incident happened. Eagle River's residential areas just about rolled up the sidewalks come nine or ten o'clock, and Kate had yet to confirm what hour the burglary and assault had occurred.

As she made her way down Vine Street, she noted a few options to easily enter and exit this neighborhood without using Main Street.

Eagle River extended only one more block east of Marie's home. The street grid quickly gave way to brush and open spaces bordering a gravel road that followed the river's west bank.

There were only a few farmhouses along that unimproved street; farther down it passed the sprawling property that housed a salvage yard and estate auction business. Going the other way, the gravel meandered north to cross the former railroad tracks that were now a paved recreational trail, then met up with the county highway.

The trail was another option for an intruder to enter town, and do so without a vehicle. The path was supposed to be closed at dusk, but there was no way to keep people from accessing it.

Kate understood why Chief Calcott had been light on specifics when he'd called Roberta that morning. There was an active investigation under way, and he needed to keep his cards close to the vest. Even so, the large number of unknowns made it very difficult to piece together what happened last night.

Kate's mind couldn't help but go back to when she'd been attacked on her route in Chicago. That incident had been simple by comparison.

The young man who'd put a gun to her temple and demanded the few dollars she'd carried in her mailbag was nabbed by quick-thinking neighbors. Several people had witnessed the incident, and been eager to share what they'd seen with authorities.

That hadn't made it any easier for Kate, however. The thought of poor Marie, struggling this morning at the Swanton hospital, brought tears to Kate's eyes.

"Stop it," she whispered to herself as she lingered at the last corner before the Lindgren house. "It's over. It's done. Just focus on Marie, do what's needed to help her."

Kate took a few deep breaths, then a satisfying gulp from her water bottle, and tried to imagine what this street would have looked like last night.

It would have been total bedlam, she decided as she walked along. There would have been an ambulance, maybe a fire truck, and at least one squad car. Flashing lights, sirens. "I doubt anyone was able to sleep through that."

Kate stopped short on the sidewalk in front of Marie's house, shocked by what she saw. Or, more like, what she didn't see.

Not one flowerpot was out of place; the white siding was immaculate, and the driveway was empty. There was nothing out of the ordinary, except for about four feet of yellow "caution" tape roping off the house's front stoop.

Kate wasn't sure what she'd expected to find, so many hours later. A gloved-up evidence team combing through the boxwoods under the front windows? Yards of yellow tape strung from one tree to the next, cordoning off everything beyond the public sidewalk? A uniformed officer keeping watch over the crime scene?

No one was there. Except a robin, who started up a song in a nearby tree as Kate opened her mailbag. There were three envelopes for Marie today along with an advertising circular. The woman's mailbox was mounted next to the front door, which meant it was included in the small percentage of this property that was now off limits.

"Neither rain nor snow, nor dark of night," Kate muttered as she tucked Marie's mail back inside the bag. "But crime-scene tape can keep us from our appointed rounds. We should be able to hold Marie's mail without an official request to do so, given the circumstances."

As she examined the front of Marie's house, Kate noticed the entrance seemed surprisingly intact given the violence that had occurred last night at this address. The metal storm door showed no dents; its screen had no tears. The fiberglass door behind it, which was painted a deep blue, was smooth and scratch-free. From what Kate could see through the storm door screen, the wooden trim near the lockset wasn't splintered or broken.

So many small-town folks, especially the older ones, clung to a deep trust of their neighbors that Kate had lost long ago. Had Marie's front entry been unlocked when the incident occurred? Did someone walk right up on the porch, ease the door open, and ...

"Hello over there!"

A female voice startled Kate out of her investigative reverie. The woman had apparently been lingering on the front porch of the next house down. Her light-brown hair was streaked with silver, and her forearms were especially tan. Kate pegged her as the gardener of the house, or at least one of them.

"Sorry, I didn't mean to startle you," she told Kate with a smile. "We were expecting Randy." She disappeared inside her screen door for a moment. "Honey, come out here! It's the mail lady."

This house was a bit bigger than Marie's, with beige siding and fuchsia shutters. Tiger lilies along the front angled their orange faces toward the sun, and a cluster of irises stood proud by one corner of the house. A ceramic frog posed by the porch's two steps.

"We made a last-minute switch this morning." Kate extended her hand when she reached the older couple. "I'm Kate Duncan."

The man peered at her through his glasses. "Wayne Burberry's granddaughter, of course! I'm Ed Moore, and this is Dorothy."

"Do you have anything for Marie?" Dorothy asked. "We can take it, if you do."

"We talked to Scott last night," Ed explained. "That's Marie's son. He asked us to pick up her mail until she ... well, until she comes home."

Dorothy looked like she was about to cry.

"Honey, don't worry." But there was uncertainty in Ed's voice as he put his arm around his wife. "Marie's a tough lady, she's going to pull through. We have to stay positive, if we can."

Kate explained the paperwork required to hold or forward

mail. "But don't worry about it. We'll just keep it at the post office for now."

Dorothy only nodded as she leaned on her husband's shoulder.

"Remember what Chief Calcott told us?" Ed seemed to say to himself as much as to his wife. "If we think of something new, we're supposed to call him. Otherwise, we should find things to take our minds off all this. Get back into our usual routine."

The Chicago police officer who'd taken Kate's statement after she'd been assaulted on her route had told her the same. As had a few of the nurses at the hospital.

But Kate knew from first-hand experience that it also helped to talk, sometimes. Share what you saw, what happened, how it made you feel.

Dorothy and Ed Moore were obviously traumatized by last night's incident. Given their age and the lack of mental health services in rural areas, they were unlikely to ask for, or be offered, professional emotional support.

Kate wasn't sure if what she was about to say was the right thing to do. But she understood what was happening here, and she couldn't just walk away.

A deeper discussion with the Moores was certain to net Kate a far-clearer picture of what happened to Marie Lindgren, but that wasn't her main motivation to take action. The agony on the older folks' faces was enough.

"Do you want to talk about it? Being so close to the scene of a crime is very scary. I know what it's like. Hearing about something like this, what happened next door ..."

Kate hadn't found the perfect words, but it didn't matter. No one had said anything similar to the Moores until now, and they stared longingly at Kate as if she were a glass of ice-cold lemonade on a hot summer day.

"We didn't just hear it. We saw it." Ed blinked and looked away. "Or at least, we saw everything right after it happened.

Scott called us, when Marie didn't answer her phone. I ran right over there."

Dorothy unexpectedly patted Kate's forearm. "Why don't you hang around for a few minutes? I think you need to get out of this hot sun."

Kate hesitated. This was more than she'd expected. Should she take them up on their offer?

"OK." She started toward the porch chairs clustered around a small table. "Yes, let's sit down and talk."

Ed looked one way up his street, then down the other. "I don't want to have this conversation out here. Please, come into the kitchen."

✳ 3 ✳

"I want to hear what happened," Kate said as Dorothy placed a glass of iced tea in front of her on the oak table. "But first, I need to tell you something."

Kate had quickly decided she should come clean about what happened to her in Chicago. Not just to encourage the Moores to open up to her, but because she wanted them to know she understood the emotions they were likely feeling.

"Oh, honey." Dorothy shook her head when Kate finished. "That must have been so terrible for you."

"Wayne never said anything about it." Ed tried to process this unexpected news. "I guess that just goes to show, you never know what people are dealing with."

Kate wondered if Ed was referencing only her situation, or Marie's as well. Had the Moores noticed anything odd about their neighbor's behavior recently, or any sign that someone unwanted was hanging around?

Kate hesitated to ask, as she felt like she was already imposing enough. And she didn't have much time; it was best to focus on last night's events.

"When did you know something was wrong?" Kate aimed her question at Ed, as Dorothy seemed to be struggling with her composure. "When exactly did this happen?"

Scott had called the Moores around nine o'clock after

trying for almost an hour to reach his mother. Marie and Scott talked every night at roughly the same time, and she always picked up when he called.

"She doesn't wear one of those medic alert devices," Dorothy added. "She doesn't need one. Marie is very agile for her age. All that gardening is good for her, I think. Keeps her active. But Scott just felt like something was wrong."

Scott asked Ed to go next door and check on his mother. Ed was a little concerned, but didn't think too much of it yet. Marie could've been in the shower, or gone to the basement for something and left her phone in the kitchen.

Ed fished out the spare key Marie kept hidden on the porch; but when he tried the front door knob, it turned easily in his hand. Once he stepped inside, he knew something terrible had happened.

"The house looked like a pack of crazed raccoons had been zooming around in there! I have never seen Marie's home, or anyone else's, in such a chaotic mess."

One of the wooden kitchen chairs was tipped over. The curtain rod on the window over the sink dangled from one of its brackets, and canned goods were scattered across the counter. One tin had made it to the tile below, and apparently landed with such force that it cracked open and flung chopped tomatoes and juice across the floor.

The living room was just as bad. The ends of some of the window-blind slats were bent, and a handful of Marie's ceramic squirrel figurines had launched themselves out of the open bookshelves. Couch pillows were everywhere, and most of the magazines were off the coffee table and all over the floor.

"I just stood there for a second, inside the door. Maybe I shouldn't have gone all the way in, should have called the police first. But I guess I was so in shock that I wasn't thinking clearly. All I could think about was that Marie was in trouble."

Ed called her name, then tried again at a louder volume. Soon, he heard an answering moan from the hallway.

"She was down on the carpet, not far from the bathroom. I didn't see anyone else," Ed added quickly. "Later, I realized the intruder could've still been inside the house, hiding in a back bedroom or down in the basement."

"You were running on autopilot," Kate told him with an understanding nod. "You were focused on helping Marie."

Ed called 9-1-1, and dispatch urged him to stay on the line until help arrived. Dorothy had hurried next door after ten minutes passed with no word from her husband.

"I wasn't going to let him face it alone, whatever was going on. I assumed Marie was sick or hurt. It never occurred to me, when I left our house, that any of us might be in danger." Dorothy put her face in her hands. "Oh, poor Marie! She was wearing her usual, capris and a short-sleeved top. Her arms, and the lower parts of her legs, had so many scratches and bruises. And she was clutching her stomach, kept saying how much it hurt."

There was blood on Marie's scalp, too. Ed and Dorothy were afraid to help Marie up, as they didn't know the extent of her injuries. Had she hit the back of her head on the floor? Did she trip and fall, or had someone pushed her? While Dorothy held Marie's hand, Ed searched for the intruder.

"He was already gone. I looked in the basement, and the garage, too," Ed recalled. "That was a stupid thing for me to do! I should have waited for the cops. If the burglar had still been there ..."

"You had to look," Dorothy told her husband. "We had to know."

Chief Calcott soon arrived, an ambulance right behind him. Dorothy and Ed were able to take a step back, but they still felt helpless and afraid. Ed had promised to call Scott back, and let him know why his mom hadn't picked up her phone. Should he do it now? What could he possibly say?

Thankfully, they didn't have to decide. Calcott made sure the house was secure, then he called Scott with the bad news. Officer Bevins soon arrived, and remained out on the lawn to keep other neighbors from rushing inside and contaminating the crime scene.

"We were already there, so we were told to stay," Dorothy explained to Kate. "But we were told not to touch anything."

Kate could imagine the distressing scene next door: Blue and red emergency lights strobing across the front of the house; Calcott and Bevins conferring about what to do next. Medics hurrying in and out, fetching supplies and a stretcher; residents gathered out front, worried for Marie and trying to comfort each other.

"Did she say anything to you?" Kate looked at Dorothy, then Ed. "You mentioned she was crying and moaning, which is understandable. But was there anything else?"

"Well, she was saying that ..." Ed stopped, and looked at his wife.

Dorothy's reaction was swift and short, but Kate caught it anyway: a slight "no" shake of her head. What was that about?

"She was upset, of course," Dorothy finally told Kate. "And you know, when people are hurt, they're not always in their right mind, sometimes. The pain is all they can focus on."

Kate wanted to press Dorothy for details, but Ed didn't give her a chance.

"She kept saying her stomach hurt, and her head. We, I ... she was crying and moaning; there wasn't much more to it."

Kate decided to let it drop, as it seemed she'd just hit a wall with the Moores. So far, they had been very generous regarding the harrowing details of last night; but they weren't going to share anything more specific about Marie's behavior.

Fair enough. Kate aimed her next question elsewhere.

"I noticed just now, when I came up the street, that her front door doesn't seem to be damaged. Did Marie have a habit of leaving it unlocked, even at night?"

"I noticed that, too," Ed admitted. "I think it was part of the reason I didn't think twice about rushing in there alone. Marie didn't worry too much about locking up, you know? This is such a safe place to live, and all."

Or it had been until last night.

No one at that kitchen table had to say it; they all felt it.

Something had changed in Kate's hometown; a sense of safety had been stolen from so many. She wondered how often Eagle River residents left a door unlocked at night, or a window open when no one was at home. If anything good could come from this horrible attack, Kate hoped people might be a little more careful. Especially since the burglar was still at large.

"Did she say anything about what the man looked like? I mean, I'm assuming it was a man," Kate added. "It sounds like the house was a terrible mess. Could you tell if anything was missing?"

Ed and Dorothy both shook their heads. But for the second time, Kate caught a look passing between the two of them that she couldn't quite read.

"Not that we noticed," Dorothy said. "Marie was crying, you know; so upset, and in so much pain, the poor thing. They started her on intravenous fluids, assuming she was dehydrated. And they gave her something to help calm her down, too."

Chief Calcott asked the Moores a few questions while Marie was tended to by medics, then urged the couple to follow the ambulance to the hospital. The police chief arrived about an hour later, Ed said, and they gave him more-detailed statements about the incident while everyone waited for Scott and his family to arrive from Cedar Rapids.

It was after midnight by the time the Moores started for home. And sleep was a long time coming once they finally went to bed.

"We're exhausted." Dorothy rubbed her eyes. "The police were still next door when we got home. I think some of the sheriff's deputies were called in to help Officer Bevins finish going through the house; it was too much for one person to handle alone. Chief Calcott stayed at the hospital to get a formal statement from Marie once the doctors got her settled, as well as talk to her family."

By sunrise, all the emergency vehicles were gone; the neighborhood was as it had been before. Except for that stretch of yellow tape strung across Marie's front door.

Marie didn't have any pets these days, so there was no one inside the house that needed looking after. Dorothy and Ed had promised Scott they'd water Marie's flowers and her garden as needed, keep an eye on things until she was able to come home.

"She's lucky to have both of you." Kate smiled at Dorothy and Ed in turn. "It must be such a relief for her that you're just a phone call away. And for Scott and his family, too, that you're willing to help Marie."

Dorothy looked down at her hands. "I just keep wondering what else we could have done. If it wasn't so hot, maybe our windows would have been open."

"Maybe we would have heard someone out there, poking around," Ed chimed in. "We might have heard Marie scream when the burglar stormed into her house. Or heard something else that would have gotten our attention sooner."

"If Scott hadn't called us …" Dorothy was in tears again. "What might have happened to her? I saw her yesterday morning, out there in her garden, when I was filling our bird feeders. She was all excited for her club meeting that afternoon, told me about a new cookie recipe she wanted to try; normal things, you know?"

Ed sighed. "And now she's like this. They think she's going to make it, but … well, who's to say what might happen?"

Kate didn't have any answers; she wished she did. But she was more determined than ever to find out who had attacked Marie Lindgren.

* * *

The rest of Kate's morning route didn't net her any significant leads in the case. Some of the folks at home weren't willing to come to their doors, even for a package. The ones who did, or who flagged down Kate from their lawns and front porches, offered mostly concern about Marie's injuries and fears for their own safety. Not one person had heard a description of the attacker.

It was the same when Kate arrived at the post office for her lunch break. Aaron had gathered similar details and theories on his west-side town route, as had Randy and the other rural-route carriers.

Kate's only new takeaway? The entire region was talking about Marie Lindgren ... except for one prominent person who had remained silent all morning.

"I keep checking my phone." Roberta gave her device another glance as she lingered in the break room with Bev and Kate. "Not one official word. No press release, and no posts about it from the Swanton newspaper."

The postmaster shook her head. "Calcott called so early, I was barely awake when I picked up. If we weren't hearing so much community chatter this morning, I could almost convince myself I dreamed the whole thing up."

Bev put down her sandwich. "If what we've heard is true, and I think at least some of it must be, this criminal is violent and dangerous. For Marie to be injured like she was, and he still didn't bother to take anything from the house ..." She turned toward Kate. "Ed and Dorothy were certain nothing was missing?"

Kate felt comfortable sharing the basics of what the Moores had told her, since it dovetailed with the general gossip going around. But Dorothy and Ed had been holding back, she was sure of it. With no clue as to what Marie's neighbors were hiding, Kate decided to not bring up that part of their conversation.

Not even with Bev. At least, not yet.

"They said they didn't notice anything missing. But then, their focus was on Marie, which was the right way to be."

"Seems like Ed used to be on the emergency medical team," Roberta mused as she continued to scroll on her phone. "He'd be able to keep a level head more than most could."

Kate hadn't shared how frightened Ed had seemed, much less Dorothy. The Moores had been gracious with their time, and bravely shared their feelings with her. She didn't feel right exposing them to any public scrutiny.

"Maybe that's why Scott has Ed and Dorothy looking in on Marie." Bev took a bite of her apple. "He knows they are capable, reliable." She chewed, thinking. "Who else lives close to Marie these days? Any ideas?"

"Randy might know." Kate reached for the last of her chips. "Here's what I'm wondering: If this person didn't steal anything, were they frightened off by something? I mean, if you didn't have a specific reason to commit a burglary, why would you barge into Marie's house like that? It would almost have to be personal ... but who would want to harm someone like her?"

Roberta finished her sandwich in two quick bites. Marge was watching the counter, but it was time to get back on the clock. "I can't imagine who would carry a grudge against that woman," the postmaster said as she pushed back her chair. "What is this world coming to?"

* * *

Kate's afternoon walk took her north of the county blacktop and into an older area of town. The northeast quadrant of Eagle River was much smaller than the southeast, and filled with compact, century-old houses in various stages of rehabilitation.

Substituting for Randy wasn't the only reason Kate spent a great deal of time in this working-class neighborhood these days. Alex Walsh's bungalow hugged one of its narrow streets; and his bar, Paul's Place, was only two blocks from his home.

Alex and Kate's relationship had hit a rough patch in the spring. They'd reconciled a few weeks ago, and Kate was glad things were good between them once again. As for how deep their connection was, she wasn't quite sure. Would it last? What might come of it?

The dating pool for Eagle River residents in their thirties wasn't much more than a mud puddle. Even so, Kate wouldn't tolerate any red flags just to have a guy in her life. She would be fine on her own, if it came to that, but it sure was nice to have Alex around.

It was after two; Alex would already be at work. The cozy bar had kept its name over the decades through many changes in ownership, and remained housed in a cinder-block building not far from the river. Its dark wood paneling and vintage decor had hung around, too; long enough to be cool again.

While Kate welcomed the opportunity to see her guy, the building's air conditioning held its own appeal this afternoon. It took her eyes a few moments to adjust to the cool gloom inside the establishment, but she soon spotted two regulars at the bar. Bob and Tom, each nursing a bottle of beer, were glued to the Cubs game on the screen behind the register.

Like the scuffed wooden bar and the neon advertising signs, Tom and Bob had basically come with the place. Both men were retirees and lived in the neighborhood. They may have worked together, even; Kate couldn't remember.

But Alex, like most bar owners, knew his customers well. The guys' current beers might be followed by a second round if the Cubbies were on a hot streak, but that would be the extent of their imbibing for the day.

"Hello!" Bob called to Kate. "Get out of that heat and take a load off, why don't ya?"

"Sure thing." With a sigh of relief, she plopped down on the nearest padded stool. Paul's Place was otherwise empty, as the after-work crowd wouldn't arrive for a few hours yet.

"It's going to be ninety-two tomorrow," Tom announced, confident about his forecast. "I wouldn't want to be walking the mail around then. Or today either, for that matter. Where's Randy?"

"He has Jack's route."

There was no sign of Alex, but Kate heard clangs and bangs coming from the kitchen. The other members of the bar's small staff didn't come in until after three.

"Walsh!" Bob leaned back as far as he dared on his vinyl seat, then to the left. "The missus is here!"

The *missus*?

Kate and Alex weren't married; and they were a long way from *that* conversation.

Weren't they? She thought so. What had her boyfriend told these two?

Alex popped through the swinging door that opened into the back of the bar. The hard line of his jaw and the hint of surprise in his brown eyes told Kate he was as blindsided by this announcement as she had been.

And then, the sun came out on his handsome face. He was a complicated individual; his mind held deep crevices and buried emotions that Kate had to admit she'd barely started to explore. But when he smiled like that, and at her, Alex was the most carefree guy she knew.

"Kate!" He slipped behind the bar and started in her direction. "Where's Randy?"

She laughed. "I had no idea he was so popular! Is that every day, or just when there's big news to discuss?"

Bob and Tom had joined in the laughter, but Kate's question brought both older men up short. The mood inside the bar changed in an instant. Even the cheers from the screen as the Cubs scored another run weren't enough to recapture the men's attention.

"I can hardly believe it!" Bob echoed the sentiment being shared all over town. "No one deserves something like that. But Marie? She's one in a million."

Tom picked at his bottle label. "You know, I'm surprised we haven't heard from the police chief yet."

His tone was far from confrontational, but Kate didn't miss the side-eye glance Alex tossed Tom's way. Ray Calcott was Alex's cousin.

Bob eagerly took the bait. "You'd think after an incident like that, Calcott would put something out there." Bob grunted with irritation as Tom nodded in agreement. "How are we supposed to help catch this lowlife if we don't know what the feller looks like?"

"They may not have a solid description yet," Alex told his customers. "Without it, a statement might cause more confusion and panic."

"Well, there will be plenty of that until they catch this dude," Tom proclaimed from his seat of judgement.

The older men began to debate the situation in earnest, as if Kate and Alex weren't in the room.

"Are you going to be OK tonight?" Alex asked her as he wiped down the bar. "I won't be out of here until two, at the earliest."

"No, don't worry about it. Or me, for that matter." She tried for a smile that she didn't quite feel. "If I wake up in the middle of the night and hear footsteps on the stairs, I'll call the sheriff. Then I'll command Hazel to pin the bad guy to the floor until help arrives."

Alex allowed himself a small chuckle, then turned serious again. Sheriff Preston ran a well-respected department; but its home base in Swanton was on the other side of Hartland County. Even if a deputy was on patrol near Eagle River, it could easily take them ten minutes to reach Kate's place. A stretch of time that would feel like an eternity if someone were trespassing on her property or trying to burglarize her home.

Nowhere was truly safe, Kate realized as her thoughts turned back to Marie Lindgren. Marie lived right in town, but it hadn't mattered. She'd been attacked and left nearly unconscious on the floor, nowhere near a phone.

"You sure you'll be all right?" Alex was worried. "I mean, not just because of last night, but …"

"I'll manage." Kate reached across the bar and squeezed his free hand. Bob and Tom were watching the game again, or at least pretending to. She leaned in as she slid a pile of mail toward Alex, and lowered her voice to a whisper. "Let me know if you hear anything interesting tonight."

Alex raised an eyebrow. "Will do. For a second there, I thought you were going to kiss me." He pulled away, then snatched up the bar's delivery stack. "Detective Duncan is on duty, like always."

✳ **4** ✳

Kate was exhausted by the time she made it home, but the strawberries couldn't wait. If she didn't pick the just-ripe ones this evening, the wild critters that called her farm home would harvest them overnight. After she fed her pets and herself, she reached for her grubbiest garden gloves and a few clean buckets.

"Charlie is the sensible one," she told Patches as they started for the rows of berries on the far edge of the garden, Hazel at their heels. "He's inside on one of his cat thrones, chilling in more ways than one. He doesn't even ask to come out here."

The calico cat refused to let Kate pick berries alone. Patches planted herself along the first row, right where Kate might bump into her if she wasn't careful; then alternated between rolling in the dirt and flicking her tail in irritation.

Kate wondered if the cat wanted attention. But every time she tried to pet Patches, her hand was batted away.

"Just so you know, I'm not letting you bring the kids out here ... ever." Patches gave a low growl, as if she didn't agree.

"No, we've been over this already. They are indoor-only kittens, and will have indoor-only homes when that time comes. You walked twelve miles to get back here; you can do as you please. But they will only know the easy life."

Patches' kittens were now seven weeks old. While she occasionally slipped in an open door to give the four youngsters some sniffs and a motherly lick or two, the calico had made it clear that her time living indoors had ended once the babies were eating on their own.

Most animal rescues and foster groups named their litters based on themes. Kate had reached for "Shakespeare" as an easy out, and came up with Romeo, Juliet, Hamlet, and Ophelia. Juliet had her mama's calico colors; Ophelia's fur was a soft tortoiseshell, gray with peach accents. Hamlet, the largest of the quartet, was an orange tabby boy; while Romeo's tuxedo markings made him look like a miniature Scout, minus Scout's long coat.

Kate harbored mixed feelings about when it would be time to say goodbye. She loved them all, but the babies were growing more rambunctious and mischievous by the day. They had their own room upstairs for when she was away; the rest of the time, her home was their playhouse. Kate didn't know how she could have managed the four of them without Hazel and Charlie to help keep the kittens entertained.

Hazel now trotted past the strawberry patch with a twig in her mouth and a gleam of triumph in her brown eyes. Once she was a few rows farther into the garden, the dog turned her back to Kate and dropped her stick. Then, Hazel pivoted to the back of the lilac bush and started to dig.

"Hey!" Kate lurched forward to get a better look, a sudden move that caused Patches to howl in annoyance. "I can see you, Miss Hazel! Just because the lilacs are almost done blooming, that doesn't mean you get to wreck their roots. And don't even think about stashing that stick in the green beans. I found the other one, along with the plants you dug up."

Hazel abandoned the twig, then retreated to her outdoor water dish by the back porch steps. Maggie, Kate's gray cat, was lounging on the nearby sidewalk, her green eyes trained on Patches. The two queen bees had declared some sort of truce in the past few weeks, but Kate wasn't convinced it would last.

Jerry was nowhere to be seen. But her orange cat with the white feet had been around at supper time, so Kate wasn't concerned. "Where's Scout?" she wondered as ripe strawberries fell into the second bucket. "He usually loves to help in the garden. He'd better hurry."

Kate had covered herself in sunscreen and bug spray, so she could last for quite a while out here if needed. But she didn't want to linger in the garden tonight, and not just because she was tired and the mosquitoes would get more aggressive as sunset approached.

Her fingers moved faster as she crawled from one strawberry plant to the next, lifting leaves and snapping off fruit while she eyed the fence line between her yard and the cornfield to the south. A quick look over her shoulder showed only the machine shed, the vacant chicken house, and the old pump shed.

During the golden hour, Kate's yard was often bustling with wildlife, both seen and unseen; but she was the only human there.

"I'm alone," she reminded herself as she moved into the last row of strawberries. "There's no one out here but me."

And then, she spotted a newcomer that made her smile. Scout suddenly rounded one back corner of the massive chicken coop, and trotted toward Kate with his bushy black tail held high.

"There you are! I can't believe you've been running around in this heat. And with that long coat." Kate set aside her berry buckets and garden gloves to meet Scout's demands for ear scratches and back rubs.

"Ouch!" She quickly pulled back her hand, as if she'd touched a hot stove. "What do we have here?"

Some sort of burr was stuck in Scout's thick fur. Kate felt down his spine, more gingerly this time, and found another. A third was enmeshed in his ruff, along with a scattering of weed seeds.

"You've been in the pasture again." Kate peered around the chicken house at the ragtag mix of vegetation on the far side of the yard fence. The emerging jungle was already two feet high in some places, and summer had barely begun.

No livestock had lived here for several years, Kate was told when she purchased the place late last summer, and nature had long ago grabbed the upper hand. While some of the weeds looked familiar, she couldn't name every invasive species in the pasture. But with the help of her nearest neighbor, Gwen Ashford, Kate had discovered a small band of prized native plants in one corner along the little creek.

With her riding lawnmower, Kate had managed to keep a narrow path clear to the waterway. But she had to take bigger action before the weeds got completely out of control.

"I'll soon need a hay baler," she told Scout. "But no one will want to buy that cover crop. It would be nasty."

Kate had a few realistic options, but she was too weary to consider those tonight. She picked a few more berries, then gave up. "Scout, meet me on the front porch in ten minutes."

She refilled Hazel's outside water dish, which was also used by the barn cats and whatever wildlife needed a drink. Once inside the house, she scrubbed the sweat off her face, filled a tall tumbler with iced tea, and reached for one of Charlie's old brushes.

Hazel and all the outdoor cats were already settled on the front porch. The dog was stretched out on the wooden floorboards, her belly turned toward whatever slight breeze was moving in from the west. Jerry had shown up in the last few minutes, and he and Maggie were now perched on the concrete-topped railing near one of the brick corner posts. Patches had claimed the top concrete step, and Scout was waiting next to the porch swing.

Kate settled in, and patted her knee. Scout jumped into

her lap, and Kate began what had become a too-frequent task this summer.

"Got it." She smoothed the spot in Scout's coat where she'd just removed the first burr. After a sip of her tea, she went after another.

"You're such a good boy; you always sit still for me. But you can't get these out on your own, and you know it."

There was a commotion inside the living room's wide front window; and Charlie, a Himalayan mix, appeared on the long, low table underneath it. Four little feline faces soon joined him to keep an eye on the porch from the air-conditioned comfort of the house.

Charlie had stepped up admirably to serve as teacher and tour guide for the kittens. In fact, he seemed especially attached to Ophelia. Maybe ...

"Nope," Kate told herself, and not for the first time. "No more pets in the house. Charlie and Hazel are inseparable these days, thank goodness; but that means I'm already outnumbered. All the kittens need to find new homes."

Once Scout's coat was free of debris, he rested his fuzzy chin on Kate's shorts. She set the brush aside, reached for her tea again, and pushed off from the gray-painted floor with the toes of her gardening shoes. The fireflies twinkled here and there around the yard, their inner lights glowing brighter as the sun slipped behind the cornfield across the gravel road.

Hazel was watching the fireflies, too; but she was too tired, or too lazy, to chase them around. Patches was asleep, Jerry and Maggie were almost there. Other than the gentle breeze, the only other sounds were Scout purring in Kate's lap, the rhythmic creak of the porch swing chains, and the final notes of the birds' songs as deep shadows gathered in the yard.

It had been a very long day. And an upsetting one, too.

But Kate had promised Alex she would be fine on her own tonight, and she was determined to make that happen.

"What else was I going to say?" she told Scout. "He's working, and will be until the wee hours. And I wasn't about to call Mom and Dad, and ask if I could spend the night with them."

Kate had chores waiting for her inside. There were dishes to wash, strawberries to trim and refrigerate. Her life was busy and full, especially during this time of year. There was no room for fear.

The daylight was nearly gone now. Kate couldn't see Eagle River, which was a mile to the west, but she reminded herself that it was there. Gwen and her boys, just a quarter mile up the road, were probably home. Kate patted the side of her shorts, felt the reassuring rectangle of her phone in her pocket.

Across the road, straight out from the porch, she spotted a sudden movement in the cornfield. The stalks were high for this time of year, and they swayed and rustled as something advanced among their dense rows.

In a second, Hazel was on alert. A low growl, then a bark. Kate felt a press of cold fear on the back of her neck.

"It's an animal," she whispered to herself. "Just some critter. A person would have to be crawling on their hands and knees to not be seen."

Hazel was on her feet now. She continued to bark, her tail rigid and her jaws snapping in aggression. Kate slowed the swing, and looked at each of her outdoor felines in turn. "It's time to go to the shed. I'm locking all of you in tonight. Hazel, we need to get inside."

As soon as Kate had raised her voice, the corn stopped moving. Hazel quit barking, but refused to abandon her guard post on the porch.

Kate blinked back a few frustrated tears as she started around the corner of the house with Scout in her arms. "I can do this," she whispered. "I can get through this night, and not be afraid."

‹ **5** ›

Despite her best intentions, Kate stared at the plaster ceiling above her bed for several hours. Rather than listening for unusual noises outside her farmhouse, she decided to put that wide-awake time to better use.

It was already the first week of June; if she was going to do something about her overgrown pasture yet this summer, she needed to act as soon as possible. By the time she finally fell asleep, long after midnight, she had a goal in mind. And an idea about who might help her meet it.

"I need to find a bunch of goats," she announced to Grandpa Wayne's breakfast buddies the next morning. "Anyone know where I can get some, and fast?"

The various conversations around the group's usual table at Peabody's came to a halt. Joan Murray, a retired nurse and part-time server for Henry and Eloise, set down her fork and knife. Grandpa nearly choked on his coffee.

But Harvey Watson just laughed. "It's about time! You've been out at your little farm for, what, almost nine months now?" He leaned toward Max Sherwood, Eagle River's retired mayor. "Pay up, man. I told you she'd come around eventually."

Max refused. "When the livestock arrive at her property, you'll get your twenty bucks." He waved away Harvey's protest. "Nope, no way. It's all talk at this point. She may not do it."

Kate couldn't believe it. "You two made a bet about me getting more animals?"

"Wayne started it," Harvey said.

Grandpa Burberry shook his head. "No; what I said was, I thought it was highly unlikely she would; that I wouldn't bet on it."

"Well, I'm glad I did." Harvey, a retired farmer, had a grin that reached from ear to ear. "Critters make country life so much fun, I've always said. Oh, you're going to enjoy this," he told Kate.

"She's got about a dozen cats right now, along with Hazel," Max pointed out. "That's plenty of animals to look after."

"I have only nine cats." Kate added cream to her coffee while she checked her math. Yes, that was right. Although sometimes, when the kittens were climbing the curtains and digging up her houseplants, it felt like twenty. "And four of them aren't permanent residents."

"What kind of goats are you going to get?" Lena Wakefield asked. She was a retired music teacher. "Milk goats, maybe?"

Joan was intrigued. "Are you going to make cheese? Oh, you certainly could. Start a little cottage industry, a side hustle. Artisanal cheeses ... do you think Melinda would want to sell them at Prosper Hardware?"

"That's a great idea," Grandpa Wayne said, "since they have a refrigerated case." He and Grandma Ida lived in Prosper, the next town to the west. "It would be great exposure. Why, everyone goes in there for milk, pizza, all sorts of things. Auggie doesn't carry that stuff at the co-op, even though he's expanded his product lines. Even the coffee shop, right here in town, might want to carry them. Austin Freitag is the head of the chamber, I'm sure he'd ..."

"OK, OK!" Kate cut off the chatter with one hand as she

partially drained her coffee cup with the other. "Let me explain: I don't want to buy any goats. This is a temporary need; I want to rent them."

"Rent goats?" Even Harvey was floored. "You can do that?"

"Do what, now?" Chris Everton, the town's pharmacist, had arrived at their table with current mayor Ward Benson in tow.

"Rent goats." Harvey was chuckling again. "Kate wants to rent goats. Any ideas?"

"Do they have to sign a lease to live in your pasture?" Grandpa Wayne couldn't help himself. "What sort of deposits do goats have to pay these days?"

As the regulars burst out laughing, a server approached the table. Kate placed her order for blueberry pancakes and sausage links, then turned back to the hot topic at hand.

"I'll be the one signing a lease. I need them for my pasture. All those weeds, whatever they are, have gotten away from me. Other than the prairie plants along that little section of creek, I want the stuff gone. Chewed down to nothing."

"How will the goats know which is which?" Chris wanted to know.

"Signs." Max was certain of that. "She'll put up little signs."

Mayor Ward ordered his usual, scrambled eggs with bacon and toast. "Well, I was expecting to talk about Marie Lindgren this morning. And we'll get to that, I'm sure. But first, I want to hear about this goat-renting gig."

While the goats would have plenty to keep them busy, Kate had her own work to do before they would arrive. She'd need to fence off the pocket of native plants she wanted to save. And clean out that oversized chicken house to serve as a temporary shelter for the goats.

It was the only building available, as half of the machine shed had been requisitioned by the outdoor cats and the other side was packed with junk. The old pump house wasn't much more than a hut; and the barn had been torn down several years ago, when it became unstable due to age and too-costly repairs.

While the goats' visit would slow the weeds' ability to grow back this year, it wouldn't fully solve Kate's problem. But it was a hoof hop in the right direction, at least.

A permanent solution would be permanent goats, but Kate wasn't ready to make that kind of commitment. Besides, while her family had raised beef cows for decades and owned some sheep and pigs over the years, they'd never had goats. This was going to be a new adventure.

"It's going to take some work to get ready for such a visit, but it'll be worth it," Kate told the table. "But first, I need to line up the goats. I found some companies that rent them out, but none of them are based super-close to Eagle River. Any ideas?"

"I didn't know anyone did that," Harvey admitted as he tucked into his scrambled eggs. "It just goes to show: You can learn something new every day, even when you're an old geezer like me. Sorry, I don't have any leads for you."

In addition to serving as Eagle River's mayor, Ward was a salesperson for a seed corn company. His job took him all around the county, and beyond.

"Everyone I know with goats keeps them at home. I don't think they'll want to share. I can ask, though."

Max gestured for Joan to pass him the jam packets. "You know, this whole thing isn't as crazy as it sounds. I can see how goats would be great at this. They will eat just about anything, and they have the stomachs to process it."

Then he chuckled. "Why, if I'd known about this when I was mayor, maybe I would have hired a dozen or two. We could have used them in the city park, and there's that green space below the water tower."

"Around the city buildings, too, as well as the library,"

Grandpa Wayne added, then looked across the table at Ward. "Goats could take a real bite out of the parks department mowing budget!"

"Minimum wage keeps going up," Chris reminded the group. "Has anyone told these goats? Do they have union representation?"

"Laugh all you like," Kate said after she joined in. "But in Chicago, goats are the lawnmowers for several pieces of public property, especially areas that don't get a lot of foot traffic. Of the human sort, I mean. I think they even chow down at the airport."

The table's conversation soon drifted toward Marie Lindgren's unfortunate situation, which had been the main topic at yesterday's gathering.

"How is Marie doing?" Chris asked Max while he spread blackberry jam on his toast. "What's the latest?"

Max and his wife were close friends of Marie's, given the Sherwoods' decades-long ownership of their furniture store and years of volunteering in the community. Kate couldn't be sure, but she thought Floyd Lindgren may have served on the city council while Max was mayor.

"Marie's holding her own, I guess; but she'll be slow to heal at her age."

"Will she ever be able to go home again?" Lena asked.

"Well, that's the worry now." Max shook his head sadly. "To get bruised up like that, and knocked to the floor? I can't imagine she's going to be discharged anytime soon."

"You wonder if she'd even feel safe, being there alone." Grandpa Wayne refilled his coffee cup, then passed the pot around. "It's bad enough this happened. But if it's the thing that puts her into a nursing home, that's even worse."

Kate knew many older people shared that fear. They preferred to stay in their own homes, be independent with a little help from friends and family. But a fall, or any health decline, could so easily take away that freedom.

"From what I've heard, it doesn't sound like the burglar stole anything." Lena drizzled syrup over her French toast. "Did they get nervous about being caught, and run out without going through everything?"

"I talked to Ray again last night," Ward said of the police chief. "I asked him if they had any solid leads. He said not yet." There was a bit of hope in the mayor's voice, but then he shrugged.

"Ray said this is a tough one. Marie was still in so much pain when he talked to her at the hospital; the meds they gave her were just starting to kick in. It was difficult for him to get many details from her. He's going back today, now that she's stabilized, to try again. The house doesn't have a security system, so there isn't any video footage he can go through."

"That's a shame." Grandpa Wayne shook his head. "But not everyone's up to date on the tech stuff like you youngsters are." He gestured at Kate and Chris with his fork, which made Kate almost laugh out loud. She was thirty-three, and Chris was in his fifties. Even so, he was the youngest regular member of this breakfast group.

Ward added more cream to his coffee. "Floyd never put in any cameras, I guess. But then, I'm not shocked by that. This is a safe town, always has been."

Kate waited for Mayor Benson to tell the group that Marie's front door showed no signs of forced entry. When he didn't, she decided to keep that to herself. It was an interesting detail, but one that might wrongfully imply Marie was at least somewhat to blame for what happened.

Of course, there was the possibility the intruder was someone close to Marie; someone who knew where to find a spare key, or even had their own.

Kate couldn't imagine that Ed or Dorothy Moore had been involved in the burglary, but she had to admit there was something they were holding back from her. Which was their right; and, if they were as good friends of Marie's as they claimed to be, they'd want to give the poor woman a little privacy if they could. Kate just hoped the Moores had been more forthcoming with Chief Calcott.

"It would be ideal if Ray could round up some witnesses," Lena was saying. "Even if it's just one. One person who saw this man prowling around Marie's home, or noticed someone who seemed to be in the wrong place at the wrong time on her street."

With so many questions and no answers, the group moved on to other news as they finished their meals.

First came an update on plans for Eagle River's annual sweet corn festival, which was still two months away but in need of more volunteers. Grandpa Wayne, who had helped with the event for as long as Kate could remember, reminded his granddaughter that the post office had yet to put forth a competitor for the corn-shucking contest.

Due to the break-in at the Lindgren residence, the breakfast group had yet to fully discuss that week's city council meeting. While nothing too noteworthy had happened, Ward was cautiously optimistic about one idea shared by a local developer.

The plan called for building two duplexes somewhere within Eagle River. The four new dwellings would bring a little variety to the town's miniscule housing market, Ward said, which was currently all single-family homes except for a few large, older houses that had been chopped into apartments years ago.

"The trouble is," Max reminded his successor, "there are no empty lots anywhere in town. We gained a few dozen when all that land was annexed for the new secondary school campus a few years ago, but it's all been developed."

"That's why I'm not getting my hopes up." Ward shrugged. "The council told the guy to come back when he had a place to put those duplexes, and we'd talk about it then."

Even as the group's focus turned to other bits of Eagle River happenings, Kate was still pondering Marie's plight. Apparently, she wasn't the only one.

Peabody's front door opened, and three new male voices soon joined the chatter of the weekday breakfast rush. When Kate craned her neck to check out the fashionably late arrivals, she noticed that Grandpa, and most of his friends, quickly halted their chatter to do the same.

But Ward shook his head as he shuffled the last of the scrambled eggs on his plate. "Oh, I wouldn't expect Ray to show up here; he knows better than that."

"Makes sense," Grandpa Wayne admitted as he turned back to his own breakfast. "The chief has to know everyone is on edge these days. And they will be until this gets resolved."

"Ray may know more than what he's saying," Max offered from across the table. "Even so, this one is certainly putting his skills to the test."

✳ **6** ✳

Lingering over her blueberry pancakes and a second cup of coffee gave Kate the fuel she needed for her weekday off. While Swanton was her ultimate destination, a family errand meant Prosper would be the first stop.

Kate's cousin Stacy Burberry was getting married the last Saturday in June, which was less than four weeks away. Stacy was an expert planner, a trait that served her well as a literature teacher at Eagle River's secondary school. But her drive to have everything picture-perfect had nearly sent the bride-to-be over the edge.

Stacy's best friend, Lauren Davis, was the maid of honor. But with Kate being the only family member among the bridesmaids, her role had quickly blossomed beyond wearing a color-coordinated dress. While the major decisions had been settled months ago, Stacy was still agonizing over table favors and seating arrangements for the reception. A week of staff development training at the end of the school year was making it increasingly difficult to cross items off her last-minute list.

So when Kate was asked to visit the reception site on her weekday off, she'd been eager to say yes. Not only to help her cousin, but to get a good look at the area's newest public venue.

Within months of its grand opening last year, the Prosper community center had become a popular event site. The historical building on one corner of the little town's Main Street housed a bank for generations, then sat vacant for several years before a team of Prosper residents renovated it into the town's crown jewel.

The structure's original oak woodwork and floors had been carefully restored, then complemented with updated lighting fixtures and period-appropriate touches. The bank's former break room had become a commercial kitchen, and the back offices converted into smaller meeting rooms and overflow space for parties.

It was quite the transformation for a building that otherwise might have faced a wrecking ball, and Kate couldn't wait to get a personal tour. Nancy Delaney, who held the dual role of Prosper city clerk and librarian, was meeting her this morning for a walkthrough of the event space.

Eagle River was considered a small town, but it was a metropolis compared to tiny Prosper, whose residents numbered two hundred at most. Grandpa Wayne liked to say that count included "every dog and most of the cats." Grandpa had served as postmaster in Prosper before his retirement; and the house he and Grandma Ida lived in, just two blocks off Main Street, had a soybean field behind its backyard.

The county blacktop brought Kate into town from the southeast, then made a bend by the water tower. As she slowed for a truck exiting the alley behind Prosper Veterinary Services, Kate spied a horse inside the tow-behind trailer.

"Karen, Melinda, and I need to get together soon," Kate vowed as she stepped on the gas. Karen Porter was one of the two vets at this clinic, and Melinda Foster worked at Prosper Hardware, her family's store. "Neither of them mind getting dirty; maybe I could convince them to help me clear out the chicken house if I'm lucky enough to find goats to rent." And then, Kate grinned.

"Karen and Doc Ogden might know someone! I'll text her when I'm done at the community center."

Several of the storefronts on Prosper's Main Street were vacant these days, a sad sight that was common in rural communities. But those that were occupied had baskets of coral-and-white impatiens swaying on the decorative light poles in front of their businesses. More baskets of flowers flanked the wide steps to the community center's double-door entrance, and the tuck-pointed brick exterior and gleaming windows added to the building's warm welcome.

Nancy was waiting inside the former bank's vestibule. Kate admired the older woman's smart eyeglass frames and chic bobbed hair, and told her so. Nancy accepted the compliments with a good-natured laugh.

"Thanks! I lived in Des Moines for two decades before I came back to the area. I guess my 'cosmopolitan' style hasn't changed."

"I understand what that's like," Kate said. "But I have to say, mine's slipped quite a bit since I returned. I always seem to be either in my work uniform or chore clothes."

The community center's main space was much larger than what Kate remembered. Freed from its old crisscross of half-wall office partitions, the former bank's refinished floors gleamed in the morning light streaming in the tall windows that lined its two outside walls.

Not a single detail had been overlooked by the center's renovation committee. Tasteful, fabric-wrapped window valances held blinds that provided privacy as needed. Soft cream paint on the repaired plaster walls set off the dark woodwork, and strips of stained glass in natural colors accented the new, vintage-style light fixtures.

Kate looked around in awe, and smiled at the sight of the Prosper post office kitty-corner across the intersection. While Eagle River was her hometown, she'd spent a great deal of time in Prosper over the years. "They have worked miracles with this building! I remember coming here when I was little, and thinking the bank was so elegant. They always had a cut-glass bowl of suckers on the front counter."

As the ladies wandered around the main space, Nancy shared insight about table layouts that left room for dancing while Kate took notes on her phone. Stacy's brother, Corey, was curating the bride and groom's playlist, so there was no need to accommodate a band.

"There will be plenty of room for all of Stacy and Ryan's guests," Nancy assured Kate. "I know how many tables and chairs they'll need. All Stacy has to decide is exactly where to put them."

Nancy rolled open a refinished set of wide pocket doors in the back of the community room.

"And this is our secret weapon; it used to be the bank manager's office. We can get four or five tables in here. It's perfect seating for families with small children. They are still part of the action, but not right in the thick of everything. Close to the restrooms, too."

Kate nodded her approval. "There are several folks on the guest list who will appreciate this space. No wonder Ryan and Stacy were so eager to rent the center for their reception. I can't wait to see the rest of the renovations."

The smaller meeting rooms were farther back in the building, along with enough storage space for stacks of chairs and collapsible tables. The ladies didn't tour the upstairs or the basement, as both had yet to be remodeled; but the original bank vault had been turned into a conversation piece.

"It's a popular spot for photos," Nancy explained. "People just love its historical vibe, how it reminds them of what this building used to be. Of course, when it comes to wedding receptions, we do hear some wisecracks about the dangers of being 'locked into a marriage' and 'putting all your hopes in one place,' that sort of thing."

The kitchen was small, but held everything a caterer

would need during an event: a double oven, a stovetop, and an oversized refrigerator, all in gleaming stainless steel. Nancy pulled out two bottles of water, and passed one to Kate.

"So, what do you think?" Nancy asked as they leaned on the quartz counter. "Is your cousin ready for her big day? There are so many last-minute details to decide, no matter how early couples start to plan."

"I think so. She got really obsessed with table favors for a while, but that crisis has passed. Now that she's settled on a theme for those, it shouldn't take long to put them together. Once we get this seating chart finalized, I hope she'll be able to take a few steps back until the big day."

Kate took another look around the small kitchen. "I know I've been raving since I walked in here, but, wow! This building has been completely transformed. And it's been so successful! Melinda says it's booked every weekend until September."

"And far beyond, for some of them." Nancy was proud, but there was an odd hint of caution in her voice. "Wedding season goes well into the fall these days. And during the week, we have several clubs that like to gather here. It saves people the hassle of entertaining at home."

"Oh, I get that." Kate had volunteered to host the post office's holiday party last year. It was a merry event, but she'd planned and prepped for weeks to make it happen. "It's so much easier to meet somewhere."

"I just hope people continue to make use of this facility." Nancy frowned. "We've put so much work into it. And the revenue has been wonderful for the town. I have five more computers on order for the library; I would have been lucky to get even one if it hadn't been for the center's rental fees."

Kate was surprised by Nancy's concerns. "This venue is so popular; I can't imagine that would suddenly change. Stacy and Ryan were so excited to snag a spot on the calendar.

Prosper can be proud of what's been done with this old building."

"Oh, we are. It's just that, you know how people talk." Nancy rolled her eyes. "Especially around here. It doesn't take long for something to get blown out of proportion."

"Don't I know it."

Kate was intrigued by Nancy's change in demeanor, and decided not to let it slide. "Did something happen?"

"I'm not sure if it did, to be honest. But some people are putting two and two together, and coming up with seven." Nancy crossed her arms. "I didn't think much of it, at first. But in the last twenty-four hours, the talk has really gotten out of hand."

The Eagle River Social Society had held its summer luncheon at the Prosper community center two days ago. The women's club was made up of mostly retirees, with a few younger ladies in the mix. While the organization was based in Eagle River, women from all over the area were members.

"They rent from us often," Nancy explained, "and usually, everyone brings a snack to share. But this was their big annual gathering, a formal luncheon they hold each year before going on hiatus for the summer, so part of the meal was catered. And that's how the grumbling started."

Nancy leaned in and lowered her voice, even though she and Kate were alone.

"Some of the ladies had, um, 'gastrointestinal distress' after they left here Tuesday afternoon. It's common, unfortunately." She shook her head in frustration. "In life, I mean; not here, at the community center. But there were enough of them, and they got sick enough, that people are starting to talk."

"Starting to talk?" Kate was floored. "How can anyone say for sure they got sick from something served at the luncheon? Even with part of the meal catered, everyone who attended brought a dish, too."

Kate thought of the cooler waiting in the trunk of her car. She needed to get groceries in Swanton before she went home, and that drive would take her almost half an hour. "It's summer; we all know transporting food in the heat can be risky. There are just too many variables there. I don't see how anyone could prove all the illnesses stemmed from the luncheon, much less say the community center is somehow to blame."

But that was just the problem, Nancy explained. No one had any clear answers for what made the ladies sick, and the only common denominator was that they'd all been at the Social Society luncheon.

When the center opened last year, two local catering companies were chosen as preferred vendors for its events. While people were allowed to bring in their own food or hire a different hospitality company, Heritage Street Grill in Swanton and The Watering Hole, which was just across the street, split the lion's share of the business. Going with a "summer picnic" theme, the Social Society officers had contracted with Heritage Street to provide fried chicken and potato salad for the luncheon.

Kate had to admit she could see where the concern was coming from. "Oh, I get it. Potato salad is a staple of summer gatherings; there's usually mayonnaise in it, or maybe sour cream. That might have been the cause, but no one could say for sure. Even so, it would be an isolated incident."

"I wish it were only that." Nancy shook her head. "But now, we have a much bigger problem on our hands."

Susan Wilson, the owner of Heritage Street Grill, had called Nancy first thing this morning, furious and upset. A handful of clients had reached out to her in the past few days, grilling her about the company's kitchen standards. Two of those concerned parties had wedding receptions scheduled at the Prosper community center.

"Susan was yelling and carrying on," Nancy told Kate,

"wanted to know what I was going to do about all this. Her name's being dragged through the mud, she says. A few of her clients have threatened to cancel their contracts with her. And that means they might drop us, too, if they think the center was somehow to blame." She gestured helplessly at the modern, spotlessly clean kitchen.

"If that happens, the only way to save our bookings would be to steer clients toward The Watering Hole. And that's not going to go over well with Susan."

With The Watering Hole being Prosper's only restaurant, and one of just a handful of businesses in town, Susan might already suspect it was getting preferential recommendations for center bookings. That wasn't true, but perception was important in the hospitality industry.

As was reputation. The young couple running The Watering Hole these days had quickly made their mark on the local catering scene by pairing budget prices with elevated menus sourcing local ingredients. Those offerings were in stark contrast to the burgers and chicken wings served at the bar, but that seemed to make them even more popular.

By contrast, Heritage Street had been under Susan Wilson's watchful eye for over twenty years. The restaurant resided in a small commercial district in the historic part of Swanton, and the catering division was known for its tried-and-true menus and experience handling larger events. Often, however, that knowledge came with a higher price tag. Heritage Street's higher costs, Kate knew, were part of the reason Stacy and Ryan had chosen The Watering Hole to cater their wedding reception.

"I can't believe I'm asking this," Kate said with a sigh, "but do you know exactly how sick the women were? The gossip barrel must be getting pretty low these days for indigestion to be such a hot topic."

From what Nancy had heard, three women had suffered only the usual symptoms: nausea, gas, diarrhea. But Helen

Weintraub, who was in her late seventies, had also vomited several times. Later that evening, Helen experienced heart palpitations that landed her at Swanton's urgent care clinic. Doctors hadn't been able to pinpoint the reason for those, but the symptoms had thankfully passed quickly.

The stress of the situation could have brought those on, Nancy suspected, when coupled with the several prescription medications Helen apparently was taking.

"Poor Helen," Kate said. "I don't know her, but I can't imagine she appreciates people discussing her health in this way. I don't think I'd want the whole county fussing over my bowel movements."

Nancy had to laugh. "Me, neither. But Susan's angry, and worried about her business. I'm not sure she understands that the more she publicly fumes about this, the more probable it is she'll lose clients. Which would be unfortunate, since it's very likely this wasn't her fault!"

"Maybe it will all blow over," Kate said as they returned to the center's main event space, where she snapped a few more photos to help Stacy narrow her seating options. "The women who got sick will definitely do what they can to change the subject, and it might be a good thing we're entering the peak of celebration season. If Heritage Street's events in the next few weeks go off without a hitch, word should get around about that, too."

Bad news always travels faster than good, Nancy reminded Kate, but she hoped Kate was right. Nancy suspected the questionable dish at the Social Society luncheon was inadvertently brought by a club member, rather than the caterer. It was even possible that one of the ladies who'd been sickened had brought it, herself.

"And they are never going to admit that possibility." Nancy nodded with conviction as she and Kate went back out into the sunshine. "Which, actually, gives me hope. As my grandma liked to say, 'Least said, soonest mended.' Even so,

Heritage Street is on the books for half of our celebrations this summer; I'd hate for any of those to fall through because of these unfounded rumors."

* * *

As Kate drove on to Swanton, her focus quickly turned to her own errands. The extra time she'd lingered at the Prosper community center had put her behind schedule, but Kate found herself pausing in the grocery store aisles to scrutinize the "best by" dates on every perishable item before she added them to her cart.

On the way home, as the corn and soybean fields rolled by, her mind turned toward Marie Lindgren. Another day had almost passed. How was Marie doing? When might she be able to come home?

Randy would have returned to his own route today, as Jack was back from vacation. Kate had Marge's circuit tomorrow, and Aaron's on Saturday. Her best opportunity to chat with Marie's neighbors had already come and gone.

By the time Kate got another chance, the burglary was likely to be classified as old news. While she shared Nancy's desire to see the crazy rumors about the Social Society meeting disappear from the local gossip menu, Kate hoped people wouldn't forget about Marie's plight.

"It's really a shame no one saw anything the other night," she muttered as the west side of Eagle River came into view. "Of course, it was dark; and by that time, most people were already inside."

As she waited at the stoplight, something occurred to Kate. She hadn't heard of any eyewitnesses to the Lindgren case, but that didn't mean none existed. What if someone had come forward in the past day or so, and talked to Chief Calcott about what they saw?

If someone had a crucial bit of information, they might not feel comfortable blabbing it all over town. There was also the possibility the police chief had urged them to stay silent, at least for now.

Kate understood. She'd been asked by law enforcement more than once in the past year to do that very thing. An element of surprise was sometimes imperative to bring a case to its conclusion. She wanted to find out who was behind Marie's injuries; but it was more important that the criminal was arrested than that Kate was the one to make it happen.

Even so, she wondered exactly what the police knew, or didn't know, about the incident. There was one way to find out: go to the police station and ask to see the report. It was public record, after all.

Under state law, certain items pertinent to a case could be redacted; and the paperwork was likely to address only the initial incident from Tuesday night. Any witness statements or leads that had appeared since then wouldn't be included. But while the report wouldn't give Kate all the answers she wanted, it was certain to offer more clues.

The light turned green. The truck ahead of Kate lingered for a moment, waited for an oncoming car to pass through the intersection before it turned left.

There was still time for Kate to flip on her own turn signal. She could go left, too; roll over the bridge, and right into city hall's parking lot. Instead, Kate pushed on toward home.

"I'd better not. Did I learn nothing from my chat with Nancy today? There's plenty of ice in the cooler; but the sooner I get those groceries home, the better."

* 7 *

"Are you sure?" Bev asked Kate the following morning as they filled their coffee thermoses in the post office break room. "It'll mean going into the lion's den."

Kate shrugged. "Maybe the lion will be out stalking speeders, and I can make my open records request to the kitty cat, instead. I just hope someone is around on a Friday afternoon." She hesitated for a moment. "Zach Bevins is a good guy, right? I don't know him at all."

"Zach is a good kid." Bev chuckled as she examined the tray of chocolate-chip muffins Marge had just left on the break room table. "Listen to me, can you tell how old I am? Zach has to be in his thirties by now. He's been an officer in this town for at least eight years, already. He's married, has his own family. Time sure does fly."

Bev chose her muffin, then pulled a plastic knife from a nearby drawer. There was more than fresh muffins this morning; Marge had brought peanut butter to spread on them, too.

"I'd gain fifteen pounds if I didn't hike a town route a few days a week," Kate said as she reached for a treat. "My jogs down the gravel road would never be enough on their own."

"Do you want me to come with you to the police station?" Bev asked. "Two against one? Or would that be too much?"

"It might be, unfortunately. I'd love the backup ... but it might get Calcott's *back up*, if you know what I mean. I just need to stop in, as soon as I get off work, and ask for a copy of the incident report. Who knows? Maybe I won't be able to get him to hand anything over."

"He has to; I'm sure of that. It's just a question of what won't be blacked out." Bev picked up her thermos. "Well, good luck. And I'll expect a full report after you get the report."

"Of course!"

* * *

Kate tried to focus on her jam-packed day, which included driving a rural route and a stop in town to cover the counter during Roberta's lunch break. But as she dropped letters in mailboxes, weighed packages, and sold stamps, a possible script for her conversation with the police chief tried to take shape in her mind.

"This is a conversation, not a confrontation," she reminded herself as she neared city hall's front door. It was just down the street from the post office, so Kate had left Bertha in her usual parking spot. "He has to give me the incident report, but it's up to him to decide exactly what I get. Just seeing his reaction to my request might tell me something worthwhile."

Mayor Benson wasn't in that afternoon, but Kate had expected that. Eagle River's highest office was a part-time role, at most; and it was a Friday, after all. Although it was a fine day, thunderstorms were forecast for the evening. Most people, as soon as they were off work, would be working in their gardens, mowing the lawn, running errands. Ward was likely doing the same.

But Kate was surprised to find Lisa Kleiner's chair vacant. The city clerk usually stayed around until four-thirty, or so Kate had heard. As with Zach Bevins, Kate only knew Lisa by name, and she felt a bit guilty about that. The city employee roster wasn't long, and Kate was a fellow public servant. She should make more of an effort to get to know these folks.

Of course, Roberta would jokingly say the post office's federal staff outranked everyone else in town. Kate was about to allow herself a chuckle over that idea when a man's voice boomed out from behind a divider in the middle of the room.

"Do you need something?"

Kate thought she recognized the voice, and she was right.

She marched behind the partition and found Ray Calcott at his desk, studying something on his computer monitor. Eagle River's "police station" consisted of Calcott's cubicle and a similar setup across the aisle that belonged to Zach. Who was also out.

The man Kate wanted to see was here, but no one else was around. She wasn't sure if that was a good thing, or not. She put on a smile she didn't feel. "I'm here to see you, actually."

"Well, then, pull up a chair." Ray's distracted expression didn't change as he gestured vaguely in her direction. "There's only one, so ..."

"Tight quarters, huh?" Kate sat down on the other side of the police chief's desk. The visitor's post was nothing more than a metal folding chair. Budgets were meager these days, sure; but Kate suspected this specific seat had been chosen to discourage folks from hanging out for too long. Or to make them uncomfortable while they were there. Probably both.

"We run on a shoestring, as I'm sure you can guess," the chief said. "Now, what can I help you with? My cousin's behaving himself, I hope."

"Alex is fine, as far as I know."

Kate wondered why Chief Calcott went right for their obvious connection. Because it was the only one? Or was he trying to create a familiarity with her that neither of them felt? She didn't know, and found it all a bit irritating. As if her entire life revolved around her relationship with Alex. As if she'd come to Ray, of all people, to vent if things weren't wonderful. Which they were.

Kate decided she might as well cut to the chase. "I'm here about Marie Lindgren. I'd like a copy of the incident report from Tuesday night, from when her home was broken into."

Ray blinked twice in rapid succession. It was the only outward sign that Kate had caught him on the back foot. He took a few beats to mess with something on his screen, but Kate could almost see the gears grinding in his mind.

Finally, he swung his chair around to meet her eye-to-eye across his desk.

"I can do that. I will do that. But first, I'm going to ask you why. You don't have to answer," he added quickly, "and I'm sure you know that. But, please, humor me for a moment. What's your personal interest in the case? Beyond the one everyone else understandably has: that our little town is considered safe, and this goes against what people expect."

Kate wasn't sure how best to respond. Her errand went several steps beyond the simple request the police chief had made of the postal carriers Wednesday morning. Leaning on that wouldn't be enough to ease his curiosity.

She could play the card about her on-the-job attack in Chicago, and how this home invasion had rattled her sense of security, because it was true. A second option was to remind the chief that, like Marie, she was a woman living alone, and far from the relative safety of town.

It was possible Calcott had heard about Chicago; if not from Alex, then from someone else around Eagle River. And he was likely to assume she was here because of the latter reason, at least partially. But both options painted her as some sort of victim, Kate realized. And that was something she didn't want to be.

"Well, frankly," she said slowly and calmly, "I'm curious about the situation because, as far as I know, your department has yet to put out a statement to the public."

As in: *I'm not convinced you are doing your job.*

It was a bold move, but Kate decided it was the one that would snare the chief's full attention.

"There hasn't been one word in the Swanton newspaper or on its website," she said, "much less anywhere else. I understand you can't share details about Marie's health issues. But what about a description of her attacker, your suspect? People are scared, and they need answers."

"I'm well aware of that." Ray's tone was flat as he absentmindedly rubbed his blond crewcut, which was going gray at the temples. "My phone and email have been blowing up since the incident occurred." He tipped his chin toward the city clerk's empty desk. "Lisa's getting calls, too; along with Ward."

None of this surprised Kate. And none of it answered her question. She waited.

The chief clasped his hands together and leaned over his desk. "Kate, look, I think I know why you're really here. You can't stay out of it; it's as simple as that. You're getting quite the reputation for unearthing evidence when something goes sideways, you and your friends."

Kate was about to nod, with a bit of pride as well as agreement; what he'd said was true. But the sharp gleam in Ray Calcott's eyes caught her off guard. She felt like a mouse being watched by a hawk.

Oh, no. Did he know something he shouldn't? Or at least suspect ...

Kate's track record was good, just as the chief said. But the last case she'd helped solve, revolving around embezzlement and fraud at the Eagle River auction barn, was one she would never take credit for.

It was too dangerous, given the situation. A friend had urged her to report what she'd uncovered in a way that didn't tie her to the information, and that's exactly what she'd done. And then, she'd put it all behind her.

Ray was waiting for her to speak. Kate knew he was good at this, that he'd sit there for an hour before he would be the one to break the silence. She'd slid back in her chair, just a bit; and knew he'd noticed.

Kate straightened her spine, and bounced the ball back into his court.

"Don't try to tell me you don't have a description," she said quietly. "Even if no one else has come forward with one, you've obviously spoken with Marie. Likely, more than once."

"Our investigation ..."

"I know, you can't divulge everything. But the only things you can legally withhold from the public are details that could hinder the investigation, or put someone directly in harm's way. I don't see how either of those could apply to a description of Marie's attacker. Why isn't that being made public? It could be your best chance to get more tips that might help solve the case." She gave him a moment to take it all in. "So, that is why I'm here."

The chief crossed his arms. "Because you think I'm not doing my job."

"Because people have a right to know."

Ray rolled his chair back a few inches. He was considering something; Kate could feel it. Suddenly, he smiled. And it was more genuine than she would have expected.

"You know, you're right." The police chief spun his chair back to the left, and tapped his keyboard. "There are some ... complications with this situation that I've been hesitant to spread all over town out of respect for Marie's privacy."

Kate frowned. Ray lifted one palm from the keyboard.

"No, I'm not going to elaborate," he said before Kate could speak. "My suspicions are just that; I have no proof of anything, either way. And at this point in the investigation, I'm not comfortable saying one more thing." As he smiled again, Ray seemed almost giddy. "But if you want to take that on for the good of the community, well, be my guest!"

Somewhere in the back of the room, a printer wheezed to life. The chief's expression turned serious again. "But I can tell you this: I'm not one-hundred percent certain there is anything further to investigate."

Kate's jaw dropped; she couldn't help it.

"You'll see what I mean," Ray told her before he rose from his chair.

Kate wasn't exactly sure how she'd expected the chief to react to her request, but his sudden generosity had thrown her for a loop. "I can come back later, like Monday morning," she called after him. "I mean, I know you'll need to go through the report, redact certain things."

"Oh, it's no problem at all." The police chief sounded ... relieved; Kate didn't know how else to describe it. "Just give me a few minutes, and I'll have it ready to go."

Ray pulled a black marker from the organizer next to the printer, and began to swipe it across the pages he'd just pulled from the tray.

"It's a rather old-school process," he said to himself as much as to Kate, who waited in her uncomfortable chair. "There's a fancy way to fix up a PDF but, well, this is how I learned to do it, back in the day. Besides, we don't get many requests like this."

"I suppose you don't," Kate said, more to make conversation than anything else.

She was surprised that the editor of the Swanton newspaper hadn't asked for a copy of the report. Perhaps the incident wasn't considered newsworthy farther out in the county. Or, if the editor had asked Calcott Wednesday morning, and he'd said there wasn't anything solid that he could share, she may have given up.

But the police chief obviously had something. And Kate couldn't wait to find out what it was.

Because Calcott had correctly assumed Kate was eager to get her hands on the report, she was careful to keep her face neutral and her posture relaxed. By the time he returned to his desk, she was waiting patiently with her hands in her lap.

"Here you go." He handed over two sheets of paper with no more ceremony than if he'd passed Kate some sugar packets at Peabody's.

"Thanks. Is there a charge?" She reached for her purse, but Calcott waved her off.

"Oh, no, don't worry about it. It's only a few pages."

Kate folded the papers in half and tucked them into her purse. The chief was still smiling as he took his seat. He apparently believed this exchange was as advantageous to him as it was to her. Maybe even more so. What Kate needed to figure out now was: why?

"If you do come across something of use, please, let me know." His demeanor had turned serious again. "I called Roberta the other morning because we could really use some help on this one."

"I'll do what I can," Kate said.

"Excellent. Let me know if you have any questions." Ray turned back to his monitor and began to type. Kate had been dismissed.

"Thanks again." She wasn't sure what else to say as she turned to leave. "Have a good weekend."

✳ ✳ ✳

Kate kept her pace slow and casual until she was across the street and down the sidewalk, in case Calcott had abandoned his computer and wandered over to city hall's front windows.

What just happened? It had started out as the tense, awkward exchange Kate had prepared for; but somewhere along the way, things had taken a hard left.

"He couldn't wait to hand this over," she muttered as she rounded the side of the post office. "I hope I'm about to find out why."

Roberta's car was the only other one in the back lot, and Kate was relieved. The postmaster probably had another half hour of work before she was done for the day; Kate could safely study this report while behind Bertha's wheel without the risk of being distracted by a coworker.

She tossed her purse onto the passenger seat, and cranked the engine so she could blast the air conditioning. Kate was sweating, and it wasn't all caused by the humidity outside or the sun-warmed heat inside her mail car. She snatched up the report and began to read.

The first part held no surprises. The emergency call from Ed Moore came in at 9:17 p.m. Tuesday night. Ed had found Marie Lindgren in distress on the floor of her home on Vine Street. Calcott was there at 9:24 p.m. Paramedics arrived two minutes later, and Officer Bevins was only minutes behind them. An initial evaluation of Marie's injuries noted scratches and bruises on her arms and legs, as well as the possibility of a concussion since she'd been found on the floor in the hallway.

"The victim was in a great deal of emotional distress as well as exhibiting physical injuries," the report stated. "She didn't know how long she'd been down on the floor. A sweep of the house confirmed the attacker was no longer inside the home."

"So far, nothing out of the ordinary." Kate's eyes slid down to the first redacted lines of the report. "I would guess these are details about Marie's ongoing health conditions and medications, stuff Calcott can't share."

Neither exterior door showed signs of forced entry, according to the report. The back entrance, which was between the basement stairwell and the driveway, was locked. Marie told Calcott her attacker had come through the front door.

Calcott then detailed the mess inside the house. His notes dovetailed with what Ed Moore had seen: The pulled-down curtain over the kitchen sink, the scattered mess in the living room, the knocked-over chair.

"The victim stated she first saw the intruder outside her kitchen window while she was getting a glass of water. She then saw him at the dining room window. By the time she turned around, the man was on the front porch and watching her from outside the living room windows."

This confirmed that Marie's attacker had been male. Even so, something seemed odd about this bit of information.

"How did he get from one window to the next so quickly?" Kate frowned. "She turns her head, takes maybe a few steps, and the guy is already around to the other side of the house? He sure moved fast!"

That was an understatement, according to what Marie next told the police chief.

"The victim stated she turned around again, and the man was back outside the kitchen window. She tried to pull the curtains closed, but lost her balance and fell to the floor. When she got to her feet, he was standing in the middle of the living room and coming toward her."

Marie hadn't been able to recall if the man had a weapon in his hand, but she had given a vivid description of the burglar: He was well over six feet tall; he wore a floppy hat covered with fishing lures, red plaid pants, and a yellow raincoat.

According to Marie, the man's skin was ... purple? And he had ... four arms, like some sort of creature?

But the strange man wasn't Marie's only unwelcome visitor Tuesday evening.

Several squirrels had appeared in the home about an hour before the man, she'd told Calcott, and they'd ransacked the house looking for peanuts. They had pink fur, were very small, and chattered at each other in German while they pawed open all the kitchen cabinets and, after that, every dresser drawer in the bedroom.

By the time Ed Moore arrived, Marie stated, the squirrels were hiding in the basement.

"The victim also warned first responders to watch out for the 'big black spiders' that were crawling across the ceilings," the report stated. "But none were found."

Marie then explained that she'd been trying to shoo the spiders out of the house with her broom when the strange man first appeared outside her kitchen window. She couldn't say for sure whether the man pushed her down in the hallway, or if she had made a misstep and fell.

"He is going to come back," Marie had frantically explained to Chief Calcott while medics stabilized her for the ride to the hospital. "The squirrels are waiting for him to return."

The report fell into Kate's lap as she blankly stared out Bertha's windshield. There was more to read, but her mind needed a few moments to process what she'd already absorbed.

"This. Is. Insane! It sounds like the ravings of a madwoman, someone who's not right in her mind. A man with purple skin and double arms? An army of pink squirrels talking in a foreign language? And no indication of forced entry."

She skimmed the next section of the report. "It's just as the Moores thought: Calcott couldn't pinpoint anything that seemed to be missing from the home. Of course, you'd have to know what to look for; only Marie could be sure of that."

Kate was pleased to see the narrative also included Calcott's initial follow-up with Marie.

"The victim was questioned again at the hospital the morning of June 4 after her injuries had stabilized. At that time, she was unable to remember most of what had occurred the night before inside her home, but maintained her description of the intruder was accurate."

"What kind of medications might Marie be taking?" Kate

wondered. "I'm not familiar with this sort of thing, but it sounds like she was tripping on some kind of hallucinatory drug. It makes no logical sense, at all."

Kate again considered the Moores' moments of hesitation as they'd shared their eyewitness accounts. Was this what they'd been unwilling to share? That their elderly neighbor, a well-known and respected member of the community, had been rambling and babbling like someone coming off a bad acid trip?

Calcott had said he wasn't sure there was more to investigate. And now, Kate understood why.

He obviously was leaning toward the idea Marie had imagined the entire situation, that it never actually happened. The lack of damage to either door, coupled with nothing missing from inside, only bolstered that theory. The mess inside the home could be explained by Marie's frantic attempts to protect herself from things that weren't real.

The police chief's quick change in demeanor also made sense. Between medical privacy laws and Marie's high standing in the community, Calcott would want to be very careful if he said more publicly about this case.

But if Kate started asking questions, shared what she now knew, it would fall on her to tell all of Eagle River that Marie Lindgren was literally out of her mind. Or at least, she had been Tuesday night.

No wonder he'd been so eager to share the report!

"Could this be dementia-related? If I had to guess, I'd say Marie's medical history is the only thing Calcott blacked out. It's possible she'd been previously diagnosed with something that might cause these ... paranoid delusions. I don't even know what else to call them."

Kate wasn't yet to the end of the file, but she decided to go back to the beginning. Now that she had a better grasp of the incident's context, she might be able to absorb more of its details.

The only new thing that jumped out to her was that Marie's account of what had happened was as vivid in detail as it was preposterous.

But at the end of the report, Kate discovered something of interest.

"When asked the next day about the state of her health before the home invasion allegedly occurred, Mrs. Lindgren said she started to feel physically unwell Tuesday afternoon. The victim stated she had been bothered by stomach upset, nausea, and diarrhea, along with a racing heartbeat. She had begun vomiting early in the evening as well."

"Oh, poor Marie." Kate shook her head in sympathy. "First she gets the stomach flu, and then this happened? She was probably very dehydrated by nighttime. Living alone, there wasn't anyone there to remind her to drink a lot of fluids, rest in bed, all the things that might have helped."

Kate felt terrible for Marie, but that wasn't all. Something just didn't feel right.

Was it only that she was still trying to process everything? That the facts of this case were completely different from what she'd expected them to be, from what all of Eagle River assumed was the truth? Maybe.

But as she tossed the file into Bertha's passenger seat and started for home, Kate sensed a piece was missing from this puzzle. It was just far enough out of reach that her mind couldn't find it, much less get a look at its edges and figure out how it fit in with purple-hued people, monster-sized spiders, and German-speaking squirrels.

"There was no burglary," she reminded herself as the east edge of town disappeared from her rearview mirror. "No bad guy lurking around the house, barging through the door, knocking Marie to the floor. Just ... a bad stomachache? Coupled with, what? Cognitive issues?"

And then, Kate had to laugh. "If any of this had been real, the squirrels would have been the real burglars, since Marie said they ransacked the kitchen looking for peanuts. It's amazing what our minds can create out of nothing."

Kate soon turned off the blacktop onto the gravel. She'd be home in just a few minutes. Maybe she should give the report another read before she called Bev with the surprising details. Between the two of them, maybe they could construct a thorough timeline of the events that occurred before Ed Moore found Marie injured inside her home.

Gwen was mowing her lawn, and Kate gave her neighbor a wave as she rolled by. And then, she remembered something.

"Wait a second! Dorothy Moore said she'd run into Marie out in the yard Tuesday morning. They talked about recipes, seems like; and then ..."

Kate tapped her brakes as her mailbox came into view.

"There was a meeting! Dorothy said Marie had some sort of club meeting that day, that she was excited to go to it. If we can figure out which one, that'll give us more people to talk to. They might have insight into how Marie was feeling, even behaving, closer to when this entire crazy situation occurred."

But Kate sighed in frustration as she collected her mail. "I can see why Calcott is so reluctant to push on with this. And why the Moores didn't say more than they did. It's all so embarrassing for Marie. If no crime was committed, why torment her by rehashing the details? Maybe I should just let this go."

Even so ... which local club had met Tuesday?

Marie and Floyd had been involved in so many initiatives over the years; it was likely she was still active in several groups in and around Eagle River. A calendar packed with meetings would be a wonderful way to socialize during retirement.

Kate could name only a few groups offhand.

"I think the historical society is the second Wednesday." She dropped her things on the kitchen counter, and prepared for cuteness overload as all four kittens followed Charlie into the room. "And then, there's the chamber of commerce ... Floyd would have been a member, I'd say; I wonder if Marie still goes? But they meet the last week of the month, not the first."

Kate handed out a few pets before she greeted Hazel, who was stretched out on the dining room's cool hardwood floor; then reached for her phone. If she looked at a calendar, maybe it would jog her memory.

Her attention zoomed in on her Thursday-morning appointment with Nancy.

"That Social Society luncheon she was talking about was on Tuesday. Those other ladies got sick at the same time as what happened to Marie!"

What were the odds Marie had been at that meeting?

Nancy's description of the other ladies' woes was similar to some of Marie's symptoms. And the Eagle River Social Society seemed like the sort of fun-loving club Marie would enjoy. Was it possible that food poisoning, coupled with one or several of Marie's medications, had caused her hallucinations?

Kate needed to reach Nancy before the weekend, and it was almost five now. She brought up the phone number for the Prosper library, knowing that calls to its front desk rolled to the adjacent city hall if they weren't answered in a timely fashion.

Nancy confirmed that Marie was a member of the Eagle River Social Society, and that she'd been at Tuesday's luncheon.

"Marie was the second one in the door," Nancy recalled. "Once I unlock the center for an event, I hang around to greet the early guests, if I can. Marie seemed to be in a good mood; she had some sort of salad to share, if I remember it right."

Kate wasn't sure how to explain everything to Nancy, or even if she should.

"I heard today that Marie had been sick Tuesday evening, before the ... incident at her home." It was the truth, if only a fraction of it. "I thought of what you'd said about the Social Society meeting."

"Two bad things in one day!" Nancy exclaimed. "Oh, that poor woman. And that makes five club members who got sick, not four. At least five! I wonder how many there were?"

Like many locals, Nancy had a personal connection to Marie. The older woman had graciously offered professional support after Nancy accepted the dual position with the city of Prosper.

"I heard she's not up to having visitors yet, so I've stayed away," Nancy told Kate. "Can you please let me know if you stumble across anything else? We have a public relations nightmare on our hands."

Two more of the center's upcoming bookings had been canceled that afternoon, Nancy said. Forfeiting their deposits hadn't been enough to keep a nervous bride, and the organizer of a family reunion, from pulling their events from the community center's calendar.

"I'll keep you in the loop," Kate promised before she exited the call. A theory was forming in her mind, but it was something she wasn't ready to say out loud.

Digesting a serving of curdled potato salad was no picnic; those discomforts could go on for several hours. The same could be said of any other heat-spoiled dish that had been brought to the Social Society meeting.

But were those likely to cause the lingering health woes that kept Marie in the hospital, three days later? Or be the basis for such vivid hallucinations? No way.

"It can't be that." Kate shook her head. "It has to be worse. Much worse."

✳ 8 ✳

"I think someone poisoned Marie Lindgren."

Alex froze, a handful of popcorn halfway to his mouth. "You what?"

Kate shifted uncomfortably on the couch, even though it was her own and she was in her favorite spot, on the left side. Maybe she shouldn't have said anything yet, at least not to anyone but Bev; but Marie's plight, and that confounding police report, had stuck with Kate for two days. Even Alex's arrival Sunday evening to watch a movie couldn't pull her mind away from the case.

"Poison." Kate nodded, as she tried to convince herself along with her boyfriend. "I think she might have been poisoned."

She knew how preposterous that statement sounded. It was something straight out of a Victorian dime novel, where the evil duke twirled his moustache as he plotted some poor woman's demise: A dramatic, agonizing ailment that could never be cured, not even with the strongest smelling salts from milady's dressing table.

But the more Kate considered this theory, the more plausible it seemed. Maybe that was because it was the only one she had.

Alex gave his popcorn a second glance before he finally

tossed it in his mouth, a gesture so quick that Kate almost missed it. She had to laugh.

"Don't worry, it's fine." She scooped up a handful for herself. "See?" she said around a mouthful of buttery, salty goodness. "I'm eating it, too."

She took a sip of her soda, then returned it to the coffee table. "I'll start at the beginning, I guess. I got a copy of the incident report Friday afternoon."

Alex's eyebrows went straight toward the old farmhouse's high ceiling, but he didn't say a word. Maybe because his mouth was still full of popcorn.

"It was an interesting meeting with Ray; more on that later," Kate promised. "Anyway, the report is ... well, it's out of this world."

"I know." Alex looked away for a moment. "I know what it says."

For a moment, Kate was surprised. And then, she realized she shouldn't be. Alex was Ray's cousin, after all; and the police chief had to confide in someone. The obvious choices were Officer Bevins and Ray's wife ... and another person with law-enforcement experience. Someone who was a professional when it came to keeping secrets.

Alex was watching her closely, as if waiting for Kate to call him out for withholding something from her. But she wasn't going to do that. They were dating, sure; but that didn't mean everything was on the table. And besides, Alex was an honorable guy. If his cousin had requested discretion, Alex wouldn't have hesitated to give it.

"Then you know exactly what I mean. The whole incident is so crazy; those are the ramblings of a delusional person. As far as I know, that doesn't exactly describe Marie these days. So, something must have caused that. And that's exactly why I'm starting to think she was poisoned."

As Alex took it all in for a second time, he seemed able to grasp the concept rather than be shocked by it. "OK, just to be crystal clear here: You're thinking a deliberate poisoning; not what we all like to call 'food poisoning,' like bad potato salad."

Kate grinned. "Is there any Midwestern dish that's as beloved, and yet feared, as potato salad?"

"Probably not. Unless it's macaroni salad, which also has mayonnaise." He wrinkled his nose. "I'm not a big fan. Of mayo, I mean. I'm a ranch-dressing guy."

Kate filed that clue away for future use. Or just some good-natured teasing. She'd never considered the possibility of having to pick sides in such a debate.

"I've pieced together part of Marie's day before she got sick, and I confirmed she attended the Eagle River Social Society luncheon at the Prosper community center just hours before her symptoms started."

Kate shared the rumors she'd heard from Nancy Delaney, including the doubt those morsels of gossip placed on the building itself.

"Now, that I hadn't heard." Alex took a swig of his soda as he considered this news. "Down at the bar, my customers have been focused on how their crops are faring, and if the Cubs can pull it together before the All-Star break. The fact that a handful of ladies got sick at a party hasn't hit their radars."

Kate understood. Those were the sort of details most women, especially older ones, would be horrified to spread beyond their own households. She wondered if some of the ladies even blamed themselves, assumed they'd caused their own indigestion by overeating. But since at least four women had become sick, five if Marie was counted among them, Kate doubted gluttony caused their woes.

"Here's the thing." Alex turned on the couch to face her. "If the food at this luncheon was somehow altered, why such a variation in reactions? It sounds like the other four ladies' symptoms were relatively minor, even if one had brief heart palpitations. Marie, the last I heard, is still in the hospital ...

five days later. And, well, you read the report. She was hallucinating big-time Tuesday night, so paranoid about her imaginary visitors that she injured herself trying to 'fight them off.'"

"Yeah; that's the part I can't figure out. Between the two catered dishes, and the others brought by the club members, so many people had their hands in this. Literally. And it's likely everyone had a taste of everything, or almost. You know how potlucks go."

She shook her head. "That brings me back to the idea that the food itself wasn't the whole problem. Or that Marie had such an extreme reaction only due to a bad interaction with her medications."

"Which you are never going to get a list of," Alex reminded her. "Unless Marie herself, or a close family member, decides to share them with you."

"I know." Kate stared out the living room's main window at the gloom-filled evening. Significant rain was on the way; and she and her garden, along with the farmers, were grateful for that. But she needed to catch a break in this case as much as she needed a change in the weather.

Hazel had taken over Kate's reading chair right after supper, and she'd barely lifted her head when Kate and Alex settled on the couch just minutes ago. Charlie had already received his evening grooming, as Kate knew she and Alex wouldn't get a moment's peace until that was done. He'd then assumed his usual post looking out to the porch, but the rustle of Alex reaching back into the popcorn bowl caused the cat to launch himself onto the closest arm of the couch.

"Hey, buddy," Alex said to Charlie. "Are you coming to sit with me?"

Kate wasn't so sure. "Only if you share that popcorn with him. There's a method to his madness."

"Popcorn?" Alex shook the large plastic bowl that sat in his lap. "This is what he wants?"

"He can have some. Just a few pieces, though. The butter's not the best thing for him. Well, the salt and the corn aren't, either. But he loves it."

Alex did Charlie's bidding. The big cat wolfed down the two popped kernels he was given, then placed one fluffy brown paw on the rim of the bowl.

"More?" Alex looked to Kate for guidance.

"Just a bit, then he's had enough."

In the front hall, tiny toenails click-clacked down the last few treads of the oak staircase. Growls, howls, and shrieks echoed from the entry as at least two of the kittens began to wrestle on the rug.

Romeo soon dashed into the living room, the black fur on his head going every which way. The kitten spotted Charlie on the arm of the couch, and decided to join him. Kate closed her eyes and searched for patience as Romeo's little claws made quick work of the sofa's upholstery during his ascent. Once he reached the summit, Romeo assumed the exact-same posture as Charlie and trained his inquisitive eyes on Alex.

"No way." Alex was floored. "The little guy wants some, too?"

"He wants whatever Charlie wants. He does exactly what Charlie does. No wonder King Charles has so easily settled into his role as proud uncle and instructor; he has a little disciple who adores him." Kate leaned toward Romeo. "No popcorn for you, sorry."

The kitten let out a pitiful whine that caused Hazel to raise her head in curiosity.

"I said, 'no.'" Kate reached across Alex and lifted Romeo into her arms. "Come here, you can sit with me. That popcorn isn't good for a little baby like you."

"You know," Alex said, "I was impressed when you brought this out from the kitchen. I'd assumed 'popcorn' meant the powder-dusted stuff people blow up in the microwave."

"My air popper should be in the Smithsonian." Kate reached into the bowl the second Romeo jumped out of her arms. Ophelia was about to ambush Juliet from around the cased opening into the dining room, and Romeo didn't want to miss out. "But I know better than to make any of this, and not share it with Charlie."

Alex had become a cat dad that spring after an oversized brown-tabby stray followed him home from the bar. Moose had been quick to adapt to the top-shelf kibble Alex spoiled him with, but he still begged for a bite of whatever protein was on Alex's menu. While Moose was now domesticated, his love of the outdoors had never wavered.

"I just wish he'd stop showing off his hunting trophies. If it's not a bird, it's one of those chipmunks or gophers. He brings them right in the door, so pleased, and drops them at my feet. I've seen worse carnage in my former line of work, sure; but I hate disposing of those critters."

"But they're always dead, right?"

Alex's eyes widened. "Of course! You don't think he'd ..."

"It can happen. We had the same, sometimes, out at the farm when I was growing up. Moose is proud of himself, and he wants you to be, too."

"Does Scout and his gang bring you some of their kills? What about Patches?"

It seemed to Kate that the Three Mouseketeers didn't bother to hunt anymore; if they did, they kept their "toys" to themselves. But she knew Patches still plotted a kill, now and then.

"Even though I've seen her in hunting mode, that girl doesn't bother to bring me anything. She likes to be petted, and I sensed she appreciated me letting her in the house when she went into labor. But I am her servant, nothing more."

Kate had noticed something interesting about her newest feline friend, and she wanted to run it past Alex. "Patches likes me, in her own way; but sometimes, I catch her staring at me with this odd look on her face."

"Like what? Moose stares at me, all the time. He stares at everything."

"They think deep thoughts, that's for sure. But this is … there's almost a note of resentment in it. Not fear," Kate quickly explained. "None of that. But I'm sure she wonders why Minnie Trowbridge is no longer here."

Romeo had moved back into Kate's lap, and she looked down into his curious eyes. "Does your mama think I did something to her friend? That it's my fault Minnie is gone?"

"I know you wrote Minnie a letter to get the nod to buy this place." Alex's tone was easy, but there was a hint of mirth in it. "Are you sure you didn't do something else, something illegal? You know, get Minnie out of the way so you could take over?"

"Is that what Patches thinks? Good thing she doesn't know how to use a phone! She'd be calling Sheriff Preston, if she could."

"Cats have dialed 9-1-1 before." Alex looked over at Hazel, who was now snoring. "Dogs, too. You'd better stay on Patches' good side."

He put his arm around Kate's shoulders. "I guess I feel safe because I know Minnie Trowbridge is alive and well, and enjoying her retirement in town. Her son comes into the bar from time to time."

"So you trust me, then, when I say I'm not a murderer?"

"I think so. At least, until I uncover evidence to the contrary."

A rumble of thunder rolled across the now-dark skies, and raindrops soon pelted the farmhouse windows. Kate and Alex both reached for their phones to see if any severe-weather watches or warnings had been issued. There were none; it was just a band of much-needed rain making its way over the county.

Kate picked up the remote and scanned through her streaming services until the agreed-upon movie appeared on the screen. As the film's opening score played, she looked around her cozy farmhouse. The gentle rain outside only added to the peace and safety she felt here.

While Marie's situation was still a cause for concern, there was a silver lining to the barrage of information Kate had gleaned from the incident report. The Lindgren home hadn't been breached by a violent attacker. Which meant it was rather unlikely anyone of that sort was roaming around Eagle River, or out in the country. She said as much to Alex.

He pulled her closer. "I'm glad you're feeling better. About that, at least."

"Still … what happened to her? Something's not right, about any of this."

Alex reached for the remote and paused the movie. "OK. Let's dissect this so we can get back to the show. You think Marie may have been poisoned; what are you going to do about it? Where do you look next?"

"I don't know. I wish I did. Leave the other ladies out of it, for a second. Let's say this was something intentional, malicious. What about blood work? Would that show anything specific?"

"You mean, like a toxicology report?" Alex rubbed the side of his face. "Technically, yes. But it's not that simple."

Blood tests that could show signs of unexpected substances were often costly, and needed weeks to get results, he said. And given Marie's symptoms that night, doctors would have been more concerned about stabilizing her physical injuries. A bump on the head or a fall, especially for someone of Marie's advanced age, could have long-term health complications. Her ramblings may have been chalked up to stress, or possibly mild dementia; two issues that could be reviewed later.

Regardless, that window of opportunity was over. Most

substances, benign or otherwise, didn't stay in people's bloodstreams long enough to appear on a blood test this far out. Five days was too late.

"That's what I was worried about." Kate frowned. "I can understand the ER doctors' priorities. But, why didn't Ray push for toxicology tests that night? If he suspected there was no burglary, no actual assault, why didn't he explore those other avenues?"

She pulled away from Alex, and crossed her arms.

"It's pretty clear he'd love nothing more than for me to run around town telling everyone Marie is a nutcase, or was tripping on illegal drugs, so he doesn't have to do it himself."

Alex stared at her for a moment.

"What do you want me to say? That my cousin, who happens to have over twenty years' experience in law enforcement, is an idiot and a fool? That he doesn't care about Marie at all?"

Kate needed to choose her next words carefully. She meant what she'd just said, but her theory certainly put Alex in an awkward position. Between his girlfriend of how-many months and his family, which side would he choose?

She was fairly certain she knew the answer, and she understood why.

And yet ...

"I'd like to think he cares." Kate shook her head. "But, I don't know. I got the distinct feeling Friday afternoon that he'd already washed his hands of the whole thing."

Alex mounted no defense on his cousin's behalf. That told Kate he suspected the same.

"This is a tough one." His tone was gentle, if firm. Kate was relieved that Alex didn't want to fight about this any more than she did.

"What you are insinuating about Marie is nearly impossible to prove. There are no other witnesses to what did, or didn't, happen at her home. As for that club meeting? I don't know who would have seen anything that could be useful. All the food, from every source, was created off-site. There would be nothing to see. And all the leftovers went into the garbage, or down a disposal, days ago."

"That's just it! If this was intentional, it's like the perfect crime. Invisible." She leaned toward him. "What do you think? Am I the one who's hallucinating now? Paranoid? Seeing things that aren't real?"

Alex sighed, then looked down. "It doesn't sit right with me, either."

Kate tossed up her hands in a gesture of relief. But he waved it away.

"I'm not saying I fully agree with this theory of yours. Just that it's a strange situation. And don't think for a moment that my cousin doesn't care. He's more invested in this than you probably realize."

Floyd Lindgren had been the Calcotts' realtor when they moved to Eagle River, Alex told Kate. On top of that, Floyd represented Alex when he purchased Paul's Place from its previous owner, and when he bought his house. Marie had brought Alex homemade cinnamon rolls on his first day in Eagle River. The following week, she issued him his library card.

"We're all connected in this community, in one way or another," he reminded Kate. "Growing up here, you know that to be true."

Gossip might net Kate more leads, Alex had to admit. But she would have to spread the negative chatter about the Prosper community center to make that happen.

"And as you know, theories are never enough. What you would need, even if you could hunt down a suspect, is a motive. Like I said, I can't imagine there's any evidence left, anywhere. And then, you'd just about need a confession to make it all stick." He shook his head. "That's a pretty tall order, if you ask me."

This case, if there was even one to solve, was complicated enough on its own. But right now, Kate had a more difficult question that needed an answer: Should she continue to involve Alex in her search?

No, she decided. Everything between them was going so well these days, and Kate didn't need any more drama in her life. Besides, family was family. The incident at Marie's home fell within Ray's jurisdiction; she couldn't put Alex in the middle like that. She loved him too much.

Oh …

That was a feeling, a realization, she'd examine later.

"I think it's time for me to stand down," she told him instead. "I should try to put this out of my mind. The important thing is for Marie to get better so she can go home."

Alex's shoulders instantly relaxed. Kate was glad she'd lied.

Because tomorrow, she and Bev were going to regroup and come up with a plan. They'd dissected the incident report Friday night over the phone, then made plans to meet at The Daily Grind first thing Monday morning. Kate had the day off, and Bev wasn't expected at the post office until nearly noon.

Bev had been eager for Kate to talk this over with Alex first, to see if he had any insight that might aid their search. His knowledge had been helpful, even if it only served to underline how difficult it would be to solve such a case. Kate wasn't sorry she'd shared her concerns with him. He was always an excellent sounding board, even though she continued to make her decisions on her own.

Including this one.

"Let's get back to that movie." She picked up the remote. "It won so many awards, it must be good."

✳ **9** ✳

Kate eyed the rows of sweet treats inside the glass showcase at The Daily Grind. Cinnamon rolls, turnovers, doughnuts …

"Another batch of blueberry muffins is about to come out of the oven." Austin explained. "Cordelia will be bringing them out shortly, if you want to wait."

Kate considered all her options again, then chose a cherry turnover. Why was it so hard to pick a pastry? She'd put a great deal more effort into that decision than the one she made last night, when she'd lied to Alex about her plans for the Marie Lindgren case.

Alex and Kate didn't live together, and they worked nearly opposite schedules. As close as they were, they didn't share every little detail of their lives. Surely it wouldn't be that hard to keep him in the dark while she hunted down more clues.

But if she was indeed in love with Alex Walsh, should she maybe …

"I'll take a mocha latte," she told Austin. That, at least, was an easy choice. "My usual."

The coffee shop was housed in one of Eagle River's many historic storefronts, and the exposed-brick interior walls and high ceiling amplified the conversation and laughter of the Monday morning rush. Kate was glad there would be plenty of background noise for this in-person chat with Bev, as the pleasant buzz would shield their strategic discussion from customers at nearby tables.

Their other public option had been Peabody's, but Kate had decided against that. The restaurant was too quiet, with too many listening ears, including those of Grandpa Wayne and his breakfast buddies. Kate had declined to meet with them this morning, and not just because of her plans with Bev. She had an off-the-record appointment with one of Grandpa's friends this afternoon, and she wanted to keep word of that interview under wraps.

Bev soon dropped her purse onto the other side of the small table Kate had scored along the back wall. "Good choice, times two." She gestured at their out-of-the-way location, as well as Kate's turnover. "Let me order, and then ... I am dying to see that report."

Kate had to laugh when Bev returned with a simple, medium-roast brew. "That's what you picked? You could have gotten one of those at the post office!"

Bev shrugged as she reached for the sugar packets. "No, my dear, you are mistaken. This packs a caffeinated punch, but it won't eat a hole in my stomach like the java Jack makes." She attacked her oversized cinnamon roll with a fork. "I don't have to be at work until midday, and I want to clean out the horses' stalls before I come back to town."

Kate slid the two folded sheets of paper across the table as if passing her friend a Cold War spy-code list. Bev pounced on the pages and began to read as Kate made quick work of her turnover.

"Oh, my." Bev set down the first page as she tried to take it all in. "I can't believe this."

"There's more. It just gets crazier and crazier."

When Bev was finished, she slid the report back to Kate, who promptly deposited it into her purse.

"And you think this is all connected to that ... meeting." Even given the noise around them, Bev was right to choose her words carefully. "I know two of the members fairly well, and I chatted briefly with another one at church yesterday. No one said anything. But then, why would they?"

"Exactly. It's not polite conversation. And for those who got sick, it's over and done with. Except for you-know-who, of course."

"What does Alex think?"

Kate stared at the lid of her coffee cup. "Well … he's not entirely convinced I'm heading in the right direction. And in the end, I told him I wasn't going to look into it any further."

She explained the situation, and was relieved when Bev nodded in agreement.

"I think that's the best way for you to go. Alex is in a tough spot, otherwise, stuck between you and Ray. It'll be easier, for both of you." Bev took a sip of her coffee. "Besides, you're still trying to convince him to be your date for Stacy's wedding, right? All the more reason to keep things on an even keel."

Alex had already met Kate's immediate family, but attending Stacy's wedding would be another step forward in their relationship. At least, Kate's relatives were sure to think so. Personally, she seesawed between wanting him to go, then having to face nosy questions from far-flung branches of her family tree; and having the freedom to focus only on her bridesmaid duties because he'd stayed home.

Or, more accurately, had to work at his bar. That was Alex's biggest hesitation about the invitation, or so he claimed. Saturday was the busiest night of the week at Paul's Place. His other concern was his accurate assumption that he'd spend most of the event, and likely all of it up until the dance, cooling his heels with the rest of the wedding party's plus-ones.

"He knows Stacy needs a final answer by Wednesday," Kate told Bev. "I'm not going to push him; it's not worth it. And there was so much else to talk about last night, it didn't even come up."

"Well, that will resolve itself, one way or another. But this case?" Bev shook her head. "I don't even know where to start."

They discussed several ideas, and discarded most of them within minutes. No matter whom they approached, however they attempted to find more information, none of those discussions would be flattering toward Marie.

"It sounds like she was tripping on some sort of psychedelic drug," Bev marveled as she dropped her voice to a whisper. "I can hardly believe it was anything like that! I've heard that some folks, even older ones, have turned to weed when seeking relief from anxiety or pain. But this is a whole other thing entirely."

Kate didn't think marijuana, whether medical grade or something harvested from beneath a basement grow light, would cause the sort of delusions Marie had experienced. "It has to be something else. But what?"

She debriefed Bev on Alex's assessment of the lack of evidence.

"He's right on that point," Bev admitted as she finished her cinnamon roll. "We certainly have our work cut out for us. It's like we'll have to disprove potential leads, rather than prove them, if we are going to make any headway at all. Eliminate the variables, if you will. It's probably our only option."

"I agree. And I hope to make a little headway on one front this afternoon."

Kate told Bev about her plans to stop at Eagle River Pharmacy and get Chris Everton's take on the situation. He wouldn't be able to speak to Marie's specific medications, much less confirm if she filled any prescriptions at his pharmacy; but his extensive knowledge of legal drugs and their potential interactions was a good place to start.

"I think that's a great idea," Bev said. "It should give us valuable insight into some of those symptoms. But I can't help but think there's more to it than that."

"I'm almost certain there is." Kate leaned back in her chair, thinking. "Beyond that, we'll need to reach out to members of the Social Society. It's mostly older ladies, right? With a few younger ones in the mix?"

"That's my impression. I think they have around, oh, maybe thirty women involved? Not everyone gets to all the meetings, of course. And the society's focus has changed some over the years."

The club, which formed during the Civil War, had initially carried a more serious name and mission. The Ladies' Aid Society supported the families of soldiers at the front, and then the veterans when they returned home. While the club had always offered a social component along with its wartime efforts, the focus had remained squarely on philanthropy until the 1960s.

As government entities rolled out more services to people in need of assistance, the women's group shifted its focus to having fun while occasionally raising money for a cause. About fifty years ago, the club's younger members urged the group to change its name to better suit its modern-day priorities.

The old-fashioned teas once hosted by Eagle River's small-but-stalwart ruling class were long gone. Instead, the ladies kept it casual with restaurant visits and group outings. Except for the semi-formal luncheon always held the first week of June.

Kate wished she knew more of the club's current members. Vanessa Archdale, a former classmate, had tried to recruit Kate to join the society just months after Kate moved home from Chicago. But Vanessa seemed as petty and childish as she'd been in high school, and Kate had shied away from her invitation. She certainly didn't trust Vanessa to show discretion if approached about such a sensitive matter.

"I could chat with Sonja Carlson and Wendy Teague," Bev

offered, "see if they mention the club's last meeting, give me an easy opener."

And then, her brow furrowed with concern. "But I don't know how to tactfully say, 'Hey, did you get sick afterward?' I think both of them would be mortified to know I'd heard about something like that."

"Nancy said the gossip is spreading, and none of it is flattering to the community center."

Kate shared her concerns about casting more doubt upon Prosper's beloved public facility, but that horse was already out of the barn. On the flip side, if they could get to the bottom of what happened at last week's luncheon, the venue's excellent reputation could be restored.

Bev agreed, and offered another motivation for moving forward.

"There's a world of difference between someone making an honest mistake, in the course of running a business, and someone deliberately attempting to make people sick. People need to have facts in hand, not rumors, if they're going to make sound decisions about where to spend their money." Bev stirred her coffee, then switched gears a bit. "Has Stacy heard this gossip yet? How does she feel about it?"

"She's relieved she picked the 'right' caterer. 'Not the one that made all those ladies sick,' as she told me."

"Oh, dear. That's exactly the kind of talk that needs to be stopped, one way or another."

Like most of Eagle River's longtime residents, Bev knew the Lindgrens on some level. But she wasn't close enough to the family to ask direct questions about Marie's health woes. Instead, she'd made gentle inquiries Saturday afternoon while working at the post office counter.

"The general consensus was that Marie's not coming home anytime soon. She became very dehydrated because of ... whatever happened. She needs constant fluids, monitoring, the whole bit."

The older woman's kidney and liver levels were concerning, Bev reported. Apparently, there was now worry about possible long-term organ damage, on top of several other issues.

Kate blinked back sudden tears. "Oh, that's terrible! All the more reason we need to track down whatever leads we can find."

"Here's another question: Do you think Calcott's truly receptive to tips at this point?" Bev waved one hand in a dismissive gesture. "I know he called Roberta first thing the other day, all hyped up for us 'public servants' to work together, and all that. But what's his temperature now?"

Kate mulled that over. "I think the chief's ducking out on this one. I hate to admit it, but I understand why. There's not much to go on, if anything. And Ray's been in town only a fraction of the years Marie has lived here. He doesn't want to ruffle feathers by telling everyone what he suspects: that she made it all up, one way or another."

Bev nodded her agreement. But then, she laughed.

"Well, look at it this way. If nothing criminal happened at Marie's home, then the scene of the crime, if you will, was actually in Prosper." She winked at Kate. "That means our official lead investigator isn't Ray Calcott."

Kate grinned. "You're right. Even so, I think we'll need something really solid before we reach out to Sheriff Preston."

"Absolutely." Bev studied the bustling coffee shop with admiration. "This is quite the place Austin has going here. Look at this crowd! Clyde and I aren't coffee connoisseurs, as you may have guessed. But we should stop in more often. That cinnamon roll was divine. We all need to support our local businesses."

Bev studied the closed stairwell not far from their table. "It seems I heard something a while back about him wanting to expand. Does he have a plan to do something with the upstairs?"

"He sure does." Kate wasn't sure where the idea stood these days, but she knew Austin was considering renovating the second floor to create not just more seating, but an area with a unique focus. He might add an event space that could be rented out, given the lack of facilities in the area; or perhaps a small bookstore or art gallery. Or some combination of the three.

"All those ideas are wonderful." Bev was pleased. "Eagle River is lucky to have someone with that kind of vision, especially one of our younger folks." Then she frowned. "Oh, I hope that's not ..."

Kate leaned forward. "What?"

"I hope none of this is true, but something just occurred to me."

Who might benefit from Prosper's event space starting to struggle? Was there any possibility that Austin, or someone else in the local hospitality industry, was behind what happened at the club meeting? Although it had been open for barely more than a year, the Prosper site was certainly popular. If someone wanted a bigger share of the market ...

Kate looked toward the counter, where a line of people waited for their orders. Austin was pushing his glasses back up his nose while he chatted with a young guy in an Eagle River Wildcats tee shirt.

Austin was the same age as Kate's brother. She'd known him long before he went off to college, then came home to be one of Eagle River's movers and shakers. But Bev was right; they had to consider every angle, no matter how uncomfortable some of them might be.

But this one was easy to set aside.

"Somehow, I don't think he's involved," she told Bev as they tidied their table. "He's so far away from having anything going upstairs. I can't see how taking such drastic action would benefit him any time soon."

"I agree, it wouldn't be worth the risk. Not to mention, I

couldn't imagine him even considering such a thing. If we are crossing leads off our list, I guess we're off to a good start."

* * *

Janet Everton didn't seem surprised when Kate entered the pharmacy early that afternoon. She just smiled and tipped her head in the general direction of the back of the building.

Kate had no qualms about asking Chris for his assistance, as well as his discretion, regarding this case. But she had wondered how they would hold a private conversation inside this bustling shop without drawing the attention of even one nosy customer. Leave it to the savvy pharmacist and his wife to devise a plan.

As she waited in Chris' neat-as-a-pin office for him to arrive, Kate's thoughts circled back to the end of that morning's conversation with Bev.

If someone was determined to undermine the Prosper community center's success, intentional poisoning would be one way to make waves. With weddings and graduations being major moments in people's lives, a club gathering would be a more palatable time to take such a drastic step. And also, the Social Society's members were generally well-connected; that would give an instigator hope the ladies might share their health woes far and wide.

Was this some sort of business-related sabotage? Kate wondered. A personal vendetta? Or maybe just someone's idea of a very sick joke?

The pharmacist arrived only moments later, pulling off his spotless white jacket as he came through the office door. "Sorry to keep you waiting. Man, has it been busy today! And not just scripts. Everyone wants bug spray and allergy meds, we can barely keep that stuff on the shelves."

Chris dropped into his chair, and gave Kate a relaxed smile. "So, what's going on?

This was going to be a far-easier conversation than the

one she'd had with the police chief, but Kate was still a bit wary. How could she get the answers she needed without spreading too much gossip about Marie's condition, or the worries now surrounding the Prosper community center and its caterers?

But there was no way around it; Kate had to tell the pharmacist everything she knew, and everything she suspected. She tried to take comfort in the fact that Chris Everton understood the concept of confidentiality, given his chosen career. And his job meant he'd surely heard it all, several times over.

"I wanted to ask you about possible drug interactions."

"Are you having issues?" Chris was immediately concerned. "Has your doctor ..."

"Oh, no, it's not for me." She should get right to her point; she didn't want to take up all of Chris' lunch break.

"I know you can't speak about your customers in any specific way. But this is about Marie Lindgren, and what I believe happened at the Social Society luncheon she attended last Tuesday."

Chris was puzzled. "Wasn't that the day, or should I say the night, that her home was broken into?"

"Yes."

Kate ran through it all as efficiently as she could. Her talk with the Moores, Nancy Delaney's concerns. Her idea to get the incident report, which made Chris grin and nod his approval. But when she told him what it said, his jaw dropped.

"You're serious? Yes, that does sound like hallucinations. To put it mildly." The pharmacist shook his head in awe. "Wow, how terrible. And she'd been at that meeting, you say? And those other women got sick, too? I hadn't heard about that."

"Maybe it was all some kind of accident." Kate was more at ease now that she'd stated her case. "But there's at least the possibility this was intentional in some way. Celebrations are a big part of life these days, when there's a party for every little thing. And they're a lucrative business, too."

"Yes, I can see a possible motive there. So, what specifically do you want to know? How can I help?"

"I want to rule out anything else that could have caused those sorts of side effects. Specific meds, for example. Or interactions between drugs or supplements."

Kate gave the pharmacist time to ponder what she'd told him. His professional knowledge was invaluable to this situation.

Psychotic episodes were possible with various street drugs and opioids, Chris said, but he agreed it was highly unlikely Marie had consumed those. "But maybe I shouldn't jump to that conclusion. I've seen ... well, let's hope that's not the case."

Severe food poisoning could be a factor with hallucinations, although not a common one. Dehydration did a number on the body, in so many ways; Marie's symptoms might have escalated if she wasn't getting enough fluids. Dementia sometimes caused hallucinations, the pharmacist said; and several legal drugs, at high enough doses, could do the same: antihistamines, anti-depressants, blood pressure medications, even some antibiotics and steroids.

"And I don't mean just the body-building kind. I mean the healing kind: anti-inflammatory drugs."

Kate was stunned. "You mean, like a hydrocortisone shot for a stiff knee?"

"Yep. But only if the dose is too strong for the patient based on their various health conditions. None of the approved drugs carry a high probability of hallucinations on their own, understand. There needs to be another factor to increase that risk. There are so many variables in these situations."

Kate sighed. "I hadn't assumed this case would be easy to

solve. But it sounds like it's more complicated than it seemed upfront."

"Sorry I'm giving you more questions than answers."

"No, I appreciate it. This is what I need to know if I'm going to pursue this."

"And I hope you do." The pharmacist crossed his arms. "Because you're the first person, a member of law enforcement or otherwise, to ask for this sort of information."

"I'm not sure where I'll go next. I don't know Marie well enough to visit her at the hospital and grill her about this. Besides, Calcott already did that, and he didn't get anything useful, anyway. Me showing up there would likely upset Marie, and she needs to focus on healing."

Chris agreed. "I can't imagine she's changed her story, if that makes you feel any better. If anything, the few details she'd initially retained are likely to fade as the days go by, given the stress she's been through." Then he smiled. "And that's all I can say about that."

"Point taken."

This visit hadn't netted Kate any new leads, but it had provided a lot of information to ponder. She was grateful for Chris's generous offer of both time and expertise, and told him so.

"Not a problem!" His expression turned somber. "If you come across anything that seems ... medically suspicious, I guess I'll call it; and you aren't sure what to do with that information, let me know. I'll walk you through it, if I can."

✳ 10 ✳

The strawberries were stemmed and chopped before Kate reached for the rhubarb. Charlie, who was supervising from the stepstool at the end of the counter, leaned so far forward he nearly toppled from his perch.

"Sorry, none for you." Kate moved the berries away from the cat's curious nose. "You don't eat fruit, and that's all I have available." She gestured at the rhubarb before she trimmed its ends and began to chop.

"Actually, this is a vegetable; most people don't know that. Charlie, you are a cat in possession of a great bit of trivia. Isn't it amazing what humans will put together and call delicious? But this is one of the best combinations of the summer. Thanks to Bev and Mom, I'll have all I can bake with for a few more weeks."

Kate had taken off a few extra days that week to tend to some chores around her little acreage, but there was always time to bake a pie. The rhubarb season was short, no more than two months. She wanted to make the most of it, even if she needed help to do so. Her little farm had come with a generous garden plot; but if there had ever been rhubarb plants at this place, they'd long ago died off or been removed.

Thursday's sunrise had delivered a beautiful morning, even if it was already stiflingly hot outside. Kate heard the air conditioner start around the back corner of the house, and felt a wave of gratitude that her old farmhouse had come with that amenity, at least.

Once she refused to share her strawberries and rhubarb, Charlie lost interest. He stared out the nearest kitchen window, lost in thought, pondering the state of the world or nothing at all.

Kate had just filled the crust and slapped on the dough lattice when Charlie made a sharp pivot and peered down the driveway. Seconds later, Hazel started to bark.

"That must be the goat man." Kate wrinkled her nose, then laughed. "That sounds like something out of a horror movie! This is the opposite. Or at least it should be, unless something goes terribly wrong while the critters are here. Am I really going to do this? Should I?"

She wiped her hands on the nearest kitchen towel, and eyed the mess she always made when she baked. Adam Fairlaine, who farmed out part of his family's goat herd for the weed-mowing services Kate needed, was likely to come into the kitchen as he wrapped up his site visit.

Kate scooped the food debris into the nearby trash can, which was of the sort proven to be cat- and dog-proof, and ran a damp sponge over the counters.

"Good enough." She pulled off her apron and adjusted her ponytail, then reached for her wide-brimmed straw hat. "Adam's a goat farmer, for goodness' sake. A little mess shouldn't be a big deal to him."

Besides, it was Kate's chicken house that was going to be under scrutiny this morning. The coop was more like a chicken palace, generously sized with a high ceiling and plenty of windows for ventilation, and it wasn't more than fifteen feet from the pasture gate. It was the perfect place to house temporary goat guests.

Doc Ogden, Karen's business partner, had personally recommended the Fairlanes' traveling goats. Even Auggie

Kleinsbach, the proprietor of the Prosper co-op, approved of this company and its animals. That was all Kate needed to know; along with the fact that goats had iron stomachs and could chomp vegetation at an impressive speed.

"Hello!" Adam called to Kate as he climbed down from his gray truck, which had a cute logo on its side. "You must be Kate." Hazel reached their visitor first, and Adam was soon accosted by four barn cats that came running from all directions.

"They've yet to meet a stranger," Kate said as she offered Adam her hand. He shook it briefly before giving all the critters pats on their heads.

Adam was in his late thirties, Kate guessed, not much older than herself. But he had the weathered complexion of a veteran farmer under his faded ball cap, and a telltale dark suntan on his forearms. He wore a tee shirt with pushed-up long sleeves, heavy jeans despite the heat, and sturdy boots.

"You have quite the little menagerie." Adam grinned as Jerry and Maggie departed almost as quickly as they'd arrived. "Our barn cats are the same; we're most interesting to them at mealtime."

Kate gestured at Scout and Patches. "These two will insist on coming with us. Unless you think I need to shut them in the shed."

"They should be fine." Adam pulled a bottle of bug spray from his truck. "Cats can always get through a fence if they choose to, so I'm sure they've been in the pasture more than you'd like them to be." He tipped his chin at Hazel. "But she should stay up by the house."

Hazel was more confused than upset when Kate reached for her collar and gently guided her toward the back steps. While she was in the kitchen, Kate took the opportunity to scrub her hands again and slip the pie into the oven.

To her surprise, Patches was in Adam's arms by the time she returned.

"I think I'm supposed to carry her," he announced with a look of amusement in his brown eyes. "She all-but climbed up my leg! Is she the queen around here?"

"It depends on the day, but she certainly thinks so."

Scout didn't hesitate to demand the same mode of transportation from Kate, and she obliged. Kate felt a bit ridiculous as she and her guest started across the yard, each with a cat in their arms. But Adam didn't seem to mind. Along the way, Kate explained how she'd come to own this little acreage. And be owned by four outdoor cats.

"It's a beautiful place," he told Kate, then gazed down at Patches. "No wonder you decided to walk home."

Kate slowed her stride as they passed the chicken house. "The coop has been vacant for over ten years, I've been told. And I don't know the last time there were cows here, or pigs, or even sheep. Which, of course, explains why you are here."

As they neared the gate, Kate cringed at the wild, unruly state of her pasture. Some of the weeds were stout, with tangled vines that meandered in every direction. Other invaders were tall and proud, emboldened by the recent rains and summer heat. Prickly leaves were everywhere, and thorns pushed out from some of the stems. Determined seed pods-in-training were camouflaged as petite flowers on some of the species, whose yellow, cream, and pink petals tried to downplay their vicious natures.

Adam, however, took it all in stride as they deposited Patches and Scout on the yard side of the fence.

"I've seen worse," he said mildly as he pulled a pair of latex gloves from the canvas bag slung over his shoulder. Then he pushed down his shirt sleeves to tuck them inside his gloves. Kate was suddenly unsure about her lightweight canvas pants and short sleeves.

"Oh, I can walk it on my own. There's no need to go in and change. Just stick to that mowed path you have there, and you'll be fine."

Kate shared her hope of protecting the prairie plants along the creek.

"That won't be a problem," Adam said as they climbed over the cattle panel that served as the gate. "That's what electric fences are for. We'll set up a perimeter around the creek. The goats won't need access, anyway, since you'll have that water station set up for them."

Having family engaged in full-scale farming was certainly to Kate's advantage when it came to hosting temporary guests. Bryan and Dad had promised to bring over buckets that would secure to the fence posts, as well as a section of metal roofing to shield the waterers from the elements.

This lone acre of pasture was just a tiny portion of what had been a larger field years ago, before the vast majority of the Trowbridges' farmland had been sold. Adam estimated a dozen goats could easily clear this small plot in just under a week. As Kate swatted away a mosquito that darted out of a clump of weeds not far from the path, she decided the cost he'd quoted her would be worth every penny.

Adam first spent a few minutes studying the waterway's native plants. "Now, these are the good guys: coneflower, milkweed, asters. You're right, you want to keep those. Have you considered planting more of them, once the pasture is cleared? They're tough plants, they could hold their own against the others if given a chance."

"I have," Kate admitted. "At least, I might plant a few more in this area. I know they benefit the butterflies and bees, and birds eat some of the seeds. One thing at a time, I guess."

Kate knew what was coming next. It was the same question she'd been asked time and again.

"I haven't decided about any permanent sheep or goats," she told Adam. "There's only room for a few out here, which is about all I could handle, anyway. Besides, that empty chicken house would have to be retrofitted into a permanent home for them, first."

"Well, one of my clients put in a flower farm after the goats did their thing. She raises commercial blooms: peonies, tulips, and the like, along with some natives. It's been very successful."

Kate shook her head in amazement. "That's so cool! But I think I'll stick with delivering the mail."

She gestured toward an especially nasty-looking plant. "What do you think that is? I've seen quite a bit of it out here, and tried to look it up, but …"

"Ragweed." Adam made a face. "The bane of many people's existence during the growing season. You can tell by the leaves. Some folks mistake it for goldenrod, which is one of the good guys. But it's far from that."

He identified a patch of poison ivy not far off the path. And a stretch of wild mustard just to its left. "A recipe for blisters, right there. Life in hell, I can assure you. That mustard is invasive, chokes out the natives. It needs to go."

Kate crossed her arms and took a small step back, but made sure to stay on the roughly mowed path. "But the goats can get rid of it? It's safe for them to ingest?"

"Oh, sure. They can eat just about anything. But there are some plants that are toxic to goats. That's what I'm looking for today. If I find just a few, I can pull them now. More than that, and … well, we might not be able to make this work."

"I wondered about that, if there was anything out here that might make them sick." She frowned with worry. "Could they die? Is there anything fatally poisonous to goats?"

"Oh, sure." His expression darkened for a moment. "They're not common, though. Especially in a plot like this where livestock grazed for years, even if animals haven't been here lately. Nope, you usually find the scary stuff in spots that have been undisturbed for decades. Hidden places, especially on the edges of forests. Or the forest floor, itself."

As Adam bravely waded into the weed-choked pasture grass, Kate's mind lit up with curiosity.

Certain wild plants were poisonous to animals; how many of those could make people sick, too?

Chris Everton had shared excellent insight regarding which drugs, prescription and otherwise, could cause the sort of hallucinations Marie had experienced. Were there botanicals that might do the same? Kate still held out hope that Marie's odd symptoms, and their unfortunate complications, had been caused by a drug interaction or accidental food poisoning. But what if someone had added something toxic, yet natural, to her food?

In the past few days, Bev had gleaned a few details about the Social Society luncheon from her friends Wendy and Sonja. Unfortunately, none of those tidbits were the red flags Kate and Bev had hoped to find.

Wendy had felt fine after the meal, and had nothing but praise for the dishes her fellow club members brought to the occasion. And Sonja, despite being one of the ladies sickened at the event, had been just as complimentary about the other women's offerings. She was certain dehydration had worsened her symptoms, as she'd mowed the lawn and pulled weeds in her garden in the heat for hours after the meeting. Some over-the-counter medicines that night, and lots of fluids, had Sonja feeling fine by morning.

Kate had already made up her mind to hire Adam's roaming goats to solve one of her problems this summer. Perhaps he could help her with a much-different dilemma if she asked the right questions.

When he'd finished his loop through the pasture, Kate was glad to note Adam's canvas bag was empty.

"I didn't find anything. You have quite a smorgasbord of weeds, but nothing that gives me any concern for the goats' health and safety."

"So, what about people?" she asked as they started back toward the gate. "What kinds of plants grow around here that people need to avoid?"

If Adam thought her question odd, he didn't let on. Kate hoped his fascination with the topic would make him eager to share his wide-ranging knowledge without hesitation.

"Now, that's a whole other thing. Nothing out there is a candidate, so you don't have to worry about that. But, yeah; there are some plants, especially in the forested areas, that fully deserve their bad reputations."

Some varieties of hemlock and oleander fit into that category, Adam said, but oleander thankfully didn't grow naturally in the Midwest. Hellebore and some nightshades were also dangerous.

And many of the plants that were toxic to goats were harmful to humans as well as other livestock.

"But here's the thing: Sometimes, only parts of certain plants are poisonous; and some are only trouble during specific times of the year. It's very complicated. People who like to forage for wild greens, for example, need to know exactly what they're doing."

Kate didn't want to press Adam for more details on poisonous plants, in case it put her in a bad light. After all, she wanted him to loan her some goats for a week; he needed to know his animals were in good hands. She'd have to look elsewhere for more information.

✳ ✳ ✳

The chicken house was dusty and cluttered with junk, and its dirt-crusted panes let in only a portion of the bright sun. But it was of adequate size to serve as a goat vacation rental, and the window sashes opened when a little force was applied to their weathered frames. Once Adam gave the space his nod of approval, he and Kate went to the house to complete the paperwork.

The farmhouse's welcoming coolness was paired with the wonderful aroma of the pie in the oven. But Kate's bare arms were coated with dust and pollen, and starting to itch.

"How do you do it?" she asked Adam while she washed up at the kitchen sink, being sure to scrub her forearms. "I didn't even wander around in those weeds, and my skin is crawling right now."

"One of the hazards of the job, I guess." Even so, he gratefully accepted the wad of soap-dampened paper towels she handed him. "It's a good thing I'm not allergic to much."

"I'm putting in another bathroom," Kate explained as she pulled a pitcher of lemonade from the refrigerator, then pointed out the torn-apart former pantry.

"I can't wait until it's ready. The only sink on this floor, right now, is this kitchen one. If I don't want to use it or go upstairs, there's only an old utility faucet in the basement."

"Old houses are wonderful, but their plumbing doesn't meet today's standards. We did the same, my wife and I, put in a downstairs bathroom. We were willing to sacrifice space for one of those."

Alex pressed the foot pedal on the trash can, then paused over the now-open cannister. "Do you have rhubarb here at your farm?"

Kate turned from where she was taking glasses from an upper cabinet. "No, my mom and a friend are keeping me supplied. The leaves are poisonous in large quantities, I know. My parents have always kept their little patch behind a sturdy fence, to make sure the cows could never reach it if they happened to get out."

"That's smart." Adam nodded his thanks for the lemonade as Kate poured one for herself, and they settled at the dining room table. Charlie wandered past, only pausing long enough to give Kate's pant legs a good sniff. Hazel barely looked up from her spot on the living room rug, one that was close to a cooling floor register.

The kittens, however, had a far-different reaction to the sight of a stranger. The pile of sleepy fluff on the couch quickly came alive with raised heads and curious eyes.

"Oh, aren't they cute!" Adam leaned over the table. "Their mom's the calico, right?"

"That's her." Kate couldn't keep the pride out of her voice. Romeo stretched one black paw in her direction, and she waved at him.

"They're eight weeks old; she weaned them a little while ago. Now we are working on socializing with our peers, the rules of indoor living, interaction with dogs and other cats, and ... well, being as cute and destructive as possible."

Adam was so taken with the kittens, Kate had to pull his attention back to the business matter at hand. "So, you have the contract with you? I can sign it now, if you like."

"Yes, of course." He reached for the clipboard he'd snagged out of his truck on the way back to the house. "I know there's a sample on our website, but why don't you give it another look, see if you have any questions?"

Kate studied the document for a few minutes before she reached for her purse, which was kept inside a nearby cabinet. She'd learned the hard way that kittens like to empty every bag and knock its items to the floor before they nestle themselves inside. "Would you like a check?"

"Absolutely! Those card fees really add up. The deposit's fifty dollars."

Kate was about to settle her payment when movement caught her eye. Ophelia and Romeo remained on the couch, but Hamlet had bravely jumped down and scampered into the dining room to study Adam more closely. Juliet wasn't far behind him.

"Those two are quite the team," Kate said before she shared their current names. "Always together. Come to think of it, the other two are the same. It would be ideal to adopt them out in pairs, if I can."

In a burst of sudden kitten energy, Hamlet launched himself into Adam's lap. Juliet was the smallest of the quartet, and she used her sharp claws to climb Adam's jeans to stay close to her brother, who was now meowing and demanding their visitor's attention.

"Aren't you friendly!" Adam gently rubbed Hamlet's orange ears, then answered Juliet's request for the same. "You, little girl, are as colorful as your mama. And there's nothing shy about you two."

Kate could hardly believe it when both kittens settled into Adam's lap and began to purr.

A few family members and friends had met Patches' crew, but Kate hadn't started a formal search for new homes. The kittens' still-young ages, paired with the distraction of this latest case and Kate's research regarding temporary goat herding, had slowed her adoption efforts.

"You like cats, I take it." It was an understatement given the joy on Adam's face.

"I sure do. So does my wife, and our two kids."

Adam's expression suddenly turned somber. "We lost our house cat, Cinders, last month. It was cancer; he was fifteen. We all miss him, but our little girl is still crying herself to sleep. Cinders always stayed on her bed until he knew she was settled for the night."

Hope filled Kate's heart. But Adam's grief, as well as that of his family, was still raw and fresh. She didn't want to push away this wonderful possibility by pushing too hard.

"Well, they need to stay with me for a while yet," she said casually as she started to fill out her check. "Doc and Karen have graciously offered to spay and neuter them at cost, but that's a few weeks down the road. And I want to find them the perfect homes."

But it was clear to Kate that Hamlet and Juliet had already made up their minds. Adam sensed it, too.

"Wow. This is a lot to take in. I expected to swing by, talk about goats and weeds, then move on to my next appointment. Which I need to do, so ..."

Juliet gave a little mew of protest when Adam reluctantly

set her down on the hardwood floor. Hamlet refused to budge until Kate came over and picked him up.

"I'll let you know which day I can bring the goats over. If not next week, it'll be the one after that." Adam gathered his things, then gave Juliet and Hamlet another admiring look. "Maybe I could bring my wife and kids along? Let everyone get acquainted, at least?"

"I think that's a brilliant idea." Kate had to cuddle Hamlet close to keep him from running after Adam. "There's plenty of time to think it over."

Adam's truck soon started down the driveway, and Kate watched it go with a mix of emotions coursing through her heart.

Her sadness about how close she was to letting the kittens go mingled with joy over possibly finding two of them the best home she could have hoped for. Adam was a kind, thoughtful person; she suspected his wife was the same. And Doc had already given the Fairlaines his stamp of approval.

No, she wasn't going to start crying; not yet.

Once Hamlet ran off with Juliet to join the rest of the litter in the living room, Kate turned her focus to the rest of her day's to-do list. Starting the laundry, weeding the garden, marinating chicken to put on the grill for supper ...

What was that smell?

"The pie!"

Kate ran to the oven, and flung open the door. The filling had bubbled through the lattice crust and dripped onto the bottom burner. The dessert's edges were too burnt for her taste, and the bottom crust surely would be, too.

But too many good things had happened that morning for Kate's disappointment to last long. If nothing else, she had a tasty strawberry-rhubarb compote to spoon over ice cream.

✳ **11** ✳

"These are amazing." Kate reached for another cheese straw, and swirled it through the chive-and-bacon dip. "And I know this spread didn't come out of a container. You made it fresh, yourself."

"Of course!" Stacy stared at her cousin in surprise. "Tonight's a special occasion. I wasn't going to serve cheap bags of chips and cans of beer."

Kate eyed the pitcher of mojito cocktails, whose ice cubes were speckled with bits of cilantro and slices of lime. Mini cucumber-dill sandwiches were carefully arranged on a tray, and the plaid tablecloth's shades of lavender reflected Stacy and Ryan's signature wedding hue. No detail had been overlooked.

"Everything looks wonderful." Kate gave Stacy the side-eye. "But this is your bachelorette party. As the guest of honor, you shouldn't have to play host."

"And I won't, once we step on that party bus. But this sets the tone for the rest of the night. And I want it to be a memorable one."

A woman with curly brown hair came into the kitchen. "We'll make sure of that," she promised Stacy, then gave Kate an unexpected hug. "It's good to see you. It's been forever!"

Crystal Smith, Stacy's closest friend from college, now

lived in Des Moines. Kate had only met Crystal a few times and was rather surprised, yet touched, by the other woman's outpouring of affection.

Stacy had picked her four attendants using carefully calibrated criteria, as she often did when making a decision. Maid of Honor Lauren, an Eagle River music teacher, was the "current best friend." Kate was "the relative," while Crystal was "the college friend." The fourth slot went to Emily Millard, Stacy's future sister-in-law, to balance out Stacy's brother Corey being a groomsman.

To round out tonight's revelry, Stacy invited a few more friends. There was room for eight in the party van she'd rented, so why not? Amber Baird, Jessica Deegan, and Kelsey Powell were on their way.

Crystal and Stacy quickly turned their focus to reliving a memorable night out during their junior year of college, so Kate was glad when Lauren arrived. She and Lauren were well acquainted, thanks to the two educators' insistence Kate join Eagle River's strolling carolers for last year's holiday open house. Kate had hesitated at first, since hoop skirts and melodramatic gestures had been involved; but the evening's romantic, if contrived, performance had brought her and Alex closer together.

"I see you got the memo about the dress code." Lauren gestured at Kate's simple blouse and casual shorts. "At first, Stacy wanted us all in frocks, heels ..." Lauren rolled her eyes. "I talked her out of it. I mean, we're going to do karaoke at a bar after we make soap and eat pizza."

Kate nodded her gratitude. "She hadn't mentioned it to me, or I would have helped you put a stop to it. I think I have two skirts these days, and no dresses at all. Except the one for the wedding."

It was a lovely shade of lavender, with a tea-length hem and cap sleeves. Simple, elegant, and not too expensive. It could have been so, so much worse.

The doorbell rang, and Stacy was soon distracted greeting two more friends.

"So," Lauren whispered to Kate and Crystal, "what's our plan to keep the happy bride on an even keel tonight? I think it'll fall on the three of us to make that happen."

While Stacy and Emily were soon going to be family, they hadn't been friends before Stacy met her husband-to-be. Ryan Millard was a dentist in Swanton; Stacy had gone in for a cleaning two years ago, and came out with a hunch that the newest member of the practice would call to ask about something other than her flossing routine. As was usually the case with Stacy, she had been right.

"She's not a big partier," Crystal said, then turned to Lauren. "That hasn't changed, right?"

"Nope. But I think she wants to let loose tonight."

"Maybe we let her drink whatever she wants to start," Kate suggested, "unless she's getting really out of hand. Later on, we may have to rein her in."

Stacy always seemed so put-together and organized, but Kate suspected it took her cousin a great deal of effort to maintain that persona. Lauren had noticed the same.

"She's nervous about tonight; she wants everyone to have the best time of their lives. If she's going to drink, we have to make sure she doesn't just pick at her food."

The last of the ladies arrived, and Stacy's small bungalow on the north side of Eagle River soon overflowed with laughter and chatter.

Kate had been looking forward to this evening, as it was a good chance to mingle with people outside her usual circle. Maybe that circle was too small, she mused as she sipped her cocktail and moved around the dining room, introducing herself to the women she didn't know. Maybe she should try to do something about that: join a club, volunteer, or something of that sort. But tonight? Kate was just going to have a good time.

"You live outside of town? All by yourself?" Jessica, who was a nurse, raised her eyebrows in surprise. "I've been nervous enough as it is, here in town, since that monster broke into Marie Lindgren's home last week. How do you manage?"

Kate realized she had another reason to watch her alcohol consumption tonight, beyond keeping an eye on her cousin and driving herself home.

She knew more about the "burglary" than anyone in this room; more than anyone else in Eagle River, come to think of it, beyond a small handful of people. It would be crucial for her and Bev's investigation, as well as Marie's reputation, to choose carefully who might hear about those details, and when.

Even so, Kate had to smile. "Monster" was a more-accurate description of what Marie had shared with Chief Calcott than Jessica possibly could know.

"I have a security system at my place," she told Jessica. "More like two, I guess. Along with the cameras, I have my dog, Hazel. She can appear ferocious when she feels like it."

"My Onyx is one fat cat." Jessica loaded a small plate with snacks. "I'm sure he'd just waddle over to an intruder and demand treats. I already have one of those doorbell cameras, but I'm thinking about upgrading to something more."

Amber, who taught at the elementary school, lived south of town. Her husband had made her promise to text him when she was on her way home so he could watch for her car.

"I don't go out of the house at night anymore," Amber admitted as she polished off a cucumber sandwich. "I mean, unless the two of us are going somewhere. I used to haul the trash out to the incinerator, check on the horses and the barn cats, whatever. Always had my phone on me, of course, and we have a yard light. But now?" She shook her head sadly. "No way. Not until this is resolved. Who knows who could be out there in the dark?"

"Well, I think we'll be in good hands tonight." Kate gestured out the window to where a party bus now purred in Stacy's driveway. "You've outdone yourself," she told Lauren. "What a nice ride!"

The small bus was outfitted with padded seats along both sides and two small tables down the middle. A built-in refrigerator had its own ice dispenser and was packed with bottled water. Lauren and Crystal carried on the rest of Stacy's snacks and a second pitcher of mojitos for the ride to the ladies' first stop.

Adelaide Beaufort, one of Melinda's neighbors, was now crafting specialty soaps to sell with her flowers and honey at local farmers markets. Adelaide had created a custom, lavender-based soap for Stacy's table favors; and when the artisan mentioned she'd started offering soap-making events for groups, Stacy had been eager to book a session for her bachelorette party. Tonight's event also included dinner, as the Beauforts had recently installed a brick pizza oven at one end of their patio.

The Beauforts' ultimate goal was to transform their historic farmhouse into a bed-and-breakfast, and the ladies exclaimed with delight as the renovated Queen Anne-style home came into view.

"Look at that gingerbread trim!" Jessica was impressed. "It's like frosting on a cake."

"A lavender-frosted cake," Crystal added, then playfully nudged the bride-to-be. "Even the house coordinates with your theme!"

Stacy laughed. "A lovely coincidence, yes. I can't wait to show you the soaps for the reception tables! Adelaide dropped them off the other day."

The ornate house was just the first of many lovely sights to absorb at this charming farm. Kate spotted two dogs, three cats, a flock of chickens and a potbellied pig before she even stepped foot in the yard. Walt, the ladies' driver, planned to remain with his bus, but Mason Beaufort encouraged him to tag along to the barn for chores.

"The goats are out back with the sheep," Kate heard Mason tell Walt. "They can't get into the front pasture, and they can't get over the fence. So don't worry, they won't tap dance on the hood of your bus."

Goats? Kate made a mental note to ask the Beauforts for tips.

Adelaide's gray-and-auburn braids were wound around her head. She wore a generous apron over her jeans and tee shirt. "Smocks for everyone are waiting downstairs," she assured the ladies as they paused in the thoughtfully renovated kitchen. "Once your soaps are started, I'll work on the pizzas."

"I need that copper exhaust hood," Stacy whispered to Kate as they made their way toward the basement stairwell. "When Ryan and I remodel his kitchen, I want a stove that looks just like Adelaide's."

As Ryan and Stacy both had their own homes, there had been debate over who would sell once they married. Stacy's bungalow was quaint, but small; Ryan's place in Swanton was larger, but older. It needed more work, but would provide enough space for a future family. It was going to be a substantial change for Stacy, who'd poured her heart into decorating her current home.

Adelaide had a second kitchen in the cellar, where a long table was set up with workstations for her guests. While she put the finishing touches on the soap base, which included milk from her goats, the ladies reviewed the countless combinations for the trio of soaps each would create. There were a variety of essential oils to choose from, and stir-ins such as dried citrus peels, flower petals, and herbs.

Kate finally settled on a rosemary-oatmeal blend with a touch of rose petals for color. "I had no idea there were so many options," she told Lauren as they put on their smocks and prepped their molds. "These are going to be perfect in my new powder room once I finally get it finished."

While Lauren and Kate chose oval molds, Kelsey had decided on rectangles. "I'm going to suggest this place for the Social Society," she told the other women as they measured their ingredients into stainless steel bowls. "We're always looking for things to do."

Kelsey and Stacy had met at a yoga class a few years ago, and continued to attend one together, but Kate and Kelsey's social circles had never overlapped until now. Kate had vowed to set the case aside, even for just one night, but this was too good of an opportunity to pass up.

"Some people think it's all older ladies, but that's not true," Kelsey explained when Kate asked about her club membership. "There are few girls around our age. It's fun, first of all; and it's a great way to connect with people, too. I work in an insurance office, and networking is important in my field."

Amber leaned across their corner of the table. "Were you at last week's luncheon? I heard there was some excitement," she added in a near-whisper. "Or at least, there was after the meeting."

Kate smiled as she sprinkled rose petals into her bowl. This was too easy.

"Yes, I was there." Kelsey passed Lauren a container of dried lemon peel. "It's too bad a few of the ladies got sick. I don't see how the caterer could be to blame, much less anything with the center, itself. If either of those had been the problem, we all would have been ill."

"What did everyone bring?" Kate kept her tone light as Adelaide ladled soap base into her mixing bowl. "I can imagine with a group of ladies, of all ages, there was quite the spread."

"We always eat well. That's never a problem."

The ladies had enjoyed the usual fruit and veggie trays,

Kelsey reported, along with cornmeal muffins to kick off the meal. "With the two main dishes catered, the rest of us focused on sides and desserts. I brought my grandma's carrot cake. Oh, and there was an amazing cucumber salad with a creamy dressing. That reminds me, I need to ask Sue for her recipe!"

Another member had brought a spinach-and-strawberry salad; there had also been scalloped corn, calico beans, chocolate-chip cookies, peanut clusters ...

Lauren, who had already heard the rumors through Stacy, raised an eyebrow at Kate as Kelsey wrapped up her recitation of the menu. No wonder some of the ladies had become sick! Sampling such a wide-ranging buffet, especially if someone possessed a geriatric stomach, was a reliable recipe for tummy trouble.

Lauren asked Kelsey if the peanut clusters might have triggered allergic reactions in any of the women.

"Maybe, but I sort of doubt it, since it was obvious there were nuts in them. From what I heard, their symptoms were just the usual problems." Kelsey tipped her head toward the bathroom across the way, and the other women nodded in understanding. "Even so, I leave the walnuts out of Grandma's carrot cake when I take it to a party, for that reason. You just never know."

There were a few other potential culprits among the dishes Kelsey had described, but Kate didn't want to appear overly interested by asking more questions tonight. And while the room was noisy with conversation, there was a possibility Stacy might overhear and be reminded of the rumors about the Prosper community center. That was the last thing the bride-to-be needed. Lauren agreed.

"She has the jitters, in more ways than one." Lauren kept her voice low. "I keep telling her everything's going to be fine." Kate and Kelsey pressed for details, but Lauren didn't have any to share.

"I don't know exactly what's behind it all, she wouldn't say. But as far as the reception goes, I told her I'd hang out in the kitchen myself, make sure the catering staff follows protocol, if that's what it takes. Nothing is going to ruin that celebration."

Kate filled her molds as she kept one eye on her cousin. Stacy was beaming, flushed with happiness, as she chatted with Emily and Jessica. Or was it just the steam from the boiling-hot soap base, coupled with a few cocktails?

It wasn't long before Adelaide announced dinner was ready. Leaving their soaps to cool at their workstations, the women adjourned to the long picnic table on the Beauforts' stone patio.

It was a beautiful evening; a soft breeze wandered across the fields, and a few faint stars appeared in the still-blue sky. Flickering votive candles dotted the table while citronella tapers kept the bugs at bay. Strings of fairy lights twinkled in the grand oak trees that shaded the back of the farmhouse.

The savory pies were layered with fresh goat cheese and sauce crafted from the garden's heirloom tomatoes. Organic vegetables were paired with meats sourced from the area's small-scale livestock herds. A layered strawberry cake topped with three lit sparklers finished off the meal.

By the time the ladies departed for Swanton, with their fresh soap tucked into cardboard boxes, Kate was in a mellow mood. The white-wine sangria Adelaide had offered at dinner was surely part of it, but so was the camaraderie shared by this group of women.

What would it be like to replicate this feeling? Kate wondered as they exited the luxury bus for the second time. Should she take Vanessa up on her year-old offer, and join the Social Society? Kelsey was so friendly; Kate was certain the rest of the group would be the same.

Lauren was eager to expand this evening's circle to include one more person. "Come with us!" she urged Walt.

"I'm sure you're quite the singer."

He chuckled. "Well, my grandchildren might think so. But my wife would tell you the truth." He pulled a digital reader from the tote bag behind his seat. "You girls have fun. Just let me know when you're wrapping up, and I'll be ready to go."

The bar was packed, but that wasn't a problem. Stacy had reserved them a large table right by the stage.

"She thought of everything," Crystal marveled to Kate as they hitched in their chairs. "Swanton may be the county seat, but it's not a large town by any means. I would have had us winging it."

"Stacy doesn't do that." Kate shook her head. "Never has."

"You're right. So, what's Ryan really like? I've yet to meet him, I've only heard about how wonderful he is."

"What you've heard is true. He's a good guy."

There wasn't much else to say. Because while Kate liked her cousin, they weren't super close; and her interactions with Stacy's betrothed had been limited to family outings and holidays. "I just hope she's going to be happy with him."

Maybe it was the sangria, or the mojitos before that, or the false sense of privacy in the darkened bar. But Kate's last statement flew out of her mouth before she could stop it.

Crystal wasn't as shocked as Kate expected her to be.

"She seems ... distracted." Crystal wriggled her left hand, and her own diamond winked in the low light. "But I was, too, when it was my turn. The next two weeks are going to fly by. And then, she can relax. I'm sure it's going to be fine."

Kate had a fleeting, troubled thought about her own wedding. And then another about her divorce. This time, she managed to keep both to herself.

Stacy was helping the server take the table's drink orders and requesting nacho platters and mozzarella sticks. Even now, during the third and final part of her special night, the bride-to-be was still steering the festivities.

While neighboring tables soon figured out this was a

bachelorette party, the rest of the bar was unaware of tonight's celebration. Stacy had begged her friends to ignore the silly trappings of some bachelorette parties, and they'd been happy to comply. There was no special tee shirt, no scrap of white netting pinned to her hair.

Lauren and Kate tracked Stacy's alcohol consumption while bar patrons, mostly in pairs or small groups, took turns on the karaoke stage. Kate played along when their table was up, and sang along, and was soon having more fun with this than she'd expected.

"I should sing a solo," Stacy insisted when their group was on deck again. The guys at the next table overheard this proclamation, and hooted and clapped their approval.

"See?" the bride-to-be told her friends. "My fans are eager for me to take the stage."

Kate motioned her forward. "Why not? Do it!"

"I'm glad she's having fun," Emily said as Stacy started toward the platform. "I don't think I've ever seen this side of my future sister-in-law."

"It's her night to shine." Kelsey cheered and whooped along with the rest of them. "Go, Stace! Make us proud!"

Stacy raised her arms in a victorious gesture once she was in the spotlight. The bar erupted in cheers, and she laughed. She soon had the microphone in one hand and the remote in the other, then flipped through her options on the monitor as patrons in various states of sobriety called out suggestions.

She finally shook her head, then approached the young staffer with a laptop on his table. He stared at her for a second, then shrugged and nodded.

Stacy strolled back to center stage, and gave the bar a huge smile.

"Most of you don't know me, but I wanted you to know: I'm getting married!"

Lauren and Kate exchanged nervous smiles as Stacy soaked up the spotlight. Who was this woman?

Lauren was a little concerned. "I didn't think she was that drunk."

"Let's give her a moment," Kate suggested. "This is her last hurrah. And maybe her only."

A song began to play over the speakers. It sounded familiar, but Kate couldn't place it. And then, she could. And then she gripped the edge of the table in worry.

"This next one's a special song, a special message." Stacy wobbled, just a fraction, as she twirled to study the lyric board.

"He's not here tonight, my beloved. But I realized, just yesterday, that this one hits me right in the feels." She patted her heart with one hand. "It's a song from one of the biggest soundtracks of all time. Ladies, this one is for all of you, and for me!"

Before Kate could set down her wine glass, the opening lyrics of "You Don't Own Me" flashed on the screen. Stacy tossed her hair, gripped the microphone, and launched into the song with great feeling.

"Come on, sing with me!" she egged on the crowd at the first lyrical pause. "I know that you know it!"

While some of the guys in the bar seemed unfamiliar with the tune, many of the women raised a glass or bottle and joined in. Emily was pale and silent at the other end of the table, staring at her future sister-in-law with a shocked expression.

Lauren grabbed Kate's arm. "What the hell? What do we do now?"

"I don't know." Kate noticed the jubilant faces of the ladies all around them. Even the servers were joining in. "I don't know how we cut her off without embarrassing her. And she hates making a faux pas in public."

"Hey, she's really good!" one of the guys at the next table shouted to Kate and Lauren. "Where have I heard this song before?"

Kate was too busy trying to read her cousin's mind to explain the dance-inspired movie so many girls had watched over and over. Or how this song had caused cultural waves when it was released sixty years ago.

"She's more wasted than I thought," Lauren said as Stacy swayed with the music. Thankfully, she was too far from the edge of the platform to topple off it. "If we try to stop her, she's going to fight us. She's as stubborn as a mule."

Kate was suddenly tired and drained. It had been a long week full of ups and downs; at home, at work, and on the case. This party was supposed to be the highlight of it, a chance to unwind. And now, this.

"Three minutes, tops," she muttered to herself as much as to Lauren. "It can't last much longer than that."

Down the way, Emily's phone glowed in the dim light as her fingers flew across its screen. Her forehead knitted with concern while she texted someone. Probably Ryan. Or, no, even worse: the mother of the groom?

The other women at their table seemed rather confused, but they all made an effort to cheer and smile when Stacy's wavering gaze paused on them.

"There's my girls!" she told the crowd as a few instrumental bars swelled through the speakers. Tears, of one form or another, started to flood Stacy's voice.

"My best friends! They're here to help me celebrate one of my last nights of freedom. Give them a big round of applause!"

The room did, and Kate waved back as Lauren urged the other ladies to do the same. Jessica was murmuring something to Crystal, and Kate's mind frantically searched for any positive way to spin this debacle.

"It's the twenty-first century," she chirped when Jessica frowned at her in concern. "Taking a stand for independence is a good thing, right? It doesn't necessarily mean she's unhappy with Ryan."

No one said anything. Kate's last statement hung in the air, a sour note to what had started out as such a fun evening. She quickly took another tactic.

"The crowd is certainly behind her! I'm sure that's why she's leaning into it as much as she is."

Tears were streaming down Stacy's face by the time the song trilled to its final crescendo. The crowd was on its feet, cheering and whistling, and Stacy soaked up the accolades with a sudden smile.

"I'll marry you if he won't!" one drunk guy yelled over the din.

Stacy almost missed the first step down from the stage. A man close by, more sober than some, swiftly moved forward to put a steadying hand on her arm.

The DJ quickly transitioned to his background music, an electro-pop tune that was modern and upbeat.

"What a performance, huh? Let's keep this party rolling! Who's next?"

Kate and Lauren edged through the crowd to meet Stacy halfway to their table, but she made a quick turn and started for the restrooms. By the time they barged through the ladies' room door, another woman was handing Stacy paper towels dampened at the sink. "Here, wipe your face. You're OK, honey. It will be OK."

"I'm not drunk!" Stacy hissed at her friends and the well-meaning stranger before anyone could say anything more. But her slurred words told a different story.

"I'm not going to be sick, and I'm not wasted. I'm just ... I'm so scared!" Stacy slid down the wall until she landed on the tile floor, then closed her eyes as the tears really started to flow.

"Maybe she needs to break it off now," the other woman whispered to Kate before she turned to leave. "If she has a bad feeling about it ..."

Kate simply nodded her thanks to the stranger. She didn't

know what to say, what else to do. She'd had no qualms when she married Ben; not one.

Lauren was on the floor now, brushing Stacy's sweaty hair out of her face. "What's going on? What's wrong?"

"Everything! Nothing!" Stacy put her face in her hands. "I'm supposed to be happy, right? Excited?"

"Do you still love him?" Lauren asked.

Stacy glared at her maid of honor. "Of course I do! I'm marrying him, aren't I?"

The door opened, and Crystal leaned in. "I texted Walt, he's bringing the bus around. I think he was in the middle of a good chapter, and we have him for two more hours, but …"

"I want to go home," Stacy said. "Why are you all staring at me like that? Can't I just go home?"

Finally, a question Kate could answer.

"Yes." She helped her cousin get on her feet. "And the sooner we leave, the better."

* 12 *

"Stand back," Kate warned her friends as they lingered on the concrete stoop of the old chicken house. "I haven't been in here for a few days. A wild critter might dash out the door when it swings open."

Melinda and Karen didn't seem too concerned. "I have a woodchuck living under my coop again this summer," Melinda reported. "Or should I say, a whole family. The little ones are so cute!"

"They won't be when they start stealing your wild black raspberries," Karen reminded her. "You'll be lucky to get a handful for yourself once they ripen."

Melinda sighed. "I'm resigned to that. It's the cost of living in the country."

Kate wanted to push up her long sleeves in the humid air, but knew better. The inside of the coop was dirty and dusty; the last thing she needed was a nasty rash or bug bite.

Or more trouble of any sort, come to think of it.

Especially when there was so much to do to get ready for the goats' arrival late next week. And then, there was the fact that Kate was exhausted, and perhaps a bit hungover, from last night's bachelorette party.

The celebration had ended on a vastly different note from how it started. Once on the bus, Crystal and Kate had kept the mindless chatter flowing while Jessica and Kelsey made sure Emily stayed as far away from Stacy as possible. Lauren had kept her focus on the distraught bride-to-be; luckily, Stacy hadn't needed the trash can Walt settled at her feet before he got back behind the wheel.

It was a relief when Emily, who hadn't had more than a glass of wine the entire night, hastily made her goodbyes once they returned to Stacy's house. Amber had made sure their bar snacks were transferred to carryout containers, and steered the other ladies out to Stacy's deck for food, water, and coffee before anyone else left.

Stacy had been sick after she got home; but even through her alcohol-induced suffering, she'd remained stubbornly tight-lipped about what was wrong between her and Ryan. All Kate and Lauren could get out of her was that their upcoming wedding meant too much change, and too fast, and she didn't want to talk about it anymore.

Thinking about last night made Kate's head pound. And it was only nine in the morning; how could it be so miserably hot out here?

Was the sun always this vicious at this hour? A line of oak trees somewhat shaded the chicken coop, but ...

"Drink up." Karen shoved a bottle of electrolyte water into Kate's hands while Melinda fearlessly opened the coop door and wedged it against the weathered wall boards with a brick.

"I'm impressed you're up and about this morning," Karen told Kate with a wry grin, "after what happened last night. In more ways than one, I might add. How much sleep did you get?"

Kate shrugged. "Four hours, maybe five?" She made sure the bottle was tightly capped before she set it on the ground, as Maggie and Jerry were eyeing it with curiosity. "I'm so glad both of you could come today, help me out. I know it's Father's Day, and we all have plans later. The sooner we start, the sooner we'll be done."

Hazel suddenly appeared from around the side of the garage. She dashed through the open doorway of the coop, making excited noises while her tail worked overtime, as the women hung back at the entrance.

"Oh, dear." Melinda looked around at the cobweb-frosted walls, then up toward the offset pitch of the tall ceiling. Far above them was a second row of grimy windows they couldn't reach. "This coop is huge. And it's going to be a huge amount of work, too."

While the interior walls had been regularly whitewashed years ago, they had since faded to a dull gray. Applying a liquid lime mixture would keep the building cleaner, deter bugs, and neutralize odors, but there was no time for that. Besides, the goats were only staying for a week, and would spend most of their time outdoors.

The Kleiner family, and then the Trowbridges once Minnie married Will and they took over this farm, had raised dozens of chickens each year for their meat-and-egg business. Rows of weathered nesting boxes still lined the long wall opposite the main windows, and wooden perches were everywhere.

So was the dirt. And bits of old straw. And a few random pieces of junk that had been left behind when the now-widowed Minnie put her longtime home on the market.

Even so, Karen nodded her approval. "This works perfectly for what you need. I'll get that roll of chicken-wire mesh; it's in the back of my truck."

"Chicken wire?" Kate asked Melinda as Karen turned away. Hazel paused her sniffing to consider whether she should follow Karen, but decided to keep investigating the coop. "Chicken wire for goats?"

"It's for the windows on this lower row," Melinda explained. The south wall consisted of modern storm windows whose lower sashes slid up to reveal screens. "So the goats don't jump through them."

Kate closed her eyes for a moment as she imagined the devastation that would bring. "This is common, I'm guessing? Sometimes they vandalize property?"

"Karen says so, and she would know." Melinda laughed at Kate's stunned expression. "You're in for some interesting days, I'm guessing. Those goats are going to pour out of that trailer like clowns from a clown car. But Adam's not bringing them until sometime next week, right? Are you having second thoughts?"

"No, because I can't." Kate shook her head. "I need to get this done. Everything's set up already. I paid my deposit. It's too late to back out."

Stacy, she realized, had uttered nearly the same words last night, several times over.

Kate tossed up her hands in frustration. "You've seen that pasture; it's a jungle. A prairie jungle. One that I need to get under control."

Karen soon returned with the roll of mesh, and two cats trailing behind. "Scout and Patches want to help. Maybe there were still chickens here when Patches was a kitten; it makes you wonder what she remembers. How old is she, do you know?"

While the big tuxedo cat was still exploring outside the coop, the calico had marched right in, tail up, to join Hazel.

"Minnie's family thinks Patches is about four years old, and that makes sense. Old enough that her birthplace made such an impression on her, but young enough that she was able to hike back here like she did."

Karen shook her head in awe as she set down the roll of mesh. "I was impressed when you told me about her journey. It's amazing how cats can find their way like that. Dogs, too."

"Since you're the critter expert, give it to me straight." Kate reached for one of the old brooms she'd brought out from the garage. "What can I expect from these goats? The owner says they're pretty well behaved, that they won't give me any trouble as long as they have room to roam, water, and shelter."

"He did, huh?" Karen barked out a laugh. "Well, he knows his crew best, I guess. That pasture is going to keep them busy, so they shouldn't get bored. That's certainly in your favor; boredom is when the trouble could start."

She pulled a respirator and wrap-around goggles from a tote, and handed them to Kate. "If you're going to sweep the underside of the roof, knock down all that dirt and cobwebs, you'll want to wear these."

Kate had assigned herself that task, the worst one in her opinion, so her friends wouldn't volunteer for it. But even with all the windows thrown open to the hot breeze, and the back door as well as the front, the shed still turned into a dust bowl. Kate suggested Karen and Melinda carry out the junk, which would give them breaks from the dirty air, until the top sections of the coop were brushed down. Sweeping the floor was a piece of cake by comparison.

As the ladies worked, Kate gave the coop a careful evaluation. She found only a few pinpricks of light on the underside of the roof, so there weren't many gaps in the shingles. The floor was almost as sound; maybe five spots needed a scrap of plywood nailed over them for stability.

"If you had animals in here all year round," Karen proclaimed as she measured the windows, "you'd want to snug up that roof. But it's really in excellent shape. This is going to be a grand place for goats for a few days."

"Maybe you'll decide to get your own," Melinda teased as she helped Karen unroll the wire mesh. "This might be so much fun, you won't want them to leave."

Kate's broom came to a halt. "Yeah, right." In the barely controlled chaos, she'd forgotten to sweep out the old nesting boxes. "I might want the same goat crew to visit next summer, but that's it. Patches, what did you find? Do I even want to know?"

The calico had been shooed out with Hazel before the dirty work began, but she'd returned once the dust started to settle. A few more squeaks came from behind the last stack of chicken crates, and then Patches appeared with a fat mouse in her jaws and a triumphant gleam in her eyes.

"Good girl!" Kate was proud; especially because the Three Mouseketeers were enjoying the shade of an oak tree, either asleep or pretending to be.

"Does she go inside to visit the kittens?" Melinda was curious. "Or is that over and done with?"

"Patches is a hands-off mom these days, has been since the babies were weaned. She's enjoying the outdoor life with Scout and his gang."

Karen snipped off a section of wire mesh. They would install it on the outside of the coop, so Kate could still raise and lower the bottom window sashes. "Wouldn't it be great if Minnie's granddaughter took the other two kittens? When is she coming to see them?"

Kate had been surprised, and pleased, to get a text from Nicole on Friday asking about Patches' babies.

"In a week or so, I think." Kate was trying not to get her hopes up. "She and her husband, and their kids, too. They want to be sure Ophelia and Romeo are a good fit, and so do I. And I have a feeling the Fairlaines will take Hamlet and Juliet. Oh, I forgot to tell you: Minnie might come out here with her granddaughter."

Karen and Melinda gasped in surprise and delight.

"You haven't met her yet, right?" Karen dropped her wire cutters to the floor and turned to face Kate. "And she certainly hasn't been back here since she moved to town."

"Yep. This will be the first time. I wrote her that letter when I made my offer, but everything was signed electronically."

What would Minnie think of her longtime home these days? Kate had big plans for the house's outdated finishes, but hadn't had the time or money to make too many changes yet. Adding a downstairs bathroom had been her biggest project by far.

The former pantry was down to the plaster walls, which were pockmarked with holes from where the old shelves and their brackets had been removed. Contractor Richard Everton and his sons were coming in a few days to run plumbing lines to the tiny room. Then, Richard would install the new sink and toilet that waited patiently in the garage.

Kate was excited to wrap up the renovations, but wondered how Minnie might feel about the destruction of the old pantry. Her friends shrugged off her concerns.

"It's your house now, and she knows that," Melinda proclaimed as she helped Karen cut another section of wire mesh. "I worried, too, when I took over at my place; but Horace and the rest of the Schermanns welcomed the improvements I made. He and Wilbur hadn't been able to do much as they aged."

"I know, I know." Kate watched Patches carry her trophy out the back door of the coop. "And besides, I think Minnie's really coming to see her calico girl. I'm glad the family finally told her Patches had returned. They didn't want to upset her, at first."

"I get it." Karen nodded. "Do you think there's any chance Patches will want to go home with Minnie?"

Patches was free to leave; she had weaned the kittens, and her spay surgery had gone well. Kate had braced herself on several mornings against the possibility of finding only the Three Mouseketeers waiting for her when she entered the machine shed, food bucket in hand.

"I think she loved Minnie, but she's her own cat." Kate reached for a snow shovel to gather up the last of the floor debris. "She walked all those miles just to get home, it meant that much to her. Which humans were living here wasn't her main motivation."

Then she laughed. "And if Minnie visits us, Patches will have to drop her suspicions that I bumped off her best friend and stole this acreage by underhanded means."

She explained the glares Patches sometimes sent her way when the cat thought Kate wasn't paying attention.

"You never know what they are thinking." Melinda picked up one end of a piece of chicken wire, and Kate reached for the other while Karen prepped her staple gun. "I have four at my farm, and they're rather mysterious when they want to be."

"Dogs are pretty simple," Karen said once they were outside the coop. "They're the easier of the two, for sure." She gestured at the bank of windows. "Let's get this mesh on here."

Hazel followed them back through the front door to sniff the now-swept floor. The shed wasn't sparkling clean, but it was greatly improved. And good enough for a bunch of rascally goats.

"It's much better." Kate grinned with relief, as she was beyond ready for a break. "Quite the transformation! It'll be nice for this building to get used again."

"But hopefully not too much." Melinda eyed the perch poles and nesting boxes. "Will the goats mess with that stuff?" she asked Karen. "Tear them up?"

"I don't think they'll be tempted by those. You know," Karen told Kate, "some of that junk we put out back could be useful. Once they chew down a section of the pasture, you could drag those chicken crates and old pallets out there. The goats would love to jump around on them. Do you have any old tires? A beach ball, even?"

There were a few left-behind truck tires in the machine shed. It was a great idea.

"I have a few things around here, sure. And Adam said his goats have several balls they really like. They take them everywhere."

Melinda laughed. "They're bringing their own toys? How cute!"

Other than hauling out the garbage bags of dust and debris, there wasn't much left to do in the chicken house. Adam would set up his own electric fencing to give the goats a path from the back door of the shed to the pasture gate, as well as construct a safe perimeter around the native plants along the creek. Bryan and Dad were bringing the water tanks over next weekend, and would help Kate spread fresh straw in the coop.

"Let's get up to the house." Kate pulled off her dusty chore gloves. "I can't wait to get out of this hot sun."

The ladies were so dirty that they decided to rest in the front porch's deep shade rather than in the kitchen. Karen and Melinda settled on the swing, and Kate passed around iced tea and oatmeal-raisin cookies before she dropped into a metal chair with a weary sigh.

She had to be at her parents' farm by four. They were grilling out this evening to celebrate Father's Day, which was extra special now that Bryan was also a dad. Kate was supposed to bring a salad, and she vowed to whip up something that could safely sit around at room temperature. But first, she would need a long nap once Karen and Melinda went home.

"So, what exactly happened last night?" Karen asked before she took a bite of her cookie. "From what little you said, it sounds like there was some serious drama."

Kate gave her friends the rundown. The more she thought about it, the more troubling last night's events seemed.

What if Stacy's worries went beyond the usual pre-wedding jitters? The celebration was only two weeks away now. Would there be an opportunity for Kate to help her cousin find clarity between now and then? Would Stacy even be receptive to such a heart-to-heart talk?

"That's a tough one." Melinda allowed Scout to jump onto

her lap. Unlike Hazel, who was trying to snag a cookie, the cat only asked for attention. "I called off my wedding, as you both know. It was so long ago, now; it feels like forever. It's like they say: water under the bridge."

Then she gave a rueful chuckle. "I'm not even standing on the same bridge these days, haven't been for a few years. It just feels like a bad dream."

Melinda recalled how several friends and family members had offered well-intentioned advice. But none of it mattered in the end.

"It was up to me, and only me, to decide what to do." She wrapped her arms around Scout. "It was hard, but I broke it off." Then she smiled. "And in the end, I got a whole new life. The right one."

"Marrying Ben felt like the right thing to do," Kate said quietly. "I had no qualms whatsoever. And look how that turned out. Can we ever really see what lies ahead?"

Karen scuffed her dusty sneaker on the porch floorboards, setting the swing into motion. "There's no way to know what's right." And then she sighed. "I don't know if Eric and I are going to make it."

Melinda and Kate gasped in surprise and sympathy.

"What?" Melinda leaned in. "I didn't know ..."

"I haven't said anything, that's why." Karen stared at the field across the road. "It's not terrible, there are no big deal-breakers. It's just that we keep talking about moving in together, and we never get around to it. I'm not sure what I want, the longer this goes on. Maybe we aren't as compatible as I'd like us to be."

"Or maybe you're just used to having your own place and space," Melinda said. "I mean, look at me and Josh."

"He has his son," Karen countered. "At least, part of the time. It makes a difference. Eric and I, well, we don't have that to manage."

"Do you think you'll marry Josh?" Kate asked Melinda.

"You two seem so happy, so well matched."

"I don't know. Everyone expects it, and we've talked about it. But I think we're both content with how things are." She turned to Kate. "So, what about Alex?"

"Oh, you mean, 'he who roams at night?' We're lucky if we see each other a few times a week. Our schedules couldn't be more different. I'm up with the chickens, even though I don't have any. And he's hanging with the night owls."

Karen was laughing so hard, she had tears in her eyes. "You make him sound like a vampire, or something."

Kate had to join in. "Well, OK, it's not *that* bad. But it's hard. We're still getting to know each other, I guess."

"There's no rush," Melinda insisted. "You have your own life, your own place. We all do. It makes a difference."

"Things are good, and that's what matters." Kate took a gulp of her tea, then held her glass out of Jerry's reach.

"I know you've both heard what happened to Marie Lindgren. Or should I say, you've heard things about Marie that aren't exactly true. Bev and I are trying to get to the bottom of it. And that's put me in a tough spot with Alex."

Melinda and Karen listened with rapt attention as Kate explained her suspicions about Marie and the Social Society meeting. How she'd obtained the incident report. Her hunch that Marie was poisoned. The conversation she had with Alex last Sunday regarding the case.

"Basically, I lied to him." Kate gave a resigned shrug. "And I'm not sure if, or when, I should tell him the truth."

"Oh, I hadn't thought of it that way," Karen said. "Yeah, he's Ray's cousin. It certainly puts him between the two of you."

"It sounds like the police chief thinks you're helping him," Melinda offered.

"And you are, but this could also expose him as lazy, or worse. He wants everyone to know this wasn't a burglary; that one way or the other, Marie 'made it all up.'" Melinda added air quotes to her last comment. "But he obviously lacks the nerve to do it himself."

Karen raised her eyebrows at Kate. "What are you going to do? Where do you look next?"

"I have no idea."

The postal carriers were keeping their ears to the ground, just as Roberta had promised Chief Calcott they would. But none of them, other than Bev, knew the truth as Kate did. They hadn't turned up any gossip that was useful to the case, which made sense given the real circumstances.

No one broke into Marie's house. No one physically assaulted her. The real crime, if there even was one, likely occurred during the Social Society's meeting at the Prosper community center.

"If someone else is behind what happened to this poor woman," Kate told her friends, "even if it wasn't intentional? We owe it to Marie to figure it out."

The ladies sat in silence for a few minutes, as if gearing themselves up to tackle the last of their goat-preparation chores. And then, Melinda had an idea.

"I know you're looking closely at the women in the Social Society, but there are a few men that I'm sure would love to help with this investigation." She turned toward Karen. "What do you think? Should Kate recruit the hardware-store coffee group to help with this case?"

"Absolutely! Two are Prosper city leaders, another can't keep his nose out of anything, and all of them are big cheerleaders for little Prosper. No one wants to see the community center in jeopardy."

"What day are you off this week?" Melinda asked Kate as the ladies collected their empty glasses. "They gather just before seven. Be sure to bring treats."

✳ **13** ✳

The parcel now waited on Bertha's front seat, an advance in the lineup from that morning's rounds. Kate eyed it again as she paused at the next rural crossroads.

"It's just a box," she reminded herself for what had to be the tenth time since Bev, with a raised eyebrow and a grin, had added it to Kate's delivery pile. Marge was off today, and Kate had her route north of town.

"I don't know what's in it, and I don't need to know. What's important is the person who will receive this delivery."

Lucille Robertson lived in the next mile, if Kate remembered correctly. If not, the one after that. This was the far-northwest corner of the Eagle River zip code; another mile out, and the Robertsons would have a Prosper address. But what mattered most to Kate and Bev was that Lucille was a member of the Eagle River Social Society.

"She prides herself on being involved in the community," Bev had whispered to Kate in the back room of the post office. "Audrey Schultz is her bestie, and Audrey has been the club treasurer for several years now. If Lucille wasn't at that meeting herself, she still knows what went down."

Bev had assured Kate that a simple "how are you doing?" would elicit a litany of woes from Lucille. And then, after commiserating with the older woman, Kate could express sympathy for what Marie was going through. The floodgates were sure to open.

"But this whole plan hinges on Lucille being home." Kate pulled away from a neighbor's mailbox, and started up the slight hill to the Robertsons' farm. "I sure hope she is."

The tan clapboard house sat rather close to the road, which was unusual given that most farmhouses were tucked at the ends of long lanes. Her home's location allowed Lucille to keep a close eye on the comings and goings in her rural neighborhood.

"She can just about read license plates from her front porch," Kate noted as she turned into the driveway. "That would come in handy, if she couldn't identify someone outright by their vehicle."

The home's significant age was visible in its narrow windows and ornate roof brackets. But the porch railings were painted a fresh white, and its light-gray floor betrayed not one dirty boot print. A maroon farm truck and a navy car, both boasting dried-mud undercarriages, rested just steps from the front porch. A brown dog of indeterminate breeding lifted its head when Kate cut Bertha's engine, but didn't seem inclined to leave the patch of sun by the steps.

Kate's curiosity kicked into high gear as she realized the odds were very good that Lucille was home. Slight movement inside the door's glass, as if a curtain had been pushed aside to give someone a better look, all-but confirmed this was true.

Which meant Kate was surprised when she rang the bell and was greeted by ... no one.

"Post office!" she called out.

The dog had finally asked for a pet, and was now sniffing Kate's left shorts pocket. It was the one stocked with doggie treats. Just as Kate started to juggle the package and a handful of letters to reward her new friend, the inside door flew open.

"Mercy me!" The woman's white hair was pulled up in a

loose bun, which was flattering to her narrow face. Her button-down blouse looked freshly pressed, and matched her sensible sandals. "Sparky can't have those. He's on a special diet; no complex carbs!"

Kate could have explained how the treats were from the top-line brand at the Prosper co-op, and worth every penny, but didn't bother. Lucille had already handed down her decree.

"Sorry." Kate put the pouch away, and gave Lucille an apologetic smile. "He seems like such a good boy."

"He is." Lucille eyed Kate closely. "And you are ..."

"I'm Kate Duncan." She handed over the parcel and the letters with another smile. "You're Lucille, I take it?"

"Of course! And you're Ida Burberry's granddaughter."

The triumph in Lucille's tone made Kate wonder if the woman half-expected Kate to challenge that notion, or praise her for her intelligence.

Kate didn't take the bait. "Yes. What a lovely day! How are you doing?"

Many folks would offer a simple answer to that question. But Lucille had much to say.

Her right hip was still bothering her, especially before a rainstorm. And there'd been so many of those lately! Her garden was filling in with weeds because of it, and it was harder this year to crouch down and pull those little rascals on her own.

"Donald could help me more than he does." Lucille rolled her eyes. "But then, his ulcer is flaring up again. That takes the pep right out of him, for sure. He's supposed to be resting, the doctor says."

"I'm sorry to hear that." Kate decided to cut to the chase, as it might take fifteen minutes to hear the full list of Lucille's woes. "I'm feeling bad for Marie Lindgren, too. It sounds like she's still in the hospital."

"I've heard the same. Can you imagine?"

Lucille switched to a whisper, even though no one else was around. Except Sparky, and he was once again nearly asleep on the sidewalk.

"You're sitting in your own home, watching your shows or whatever, and a masked intruder bursts through your front door and tackles you to the floor!" Lucille gasped. "I'm sure this evil man, whoever he is, was after all the money Marie keeps in that safe."

Kate had heard nothing about cash stashed in Marie's house. "She doesn't trust the banks, then?"

Lucille shrugged. "Who knows? Floyd was the one who insisted on that." She nodded with certainty. "Oh, yes; he was tight-fisted with his dollars, that one. But then, he made a small fortune with that real estate *business* of his."

Kate noted the sarcasm, but let Lucille roll on.

"I told our daughter and son-in-law, several times: You don't want to work with Floyd Lindgren. Find another agent! They're everywhere you look, even around here. Why they used him to buy their place all those years ago is beyond me. You wouldn't believe the problems they found in that house once they closed!"

Kate understood real estate enough to know the blame for such issues ultimately landed on the seller, not the agent; and "buyer beware" was wise advice when purchasing property. What she found interesting was Lucille's less-than-rosy view of Floyd, and perhaps Marie by association.

Kate hadn't known either of the Lindgrens well, but she couldn't recall a bad word spoken against either of them. Until today.

"Did other people have bad experiences with Floyd?" she asked mildly.

"Oh my, yes! Sure, the Lindgrens donated an awful lot of money to charities over the years, including the Eagle River Social Society's causes. You've heard of it, my dear?"

There was a hint of challenge in Lucille's tone.

"Of course! Are you a member?"

"I've given several decades of service to the club," Lucille said proudly. "But, oh, about the money. It's no wonder Marie and Floyd always had extra cash for this or that. He'd pinch a penny until it squealed, that one. Would haggle someone mercilessly to save himself a few bucks, if he could. It was all about the *win*, you see. But Marie paid a high price for being with a man who was that successful. He couldn't keep it zipped, if you know what I mean."

Kate only nodded.

"You can't blame Marie for stepping out on him like she did." Lucille's tone was suddenly much more sympathetic. "He was always out and about, all hours of the day and night. Realtors are like that, you know. Poor Marie! She never knew if his absences were due to business or pleasure." Then Lucille chuckled. "Maybe both!"

This was more information than Kate had expected to hear; she'd process it later. For now, she tried to steer Lucille toward the recent club meeting.

"I hear the June luncheon is the highlight of the club's calendar. Were you able to attend this year?"

"We were out of town. How I hated to miss it! But I heard it was a wonderful time, as always; and the meal was splendid! It's the one time of the year that we do things properly, the way they used to be. The club has leaned more into the 'fun,' rather than 'fundraising,' the last how-many years."

Lucille's mother and one of her grandmothers had been active in the club. She was rather nostalgic about how things were done back in the day, when everyone dressed up for the monthly meetings that were held in members' homes. The focus then was squarely on philanthropy, she informed Kate, not the "running around and being silly" that today's younger members considered a priority.

"I know people can donate online these days." Lucille

waved that away with one hand. "But the Social Society has always been an important part of the culture around here, and we need to take that seriously."

It was becoming clear that Lucille didn't have anything of note to share about the luncheon, but Kate decided this extended stop was still worth her time. The older woman's chitchat about the inner dynamics of the club could come in handy when trying to pinpoint a suspect.

"I can see how different priorities could cause strain among the members." She gave Lucille a sympathetic nod. "Have there been times when they couldn't agree on a project?"

"Absolutely! We're down to maybe two charitable drives a year. A lot of this really started to change when Marie was president, by the way."

Marie had held the top spot in the club for six years, and had remained an officer until about a decade ago, Lucille reported. During that time, she had been vocal about declining some of the charitable proposals presented by certain members of the Social Society.

"Some of the ladies were pretty upset. But Marie kept reminding us veteran members that we needed to evolve to attract the younger ladies. I have to say, she was right about that. That club has been around for over one hundred-and-fifty years, in one form or another. We can't let the ship go down while we're still at the helm."

Kate was eager to hear who'd had their feathers ruffled, but decided to take a step back. In the coming days, Lucille's stream of gossip was likely to include the chatty, curious carrier who'd brought the mail on Marge's day off, and how she'd asked oh-so-many questions about the society, Marie, and its other members.

Discretion, and perhaps deception, would be needed if Kate and Bev were going to comb through the club's ranks without setting off alarm bells. The last thing they needed was for the perpetrator to realize someone was on their trail.

"I'm glad to hear the Social Society is thriving," Kate said before she turned to leave. "You can all be proud of what you've accomplished over the years. And let's hope Marie feels better soon."

* * *

As she piloted Bertha from one farm lane to the next, Kate sifted through the crumbs of information Lucille had tossed out on her porch.

If Marie had indeed been poisoned, it had to be personal. And after the earful of speculation Kate had just received, she had to admit she barely knew Marie at all. That needed to change if Kate could have any hope of getting to the bottom of this situation.

But where could she find those answers? Who might be willing to enlighten her while keeping to themselves what Kate told them in return?

As she continued with her route that afternoon, Kate decided to approach Kyle Gibson, the director of the Eagle River Public Library.

Kyle was a younger, newer resident who didn't seem to feed his observations and conversations into the town's gossip mill. Even better, Kate knew he'd been befriended by Marie. The longtime library volunteer had stepped forward last year to help Kyle, who'd moved from Cedar Rapids with his young family, settle in at his new post after the previous director moved away.

Marie was a longtime pillar of the community, and Floyd had been the same. But no one was perfect; like most people, they'd surely made some missteps in life. And it was now clear that fallout from Marie's relationships, of one form or another, was likely behind this attack.

She started with the idea of jealousy playing a role in what happened to Marie.

Whether the Lindgrens had made joint professional decisions, or Marie had simply helped her husband with his bookkeeping, the region's residents had seen them as a team. Some people assumed realtors were shady and untrustworthy because they only worked on commission. That might account for some of the hostility toward Floyd, but could extend to include Marie as well.

Thanks to her husband's success, Marie had enjoyed a wealth of freedom and free time that few people could count on. She had been a stay-at-home mom when their two children were young, a traditional way of life that had become a luxury for many as the cost of living skyrocketed over the years. Even once their son and daughter were out of school, Marie had been able to accept a part-time volunteer position at the library, rather than having to find a job that helped pay the bills.

The Lindgrens' apparent financial wealth and untraditional work schedules, in turn, were what allowed them to give so much back to the community. Having a high public profile surely brought in more clients for Floyd's business, but it had also given both Lindgrens access to a wider social network than most people enjoyed.

Which brought Kate to Lucille's gossip about infidelity. Of course, Floyd had already been gone for a few years now; and at eighty, Kate suspected any dalliances Marie may have enjoyed were long over, as well. But it was also true that resentment could simmer for years. Had someone been biding their time, looking for the perfect chance to strike?

✳ ✳ ✳

The Eagle River Public Library had always been one of Kate's favorite buildings in her hometown. It was one of the historic Carnegie libraries, with generous windows, wide front steps, and a bracketed tile roof. As she pulled open one of its heavy front doors, she was met by the refreshing coolness the library always offered on scorching summer days.

While the change in temperature was welcome, Kate had to tamp down her expectations for what she might uncover inside the library this afternoon. Kyle would be receptive to what Kate wanted to discuss with him, she was sure of that; but there was a chance he wouldn't have leads to share.

As for where she'd go from there, who she might approach next ... Kate would deal with that later.

Before she approached Kyle, she had another, if related, errand within the library's stacks. Kate was still considering how best to approach that task when she saw Chief Calcott striding in her direction.

He'd already spotted her, of course, lingering just inside the entrance with a canvas tote bag in one hand and her purse in the other. Kate hadn't bothered to change at the post office; like the police chief, she was still in uniform.

Ray Calcott gave her a small smile as he approached. But there was a knowing look in his eyes, as well. A bit of friendliness, too; and perhaps a hint of triumph?

She would like to see some gratitude, but maybe that was too much to ask for.

"Kate," was all he said as he edged past her with a nod, never slowing his stride as he neared the doors.

She nodded back. "Chief."

What Kate really wanted to say was more along the lines of, "when are you going to tell everyone that no one broke into Marie's house?"

But Calcott had already passed through the vestibule and out into the sunshine.

What a strange coincidence it was to run into the police chief at the library, given the reasons for Kate's errand. If she'd been forced to admit it, she was feeling a bit paranoid after an online search she'd attempted last night at home.

As she started toward the bank of catalog-search computers, Kate reminded herself it was impossible for Eagle

River's law-enforcement leader to have any idea what she was up to this afternoon. So, what was Calcott doing here? This didn't seem like a place he'd hang out at much, if at all. But the library was one of Eagle River's handful of public buildings. Really, she shouldn't be so suspicious.

But wasn't that the only way she was going to solve this case?

Her fingers hesitated over the keyboard as she inwardly cringed over what she wanted to type into the search field. The guy at the next station was focused on the screen in front of him, a stack of books already next to his elbow on the counter. He would have to make a serious effort to get even a glimpse at what she was doing. But still ...

Kate turned away and aimed for the nonfiction stacks, then browsed until she found the medical section. There was more to peruse than she'd expected. For being in a small town, and having a tight budget, the Eagle River Public Library had an impressive array of titles on its shelves.

Even so, Kate wasn't sure any of these books could offer what she needed. Maybe she should check the natural history section? Or gardening? Or ...

"Hey, Kate." Kyle appeared at the end of the row, two books in the crook of his arm and a packed-full wheeled cart in front of him. "Can I help you find something?"

There was no easy way into this conversation. Kate made sure no one else was near, then leaned over the cart of books.

"I'm looking for information on, well ... if you wanted to poison someone, how would you do it? I mean with a plant or weed, something natural like that. What might you use?"

Kyle's eyes registered surprise, even though his overall expression remained carefully neutral. As a library director, he was used to fielding wide-ranging requests from patrons.

"I'm not going to try it," Kate added quickly. "I would never! But I'd like to find out how. I tried to look it up online, and the search engine's chat bots refused to give me any information. They urged me not to hurt myself or someone else, and then showed me the phone number for the poison control center."

She shook her head in frustration. "I kept looking, of course. I tried to ferret out something from the search results themselves. But I only found information about native plants that could sicken animals, especially livestock."

Kyle considered the situation while she rambled to a halt. "Well, this is a new one for me."

"I feel so weird even asking. I didn't even want to type it into the catalog." She gestured toward the bank of computers. "And I would never check anything out! I'd just look at it here."

"Your list of borrowed library materials is not public record," Kyle assured her. "Never has been. Someone would have to get a warrant, or something of that nature, to force us to reveal it."

A smirk played at one corner of his mouth. "You're not concerned the police are going to ... get involved in whatever's going on, right?"

The irony of Kyle's question made Kate want to roll her eyes. Because from what Kate could gather, Chief Calcott seemed determined to stay as far away from this case as possible.

"Don't worry, I'm not going to be on their radar."

Or at least, Kate hoped that was true. But the way Calcott looked at her just moments ago said she wasn't completely off the chief's mind these days.

"The truth is, I wish they'd get more involved in something. That's why I'm here."

She leaned closer, and Kyle did the same.

"It's about Marie Lindgren," she whispered. "I need to talk to you about it. I know you know her, better than I do. Something's not right; I mean, about what happened that night at her house. I got a copy of the incident report and, well … things aren't what they seem to be. Not at all."

Kyle tipped his head toward the other side of the library. "Meet me in the office in a few minutes."

Kate wandered in that direction, then busied herself at the hallway water fountain. Once Kyle arrived, she took the chair across from his desk as he closed the door behind them.

"I knew it!" he said to himself as much as to Kate. "The whole thing feels so … odd. And they haven't caught the guy. Not one person saw anything, or had anything on their doorbell camera, as far as I've heard."

"There was no intruder. I'm certain about that."

Kate wished she had her copy of the police report handy, but it was tucked away at home. Kyle was going to have to take her word for what she told him next. Thankfully, she knew him well enough to think he would.

As she explained what was in the paperwork she'd obtained from Chief Calcott, Kyle was surprised, of course; and then, he was visibly frustrated.

"Poor Marie! That's terrible!" He crossed his arms. "Calcott was just here, not fifteen minutes ago, and didn't say one word about this to me."

Kyle had contacted the police chief because several senior-aged patrons had expressed concerns about home safety after what happened at Marie's house.

"We're always looking for ways to serve the community, offer relevant programming. I'd suggested a short forum where he or Officer Bevins shared safety tips to put residents' minds at ease. People are still talking about it even though as of tomorrow, it'll be two weeks since the … incident."

Kate surmised Kyle had been about to use the word "burglary," but stopped himself just in time.

"The chief was very eager to set something up. Sure, it'll be useful information, no matter what's going on with Marie. But he had several opportunities to enlighten me, and he didn't."

"I wondered why he was here," Kate said, then explained her hunch about the police chief's motives.

"So he's balancing the community's concerns with the fact that Marie made this up, one way or another." Kyle nodded slowly as he considered this. "And you think she might have been poisoned, given the symptoms she experienced? Who would do such a thing, and to Marie, of all people?"

"I don't know. But that's what I'm trying to find out."

Kyle turned toward his monitor and started to type. "Hmm. Looking through the catalog, I'm not sure we have what you need. Yeah, 'native plants of Iowa' is about the closest topic. But you can find that on the internet, like you said."

Kate shook her head. "I've never had a search engine give me a warning message like that. Every click online is tracked these days, one way or another. I half-expected to see a sheriff's deputy roll up my driveway."

"I'd feel the same! But I doubt the chat bots actually care if you're plotting to off someone. It's just that their masters don't want to risk being sued if something happened. So, what do you want to know about Marie? I'll help if I can."

Kate didn't reveal her source, but gave a general explanation of the gossip Lucille had shared earlier that afternoon.

"It's the best tip I have at this point, and it's not much. There would have to be someone in the Social Society who has it in for Marie. And bad enough that they'd try to make her sick, or worse."

"I haven't heard any of that. But then, we're still new to town, even though it's been just over a year now. And, I hate to say it; but I'm a guy, so ..."

"No offense taken. You're right, the ladies love their gossip."

The library director tapped a pen on his desk as he mulled over the situation.

"I wonder who it might be? Marie has never said a bad word about anyone. To me, at least. What I know of her is what you've heard; she's kind and friendly, and seems well-liked by everyone. But of course, people are complicated. And you think this might have something to do with Floyd?"

Kyle had never met Marie's husband, but his friendship with Marie meant he was knowledgeable about the Lindgrens' specific roles in the community.

Most of what the library director had to share were things Kate had heard or suspected, but one observation about the couple's business dealings did catch her attention. Not because it hinted at scandal; in fact, it was the opposite. While Floyd and Marie had regularly donated money to various causes, they had also taken action years ago to save a piece of Eagle River history.

The Lindgrens purchased the land that included the town's vacant train depot for next to nothing, Kyle reported, possibly at a sheriff's sale or via other channels after the railroad halted passenger-train service through Eagle River.

Marie had mentioned there was a trust set up for her and Floyd's financial affairs, and Kyle believed the Lindgrens still owned the depot. Their son Scott, who had been in Cedar Rapids for many years, was the trustee; their daughter and her family lived out of state.

"I don't know what they planned to do with the building. If I remember it right, Floyd bought it almost on a lark. It was a sentimental purchase, I guess, given its history and the fact no one else wanted it."

"Maybe Floyd thought he could find a buyer," Kate suggested, "and turn a nice profit on it. But no one ever came along."

The railroad eventually abandoned its line through Eagle River, and Hartland County acquired the right of way once the tracks were removed. After a few years of fundraising and grant writing, county leaders succeeded in turning the corridor into a paved path that linked to the region's recreational trail system.

Kate had become acquainted with Eagle River's newest outdoor amenity when she moved back last year, as her Main Street apartment had been less than two blocks from the trail. Even now, she enjoyed hitting the path after work or on weekends, sometimes with Hazel in tow.

The depot was still standing, but it was in a terrible state of disrepair. It would cost a small fortune to fix it up after being vacant for decades, and probably just as much to tear it down and construct something else on the site. While the parcel wasn't of use to anyone these days, it gave Kyle an idea.

"It makes me wonder what other properties the Lindgrens might own around here. Given what you've heard about Floyd, I could see where there might be some bad blood over a land deal. Worth a look, I'd say."

"That's a great idea!" Kate was feeling energized by this conversation. She'd hoped Kyle might offer a fresh perspective, and he'd come through with one. "I'll look into that. Property records are easily accessible online." Then she grinned. "It's a much-safer search than digging up how to poison someone with toxic plants."

Kyle agreed. Then he asked Kate if he should pass on her theories about poison to Marie's family. "I won't say a word to them, or anyone else, unless you think it's the right thing to do."

Kate considered it, then shook her head.

"At this point, I'd say no. Bev and I have been back and forth about that. We just don't have anything solid to go on; it's no use upsetting anyone further when it's already such a stressful time for them. Especially when, medically speaking, we are long past the point of being able to prove she was poisoned. If that's even what happened."

Kyle reported that Marie had been moved to a rehabilitation facility in Swanton late last week. Not because she was improving, unfortunately, but because insurance companies didn't want patients taking up hospital beds unless that was absolutely necessary. He'd spent a few minutes with her over the weekend, and confirmed what Kate had heard: Marie was in frail health; and, while she was expected to live, hopes for a complete recovery were dim.

"I don't think she remembers anything that happened that night. Or that day, given what you suspect. She's experienced so much physical discomfort, and been uprooted from her home. This has been a terrible ordeal for her. And her family."

Kate knew Chief Calcott had returned to the hospital the morning after the incident to interview Marie a second time, and she wondered if he'd attempted another such visit since then. Was he, even now, working some angle Kate didn't know about?

That was possible, and Kate sincerely hoped it was true. Because she didn't have much to go on.

But Kyle had been a great help, and she told him so.

"Please let me know if you find out anything else," the library director told Kate before he opened the office door. "I'll keep my ears open, in here as well as around town."

** 14 **

The pan of fresh blueberry cinnamon rolls, perched on the passenger seat, filled Kate's car with a heavenly aroma. She took the bend in Prosper's Main Street with one hand on the wheel and the other hovering over the pan's aluminum foil cover.

"They aren't Miriam Lange's famous pecan rolls, but they'll have to do." And then, Kate laughed. "What am I saying? These guys will eat just about anything, according to Melinda. And they'd be eager to chew over theories about the community-center incident even if I didn't offer snacks in return."

Melinda's idea to have Kate hang out with the Prosper Hardware coffee crew was a brilliant one, and couldn't have come at a better time.

It was Wednesday, Kate's day off that week; but she had Thursday free as well, because tomorrow was Juneteenth and the post office was closed. With two open days in a row, Kate hoped to make some headway on the case as well as countless things that needed attention at home.

Kyle's theory that Floyd Lindgren's business dealings might be behind what happened to his wife was an interesting one, but Kate had yet to uncover anything within county property records that pointed in that direction.

The library director was correct that Marie's longtime home was held within a Lindgren family trust. The former Eagle River depot property was still part of it, as well. The only other tracts of land the entity now owned were a four-acre residence southwest of town, complete with a renovated old house, barn, and the usual outbuildings; and more than five hundred acres of farmland in the general area of the rural residential property.

It was a common practice for families who no longer wanted, or needed, to live "at the old home place" to maintain the property as a rental; either at a steep discount for a relative who needed it, or for another tenant to generate income. With fewer people farming these days, families often retained ownership of their productive acres for the same reason.

So while there was still the possibility of a long-ago transaction causing trouble for the Lindgrens, nothing in the current land records offered a possible motive for the attack on Marie.

The Prosper coffee guys were aware of Marie's continued suffering, Melinda had told Kate, but none of them knew the truth about what happened that night at the Lindgren home. And, given their various roles in Prosper, the men were anxious about the reputation of the little town's event space.

Kate had decided to focus on those two topics, and not attempt to make inquiries into Marie's personal life. She had only an hour with the guys before the store opened, and she had to keep their discussion on track.

"It's like Bev has been saying," Kate reminded herself as the community center came into view, "our best bet may be trying to disprove things so we can set them aside. We'll keep narrowing our focus until we stumble upon the answers we need."

Even though Kate had a short agenda for this meeting, she had high hopes the men would have plenty of insights to share. Because despite their faded ball caps and folksy ways, they held a wealth of knowledge about everything happening in Hartland County.

Mayor Jerry Simmons would certainly have a lot to say, since much of the gossip swirling around the community center landed on his plate.

A retired principal, Jerry was well known in the area and had guided the city council through the acquisition and renovation of the former bank property.

Melinda's uncle, Frank Lange, was a current member of the council as well as the center's steering committee. George Freitag, who was in his mid-eighties and the group's elder statesman, didn't have a hand in civic business but had decades of observing people's behavior under his belt.

John "Doc" Ogden, the senior partner in Karen's veterinary practice, could prove to be a valuable source this morning. And not just because he was known to stay calm when drama came to call. Doc's medical background, even though it was based in the animal field, might come in handy. Also, as a former member of the city council, he had insight regarding leaders' long-standing goal of creating a community center.

Along with Bill Larsen, who was the store's second full-time employee and a volunteer first responder, the coffee circle would be rounded out by Auggie Kleinsbach, the proprietor of Prosper's co-op.

Auggie's business traded in hearsay as much as it did in corn, soybeans, and animal feed. Kate knew Auggie well; he'd be a thorough source no matter which direction this conversation took.

Melinda had suggested that Kate park in front of the store. True to form, Auggie's truck was already angled along the curb.

He still had keys to Prosper Hardware from working there in high school over thirty years ago, which spoke to how close he was to Melinda's family. He put the coffee on in the morning, six days a week, and set the folding chairs around the store's antique sideboard before the group gathered.

Juggling a pan of cinnamon rolls while opening Prosper Hardware's front door was going to be Kate's first challenge this morning, but Auggie swiftly stepped in. He was halfway out the metal-framed screen door before Kate reached the store's dark green awning.

"Our special guest has arrived!" Auggie exclaimed as he reached for the rolls. He was trying to help, but Kate knew he also wanted dibs on the first treat off the tray. "No deliveries for you today, huh? Tomorrow, either. What's the plan when you leave our little party?"

"Not much, if I can help it. I'm hoping to tackle some stuff at home, though."

Kate set her purse on one of the folding chairs, which were already in place. Auggie gave her a slight frown, and pointed two spots over.

Assigned seats? Kate knew the guys had a routine, but ... really?

"The goats are coming next week," she said as she changed spots, "and I'm relieved to say I'm just about ready. The old chicken coop is cleaned out, thanks to Melinda and Karen. That was most of the battle."

"I know that coop," Auggie crowed as he poured himself the first cup of coffee. This was a serve-yourself sort of gathering, so Kate did the same.

"The Trowbridges had quite the egg business going for several decades," Auggie shared. "Minnie's parents started it, way back during the Great Depression. They wanted only the best for their birds, and they were right: a good setup can generate a great product. That chicken house is one of the finest around. That's still standing, anyway."

Auggie perched on what had to be his usual chair. It was the one closest to the plate-glass window on that side of the store, and gave him the best view of Main Street's comings and goings.

There wasn't much, especially at this early hour, but Auggie couldn't stand to be left out of anything.

"Oh, don't let me forget," he told Kate before he took a bite from his roll. "I have two economy-size bags of cat food in the back of the truck."

Auggie had stepped up when Kate took in the Three Mouseketeers last year. "I'm not quite out," Kate said as she nodded her thanks. "But I'm always headed in that direction, with four mouths to feed in the shed these days. The kittens are in the house, of course; they're on a different diet."

Kate had to admit: Auggie knew how to do coffee hour right. Plates and disposable napkins were arranged on the sideboard, along with white ceramic mugs and a selection of silverware. These were paired with a bowl of sugar packets and a half gallon of whole milk from the refrigerated case, which had "store use only" scrawled across its label. The "creamer" had its own spot on the fridge's second shelf, Melinda had told Kate.

"Have you found homes for all the kittens yet?" Auggie leaned in Kate's direction from across the circle. "Those photos you showed me a while back? Man, are they cute. I'm sure that …"

"Good morning!" Melinda sang as she came up the main aisle from the back of the store. "Auggie, what did I tell you about the kittens?"

Auggie frowned before he sipped his coffee. "Kate has people lined up."

"And?"

"I have enough cats."

Melinda prompted him to continue.

"And my wife agrees with you that I have enough cats." Auggie's brown eyes snapped with mischief behind his dark-framed glasses as Melinda laughed. "But I beg to differ."

He turned back toward Kate. "You know Dan's a cat guy, like me. We could take a few more at the co-op."

"I appreciate the offer. I'll let you know if something falls through."

Kate tried her coffee, and nearly choked. It needed a hefty dose of sugar, and a few ounces of water.

What was it with older guys making java so strong it could strip paint? Jack was probably loading the Eagle River post office percolator with an overdose of coffee grounds at that very moment.

Melinda caught Kate's eye as she wiped down the antique oak showcase that served as the counter. She jerked her head toward the back of the store. "The utility room's that way."

By the time Kate returned with her watered-down cup, Jerry and Frank had arrived.

The expanding group's conversation turned to how the recent rains had affected the local crops. Melinda had warned Kate there might be a few important "items of business" before she could turn the men's focus toward the community center down the street.

Doc soon came in from the back, with George in tow.

"How is Patches doing?" Doc asked Kate as he took a roll from the tray. "She wasn't too happy with me when I took her into the surgical suite that morning. Even when I was done, and the pain meds had her lulled into a stupor, she was still giving me the stink eye."

"That cat has the right to put on a queen's act," George proclaimed as he carefully lowered himself into a chair by Kate. It was next to the sideboard, which gave the elderly man an easy place to rest his cane. "She walked home, all that way! I could hardly believe it when I heard the news."

Patches' antics were soon overshadowed by questions about a herd of very-different critters about to arrive at Kate's little farm.

"The goats are supposed to be very docile," Kate reported.

"Adam promises they should settle in easily, as they are used to moving from place to place. He's going to string up the temporary electric fences that'll keep them where they're supposed to be, and nowhere else. They're big eaters, which is exactly what I need them to do."

It was a relief to see George, a retired farmer, nod in agreement.

"They'll clear that pasture, you won't have to worry about that. Goats are smarter than most people think, and they know to leave those live wires alone. Just make sure the lines stay juiced. Otherwise, you could find yourself in big trouble."

Auggie guffawed. "More like, having to replant your entire garden."

The men were generous with their praise for Kate's baking skills as they alternated between bites of blueberries and frosting, and grumbling about summer being road construction season. And then, they turned to the subject Kate was eager to discuss.

"What can you tell us?" Auggie was nearly on the edge of his chair. "Melinda says you have some big news to share on the community center front."

"I do." Kate set her paper plate by her feet. "So, you've heard four women got sick after the Eagle River Social Society lunch two weeks ago. I believe that to be true. The trouble is, a fifth person became ill, too. Extremely ill, in fact. And it's someone you all know."

Forks halted around the circle as Kate shared the highlights from Chief Calcott's incident report.

By the time she got to the pink squirrels and the purple-hued man with four arms, the men were staring at her in shocked silence.

Kate understood. After two weeks of continued speculation about a burglary happening in Eagle River, it would take a significant mind shift to process what she had just told them.

Mayor Jerry was the first to find the words. "So what you're saying is ... those two incidents are related? The stomach bug those women got at the club meeting, and the burglary at Marie's home?"

"No burglary," Auggie interjected. "That didn't even happen."

Frank shook his head as he tried to absorb this news. "OK, right. Marie imagined it all, huh? Not one bit of that was real."

The color was starting to drain from the mayor's face. "Except for the part where Marie Lindgren was made so ill during an event at our community center that she hallucinated about pink squirrels ransacking her kitchen."

Jerry put his mug on the floor, and his head in his hands. "And we're not talking a little discomfort here, like the other ladies. These are serious medical issues."

"And she's not getting better. If anything, she's worse." Auggie's blunt assessment caused the mayor to groan. "That poor woman's going to end up in a nursing home before this is over, I'm afraid."

Melinda gave Kate a worried glance. "Is that true? Auggie, what have you heard?"

The latest gossip was that Marie's overall health had been permanently compromised. Various internal issues were taking their toll. It was likely she might never return home.

"Could she die from this?" George's voice trembled with emotion. "Poor Marie! When you get up in years like us old folks, it doesn't take much, sometimes, for everything to go haywire."

"I can't believe it's this bad." Doc was stunned. "I mean, I do."

He nodded at Kate. "I know you're telling us the truth. Good thing you asked for a copy of that report."

Auggie was suddenly more angry than concerned.

"So, when was Calcott going to get around to setting everyone straight? Hiding the truth from people! What kind of nonsense is that? Just because he's worried about embarrassing Marie. Someone should put a stop to it!"

He looked at Jerry. "I'd like to think you'd never let something like that happen."

The mayor sighed. "No, I wouldn't. But then, Prosper doesn't even have a police chief for me to supervise; we rely on the county. And with all the health privacy laws, I guess I could see where things might get sticky. But some of the details are public record, if people bothered to ask. Like Kate said, Calcott didn't redact all of them."

"Sheriff Preston wouldn't go for this nonsense." Frank was certain of that. "He'd level with people. Too bad he's not in charge of the situation."

"He can be," Kate told the guys. "But he'll need something solid to go on. Solid evidence that a crime was committed at the community center that day. That's why I'm here. Any ideas?"

The men looked at each other, worry and frustration visible on all their faces. The injustice of the situation had caught the coffee guys' full attention. Every one of them seemed determined to dig deep to generate leads.

Not just to salvage the reputation of their little town's community center, but to find answers for a woman who'd been terribly, perhaps permanently, harmed by what happened.

"I'd be looking at that caterer," Auggie offered before he took a bracing gulp of his coffee. The shock had worn off; it was time to start pointing fingers in hopes of finding the right target.

"Heritage Street's been around forever, but that doesn't matter. Susan Wilson's above board, I don't mean her. Word is her assistant, Colleen Rigby, wants to buy Susan out, but Susan's in no hurry to retire."

Melinda raised her eyebrows as she swept the door mat. "You think Colleen would stoop to something like this? It would let her buy the company for a song, I suppose. She could tout that it's under new ownership, make a clean break from the bad gossip."

"No idea." Auggie shrugged. "Just sharing what I've heard."

The owners of The Watering Hole weren't likely to blame, Jerry said with a sigh of relief. Not just because Jessie and Doug Kirkpatrick were such wonderful people, but because the catering arm of Prosper's only restaurant was so in demand the Kirkpatricks could hardly keep up.

"They can't take on any more jobs," the mayor told the group. "Nancy's had to all-but beg Jessie to take events for people who'd contracted with Heritage Street through us, and are looking to switch caterers."

Three more bookings had been lost in just the past week, Jerry said. Even some clients who'd signed with The Watering Hole were at risk of canceling their events, as gossip about the incident had inevitably expanded to question the cleanliness of the community center along with Heritage Street's food-service practices.

The venue's health inspections were all current, and posted in the kitchen. Nancy was doing her best to ease clients' concerns; she was offering extra volunteers at events to keep a closer eye on the caterers and the kitchen.

"But our clients are like a bunch of scared rabbits." Jerry rubbed his face with one hand. "A few decide to bolt, and the others panic and do the same."

"I can see where they're coming from," Doc admitted. "I mean, you're inviting dozens of your friends and family members to a party. Even the possibility of something like this happening would ruin the whole thing."

Bill had been the last to arrive, but he'd heard what Kate had to share. He added his two cents while he dished up a cinnamon roll.

"And the people who've canceled don't even know how

bad the situation really is! Imagine what would happen if they did. If that luncheon caused Marie to get that sick ..."

"The event itself wasn't the problem," Doc put in, then shook his head. "See? That's just it! The food at the event was the problem. Someone tampered with it; accidentally, or otherwise. This could have happened anywhere."

"But it happened here." Jerry frowned. "And it's our mess to clean up."

With her opening tasks done, Melinda was free to join the circle. "I'm worried about Marie, of course. But beyond that, what you have here is a marketing problem, an image problem. Even proving the center wasn't at fault might not be enough for some people. Once they get an idea in their heads, it's going to be hard for them to let that go."

Kate knew Melinda was right. "What does it take to get the blame off the community center, and the city? Do you cut ties with Heritage Street? Bring in new catering options?"

Frank hesitated. "I'd worry that would backfire. We'd be implicating someone with such a move, even if nothing was stated to the public."

"You could get sued," Auggie grumbled. "I know those two caterers are only suggested to the renters, they can do whatever they want. There'd be no breach of contract for the city, but you'd be insinuating Heritage Street ran a bad kitchen if you dropped them now."

No matter what anyone suggested, there were no easy answers.

"What exactly are you hearing about the building itself?" Kate asked Mayor Jerry. "Is there a way to halt those rumors, at least?"

Along with general concerns that the kitchen wasn't clean enough, Jerry said, there were whispers that its fixtures weren't up to par.

Frank admitted the appliances were purchased at a scratch-and-dent shop in Mason City to ease the renovation budget, but insisted there was nothing wrong with any of them.

"They're all brand new, and the others were double the price," he reminded the group. "We were excited to get ones as nice as we did for the money we had. And that workspace, and the whole center, is scrubbed top to bottom after every event."

Other concerns had been voiced about the age of the building, Jerry reported, and the fact that it sat empty for decades before the city purchased it for a song. While the main floor and all its event spaces had been transformed, the basement and second floors were still in rough shape. The roof was serviceable, but it would need to be replaced in a few years. The plumbing and heating-cooling systems were decent, if dated.

"It's an old structure." Jerry tossed up his hands. "Over a hundred years old. We can't do anything about that. But it's not like the thing's about to fall over and crumble into a pile of bricks."

Frank added sugar to his second cup of coffee. "Its age is part of its charm. This isn't some beige box; it has character. That's what we decided we wanted."

Plans for the Prosper community center had been set in motion while Kate was still living in Chicago, but she'd heard about the project through Grandpa Wayne and Grandma Ida. "Wasn't there talk about doing something else, at least at first?"

"Jake Newcastle wanted to build new," Jerry said of one of the Prosper council members.

"He made a hard sell, and had some folks backing his idea. But in the end, the old bank was a better economic choice. And it's right in the heart of Prosper. Anything new would have been on the edge of town, you see; guests would have been parking along the residential streets. Some homeowners were against that idea."

A possibility occurred to Kate, one that Frank and Jerry might not want to hear.

"Do you think," she said slowly, "that someone is taking advantage of this bad situation to spread malicious rumors about the center? Maybe they wouldn't have, otherwise," she added quickly, as Jerry's eyes had widened in surprise. "But once those ladies became sick, they saw an opportunity."

Jerry and Frank stared at each other. Auggie didn't hesitate to jump in.

"Jake is a first-class jerk; and I know he was fit to be tied when he didn't get his way, but ... man, that would be low, even for him."

George was willing to consider the idea. "Jake certainly likes to stir up trouble."

The rumors about the old bank went beyond its kitchen and mechanicals. The mayor had fielded overblown concerns about everything from mold to poor ventilation, and the possibility of vermin living inside.

"Every old structure is at risk for mice," Auggie said. "It can't be helped. I buy traps in bulk for the co-op. That's where the cats come in," he told Kate with a grin.

She spoke up before Auggie could mention Patches' kittens again. "I'm sure the city has that under control."

"We sure do," Jerry promised. "But that's not the worst of it. Just yesterday, somebody asked me if it was possible the social club women got sick because of rat droppings."

"Rats?" Melinda gasped.

"You mean hantavirus?" Doc was so shocked, Kate wondered if he might burst out laughing.

"Now, hold up." The veterinarian put his mug on the sideboard, which was behind his chair. "That's a real thing, sure; but hantavirus requires repeated, extended exposure to rat feces to even have a chance of getting sick. Two hours inside a building, even if there were rat droppings anywhere in the structure, would never be enough to cause that. Not to mention, its symptoms aren't exactly what these women experienced."

"But you see?" Frank told Kate. "This is the problem we're facing. Medical ignorance, lack of knowledge of the situation itself; it just goes on and on."

"I hate to ask," Kate said. "But are there rats?"

"None." Jerry seemed confident in his statement.

George wasn't so sure. "Well, they're around. You just don't see them. Why, out in our barn, we'd often ..."

"Just because we had bats in there," the mayor said, "that doesn't mean we have rats!

"There were bats?" Kate wondered if this could get any worse. "When?"

"Oh, they've flown the coop," Auggie told her. "A team of guys came out, way before the renovations even started. Scooped them into cages, cleaned all the droppings out of the attic."

"Did many people know about that?" Kate asked.

"Of course!" Auggie shrugged. "It was quite the show, the day they were here."

"I remember." Melinda said wryly. "There was a crowd out on Main Street," she told Kate. "It was the biggest happening around here in a month, at least."

"Most of this state's bat species are designated as endangered or vulnerable." Doc paused to finish off his roll. "That company was amazing, by the way. The bats were released into a safe environment. The guys plugged all the holes in the attic, sealed them so no more could get in."

"The smell was totally gone once they were done," Jerry said proudly.

No wonder such awful rumors were going around about the Prosper community center, Kate decided, because they were inspired by facts. Even if those facts were now history.

The cinnamon rolls were more than half gone, and the group still didn't have any solid answers for how the women might have been sickened. Or the best way to combat the smear campaign against the community center.

"What can we do?" Frank crossed his arms. "Just stay quiet? If we remind everyone the bats are long gone, for example, it might make everything worse."

"Maybe the gossip will die off on its own." Jerry seemed to be reaching for any small hope he could find. "But that's a big risk to take, in its own way. And it does nothing to help Marie Lindgren."

As usual, Auggie was ready to weigh in on the situation.

"At minimum, I think you need to show, one way or another, that this whole mess was not the center's fault. The caterer made a mistake, one of the ladies brought a dish that couldn't handle the heat, whatever. But the city needs to wash its hands of this."

"How many people know Marie's condition was likely caused by that luncheon?" Doc asked Kate. "Because if word of that gets around, this storm of gossip is going to get worse, not better."

"Only a few people." She hesitated to give names. "But everyone is discreet, I can assure you of that. They understand how important it is to keep this quiet."

That seemed to ease Jerry's mind. "And the police report says nothing about Marie's time at our community center, earlier in the day?"

"Correct. There's a line noting she felt sick for several hours before this 'burglar' invaded her home. But that's it."

Frank sighed as he glanced at the clock above the sideboard.

"The store's going to open soon. We'd better wrap up." He paused with his mug still in hand. "I mean, no more talk about this today. You can all hang around for a while, like always."

George offered to pass the rest of the cinnamon rolls around, and the men's chatter quickly turned to other topics.

Melinda promised to wash Kate's pan and get it back to her sometime soon, and Kate gathered the rest of her things.

Auggie wiped his hands on a paper napkin, and stood up. "I'll follow you out when you're ready," he told Kate. "I'll put the cat food in your car."

Melinda ducked behind the counter and pulled out a canvas tote. "Before you go, I have something, too. It's on loan from the Horace Schermann Private Library; your checkout period can last as long as you need it to. There's no fine for a late return."

"I'll give it a look." Kate was thrilled as she reached for the heavy bag, and the antique book inside it. "Who knows what I might find?"

✳ **15** ✳

That afternoon, Kate settled in at her dining room table with the hefty reference volume Melinda had passed her at the hardware store.

The vintage book carried a musty, mysterious scent that even Hazel wanted to sniff. But while the dog soon returned to her cool spot next to a floor register, the cats were eager to investigate.

"It's so big, you could use this as a doorstop," Kate told Charlie, who'd ignored her admonitions to not jump on the table.

He usually did as he pleased; and the kittens, of course, were right behind their leader. Kate had borrowed a thick tablecloth from her mom when the kittens moved up from the basement, and she was glad she had. It was going to save the finish on this piece of furniture.

"No, Ophelia! That's not a snack." She gently pushed the curious kitten back a few inches. "Don't chew on it. You have no idea where this thing has been."

Well, maybe that wasn't true. "More like, I can't imagine the things this book has seen over the years. Even if it spent all its life parked on a shelf in the Schermann family's farmhouse." She shook her head in wonder as she checked the front flyleaf. "It's well over a hundred years old!"

The historic volume had three thick sections: Recipes, human medical information, and a veterinary guide.

Somewhere in its vast scope of knowledge, Melinda had hoped, would be the botanical information Kate was looking for. Kate quickly realized those details could be hidden in any of the sections.

"The cooking division might cover which plants are safe to eat, if they are even referenced in such a way," she mused as she began to carefully turn the yellowed pages. Various notes about household matters were scrawled in pencil here and there in the margins, and some of the recipes had check marks and long-ago dates next to them.

It was a window into the past, and Kate was fascinated by it. But she needed to stay on task. Later, a deep dive into this book would be an enjoyable way to pass a few hours.

"I would guess the veterinary part has the sort of details I've already found online regarding livestock."

She turned to the index in the back of that section.

"Oh, look: 'Household Pets' has its own chapters. And 'Dogs' is listed before 'Cats,' which is interesting since that's not alphabetical. They had their priorities back in the day, I guess."

Charlie stretched out one fluffy brown paw and laid it across the page. "Yeah, you're in charge, you come first. This is your house."

This massive book had been the internet of its time, Kate decided as she flipped through more pages.

Melinda, who had researched the title, explained that updated editions were printed several years in a row. It was so commonly used a century ago that copies of it were still relatively easy to find.

But many were in poor condition, and didn't hold much monetary value these days. And some of this information had likely been proven wrong by modern medicine decades ago. No wonder none of the Schermanns stepped forward to take this book when they sold their farmhouse to Melinda.

Even so, the information Kate sought within its pages would have stood the test of time. This book would prove priceless if it had what she needed.

Hamlet jumped into Kate's lap, and she absentmindedly rubbed his orange ears while she studied the wealth of information before her.

Her jaw dropped when she arrived at the medical section index.

"Oh, look at this! There are tons of herbal remedies. And, here we go: poisons. More like, antidotes for poisons. But that'll tell me what I want to know."

A chill crawled down Kate's spine as she flipped to that part of the old book. Nearly ten pages were devoted to every sort of danger people could have encountered back in the day, from botanicals to drug overdoses to toxins such as arsenic.

All of them carried cringeworthy descriptions of what symptoms to look for. Most offered suggestions on how to combat the poisons, although success was not guaranteed.

A few simply noted some substances, especially in large amounts, were fatal.

"Well, this is what I wanted to find. I don't even know where to start."

So many of the toxins presented similar symptoms in their victims; most of those were digestive in nature, which was to be expected.

Page after page told Kate how dangerous life used to be long ago, and still could be today if someone possessed the right knowledge, a source for those items, and a vicious intent to pair with them.

But there were countless choices here, too many to sift through.

And none of them could tell her what she really needed to know: Who had done this to Marie, and why?

"It's not going to be like that board game," Kate explained

to Ophelia, who'd dialed down her energy and now rested her furry chin on the open pages. "This book can't tell me that it was 'Mrs. Smith with the belladonna in the spinach salad,' or whatever."

Kate closed her eyes in defeat.

"It's too late for toxicology reports. Marie apparently doesn't remember much, if anything, from before her hallucinations began. Even if I found a possibility in here, there's nothing to back it up."

And then, she cringed for another reason. "And I'm still hiding what I'm doing from Alex."

What had surprised Kate in the past week or so was how easy it had been to keep that secret. There was always something else for her and Alex to talk about, and he had yet to question her vow to leave the case alone. Whether he'd taken her at her word, or suspected otherwise but kept silent, she didn't know.

As she stared at the musty pages of the old book, Kate had to admit there was a chance this case couldn't be solved. The criminal would spend the rest of their life privately gloating about how they'd planned, and then executed, the perfect crime.

Or maybe, Chief Calcott's hunch was the correct one: There had never been a crime in the first place.

"We all need answers, so I'd better come up with something," she told Charlie as she closed the massive volume and stored it in the nearby cabinet.

As worried as she was, Kate had to allow herself a few chuckles as she fetched a glass of iced tea.

"The hardware store guys were certainly full of information this morning, even if it wasn't all directly related to Marie's situation. Rats and bats both! Well, OK, they didn't really admit to the rats; but George is probably right, they surely had been in there. You know the place had to have been full of mice, either way."

She returned to the table, and her evaluation of what else she'd heard that morning.

"No wonder that one guy on the council pushed for a new building. It's amazing they were able to salvage the old bank at all, and that people are willing to pay good money to ask their friends and family to dine there, if you look at it that way."

Kate still wondered if Jake Newcastle was taking advantage of the community center's woes to spread a few "I told you so" rumors. But she agreed with the men's assessment that Jake wouldn't resort to outright sabotage by poisoning people at an event.

The project was already done, and the facility was the crown jewel of little Prosper. And, probably most important of all, Jake held an office that required voters' support to keep. Someone like him, if Kate was reading him right, wouldn't risk losing his community clout just to get back at those who'd disagreed with him on one issue.

The theory about Susan Wilson's assistant was an interesting one. Colleen would have had easy access to the restaurant dishes that were served at the Social Society luncheon. Even so, such a rash move would be more likely to tarnish the company's name than offer Colleen an underhanded opportunity to take control.

What about other caterers in the region? Or other places that counted on event-rental fees to make ends meet?

Neither type of business was common in such a rural area. Kate knew Stacy and Ryan would have had only a handful of options if they hadn't secured a date at the popular Prosper community center.

It was likely the owners of some other venues were green with envy over the Prosper site's out-of-the gate success.

But it would have been nearly impossible for people affiliated with any of those companies to be present at the Social Society's private luncheon, much less get close enough to the food to slip something toxic into one of the dishes.

Unless they'd conned someone into doing it for them. A mother, a sister, an aunt; perhaps a close friend? The criminal even could have been present while the dish was being prepared, doctored it themselves, then made their loved one an unwitting accessory to a crime.

It was a long shot, sure. But as Kate stared out at the warm sunshine, and contemplated the weeds that needed to be pulled in the garden, the laundry piled up in the basket, and the dust bunnies that popped out from underneath the sofa every time one of the kittens attacked an unsuspecting sibling, it was the best new lead she had.

Even better, it was the perfect way for Kate to occupy her mind as she tackled mindless chores around her little farm.

Could she and Bev, perhaps with Nancy's help, reconstruct the luncheon guest list? And then figure out which, if any, of the ladies have a loved one connected to a company that might see the community center or Heritage Street as their competition?

"No matter which theory I consider, everything keeps coming back to the inner circle of the Social Society." Kate reached for her phone, and started to text Bev. "If we start now, perhaps we can figure out all the connections before the week is out."

* * *

Bev was on board with their next assignment, and a quick call to Nancy had the Prosper city employee drawing up a list of names.

In a wonderful bit of subterfuge, Nancy had the idea to concoct a story about a lost item recently found at the community center. The "stray earring" could easily have been left by one of the Social Society ladies, Nancy reasoned, which would give her an excuse to reach out to the club's president and verify who attended the luncheon.

While work progressed on this new effort, Kate decided to wrap up a different loose end by attending the Eagle River farmers market Thursday afternoon.

This was the first year she'd planted a garden at her new home and, while she had likely planted more than she could use, the early vegetables weren't ready to harvest. She hoped to score some early season produce from the gardeners who'd started their plants indoors, along with digging up some local history with the help of one of the vendors.

The parking lot at the elementary school was half full by the time Kate arrived. Portable awnings kept the brightest of the sun's rays off the vendors and their wares.

Shoppers wandered from one table to the next, admiring the wealth of fruits and vegetables on display. A few stalls offered cut flowers and crafts, while one participant sold honey and jars of jam.

On the far end, a food vendor tended to a line of children waiting for snow cones, and the tempting aroma of seasoned beef wafted from the walking taco stand.

It was a small farmers market, compared to those held in the larger towns in the region. But local residents welcomed the chance to wander in the fresh air, walk their dogs, and greet friends as much as they came to stock up on fresh produce.

Kate was tempted to linger at more than one table, but was also eager to get home. Richard Everton had been at her farmhouse for most of the day, working on the downstairs powder room; when she left just before lunch to run errands in Swanton, he'd promised big changes by the time she returned.

She had previously known Fred Winthrop from his years teaching history at the high school, but they'd reconnected last winter as members of the holiday celebration's strolling choir. His market table was on the far end of the second row, which fit perfectly into Kate's plan.

She needed to chat with him about something tied to his role in the historical society, rather than the produce he had on display in his booth. But given the crowds milling around, Kate would have to choose her words carefully.

"Hey, Kate!" Fred's white hair had been buzzed to beat the heat, and his scalp was protected by a faded Eagle River Wildcats cap. "What are you looking for this fine afternoon?"

"Well, I could use some strawberries."

Kate had plenty of those at home, thanks to Minnie Trowbridge's long-established patch. But she needed information, and considered it a fair trade.

"And maybe two zucchini." That upped the ante, as Fred's eyes lit up with glee. "I'm impressed you have some this early."

"I have a little greenhouse going," he said proudly. "You know, if you want more later in the season, I could always drop some off at the post office. They multiply like rabbits."

Kate was quick to block that offer. "Oh, no, that's OK! I just have a zucchini chocolate cake I want to try," she said with a smile.

"So, I had the mail route through this neighborhood the other day. As I walked by the old depot, I couldn't help but imagine how it might be fixed up into something new. It's rough around the edges, but it has so much history."

"You're right about that!" Fred stepped aside to let his wife help another woman choose her cucumbers, and Kate followed him to the edge of the table. "The historical society has big plans for the old depot if things ever work out in our favor."

Fred quickly confirmed everything Kyle told Kate about how Floyd and Marie Lindgren acquired the property.

"Our group would love to turn the structure into a museum. As you know, we only have that window display in an empty storefront on Main Street. The Lindgrens have been so kind and patient, holding on to the parcel for us for all these years. It's not worth much, given the condition of the old depot, but still."

Historical society leaders set aside money for the depot project whenever they could, Fred reported, but the building's sorry state meant repairs would be very expensive. The parcel's tax bill wasn't much, given the depot's current condition, but it was more than the nonprofit wanted to shoulder until they knew they had enough funds to turn their longtime dream into reality.

While Fred was enthused about the project, it was clear he had doubts it would ever come to fruition.

"Grants are an option, of course. I've been looking into those, since the site has historical significance for our town. But it doesn't qualify for the national register, given all the remodeling the depot saw over the years before it was shuttered in the sixties."

Kate picked out two zucchini, and Fred added them to her bag. With a grin, he threw in a third. "On the house. Make a second cake for the mail carriers, if you like."

He gestured at the bustling scene around them. "The old depot property has more future uses than just as a museum. This market could be held there, too. There'd be plenty of parking, which we really need. As you know, the first month of this market happens when school is in session, and the last two months are the same. There's often quite the traffic jam when parents are picking up their kids, or there are after-school activities going on."

Kate hadn't considered that, but Fred was right. "I hope you can get the money together someday. It would be such an asset to the community."

She paid for her produce and returned to her car. It was stiflingly hot inside, even though it hadn't been sitting for more than twenty minutes.

As Kate blasted the air conditioning, she reviewed her brief conversation with Fred. "There's nothing there of note.

I'm not surprised, really. Everything is just as Kyle had heard from Marie."

But as she made her way back toward Main Street, Kate had a reason to get excited.

"What am I going to find when I get home? I can't wait to see how far Richard got this afternoon!"

* * *

Richard's truck was still in the yard, parked in the shade up by the house. Kate hoped that meant her contractor was making progress on the new bathroom's plumbing, rather than he'd uncovered yet-another confounding difficulty or delay.

This brick farmhouse, while well-built and sturdy, was a hundred years old. Richard suspected the upstairs bathroom had been added in the 1950s; and, he'd told Kate with a sorry shake of his head, that was the last time updated pipes had been run to the kitchen, as well. There'd been more than one repair that needed to be addressed before new water and sewer lines could service the former pantry, and Kate had often felt like she was pulling stacks of twenty-dollar bills from her purse and lighting them on fire.

But it would all be worth it in the end. Not only would the first floor finally have a bathroom, but the repairs this project had brought to light should keep her plumbing in fine shape for years to come.

Today, at least, she hoped to see major, visible proof that renovations were finally coming to a close. When she peered in through the powder room's open doorway, she squealed with delight.

"It's a beauty, isn't it?" Richard grinned as he gave the shiny new toilet an affectionate pat on the top of its tank. The fixture was standard white, and nothing fancy; the pedestal sink parked next to it was the same. But Kate felt like she'd won the lottery.

"I love it, both of them! And the vanity light fits perfectly."

"I'm glad you went with that smaller size," Richard said of the three-light bar now secured over the sink and an oval mirror. "To say this is a tiny bathroom would be an understatement. Anything bigger, and everything would have been crowded."

Kate gestured at the vintage-style, single-light fixture over their heads.

"Much better than a bare bulb on a string, huh?"

"That's for sure. And safer, too." Richard grinned as he flipped the new light switch up and down for dramatic effect. "Look at that! It's come a long way since we started."

Kate had noticed that the kitchen, as well as the adjacent dining room and front hall, were suspiciously vacant. "Where are your assistants?"

"Charlie's been through a few times to check my work, but he's napping on the couch now. I think Hazel's back upstairs, stretched out in front of the kittens' room. She can hear them playing in there, of course."

Since doing renovations with kittens clocking your every move would be a bigger challenge than splicing into old plumbing, Patches' brood had been settled in the spare bedroom since that morning.

"I'll reunite them once you've wrapped up for the day." Kate swallowed the lump that had formed in her throat. She wasn't the only one who was going to miss the babies when they moved on to their lifelong homes. "And I can't thank you enough for what you've done with this space! Alex and I can handle the painting. And the decorating, of course. Well, I'll be in charge of that."

Fresh hand towels waited in a tote upstairs, along with the lone bathmat that would just fit in front of the sink. Kate couldn't wait to set her new soap dish on the sink rim, and drop in one of the custom bars she'd molded at Adelaide's.

Richard pointed at the box of sink fixtures still sitting in one corner. "Another half day or so, and I'll be done."

He grinned with satisfaction as he looked around the little bathroom. "You know, these small projects are just as meaningful as the big ones. It's rewarding to see them come together."

But then, his expression darkened. "All the hard work is worth it when the customer is happy."

Everton Construction had been chosen by the city of Prosper to overhaul the old bank building last year. From plumbing and electrical to tearing out walls and refinishing flooring, Richard and his adult sons had put countless hours into the project. Some of that labor had been free as part of Richard's bid to keep the project affordable, along with securing the materials at cost.

But now that people were whispering about the building, especially the new kitchen that had been retrofitted into an old space, a harsh spotlight had fallen on the Evertons' substantial work at the community center. It didn't help that Richard and Nancy were romantically involved, even though they were both free to do just that.

Their personal connection only fueled whispers of favoritism during the bidding process and lax supervision of the work.

Nancy and Richard had barely known each other until the community center project had thrown them together, and they hadn't begun seriously dating until after it was completed, but that didn't seem to matter.

"Prosper's city leaders are thrilled with the work you did at the community center," Kate reminded Richard. "That's not the problem. Nor is your relationship with Nancy."

"Yeah, I know; she says the same. But all the gossip hasn't exactly made things easy these past few weeks."

As Kate admired the contractor's fine work in her home, the care Richard had taken to modernize the former pantry while maintaining the house's integrity and character, she felt a renewed determination to get to the bottom of what happened to Marie.

If she could clear the name of one of the most talented tradesmen she'd ever encountered, along with getting justice for the older woman, it would all be worth it.

"Maybe something will come to light, and soon," she told Richard as he packed up his tools for the day. "Then we can put all those rumors to rest."

Kate certainly hoped that was true. If only she could figure out how to make it happen.

∗ 16 ∗

"So nothing new, huh?" Bev sighed as she eyed the post office's lush lawn and the cheerful phlox Roberta planted by the front entrance two years ago.

There was not a cloud in the sky on this Tuesday afternoon, but Kate shared her friend's dim outlook.

"Nope." She reached for the broom kept in one corner behind the counter. "I don't have a single worthwhile tidbit to share."

The floor wasn't that dirty, as it wasn't mud season or snow season, but Kate attacked the tile with gusto. Her day's route was done, so she was keeping Bev company until the front counter closed in half an hour.

They had the lobby to themselves and, based on the lack of traffic outside its windows, that was likely to continue. Roberta was off, and the other carriers who weren't enjoying a vacation day had either gone home or were still wrapping up longer routes.

"I'm glad we put that luncheon list together, though." Bev reached for a dust cloth and began to buff the counter. "Nineteen ladies makes for an awful lot of relatives and friends to sift through, but we knew that when we started."

Then she laughed. "Nancy's idea was brilliant, if you ask me. All she had to do was call up Carolyn Dahlberg with that nonsense about finding an earring, and the president was happy to hand over her attendance roll from the luncheon."

Kate reached for the dustpan. "It's a shame we couldn't pick Carolyn's brain further, ask about any club members with connections to caterers and event centers in the area. But that was too risky."

"Carolyn's not the chatterbox Audrey Schultz is, or Lucille Robertson," Bev proclaimed. "Even so, I don't think we should have the club president helping us out. You just never know who's behind this, or what Carolyn might say to someone."

"I agree. And we need to keep Nancy out of this, going forward. She's in enough hot water with some people as it is, and unfairly so."

Nancy had offered to put out feelers about other caterers in the region, but that would be a disaster. People would wrongfully assume she was attempting to replace the center's current vendors. And the folks behind Heritage Street and The Watering Hole would worry that their offerings had been deemed subpar, and that they were likely to lose business in the future.

"I spent several hours again last night," Kate told Bev, "studying that list and trying to figure out who was who, for our needs." She shook her head. "Being away from here for a decade certainly didn't help me any. I recognized maybe half of the names, but couldn't always come up with faces to go with them. As for connections? I think I recalled a few of the women's daughters, and that was it."

Kate had almost reached out to Stacy with her conundrum, but decided against it.

Her cousin had been back in Eagle River since college, and knew many more people in the area than Kate did. But to say Stacy was distracted these days was an understatement, and Kate didn't want to worry her with anything that wasn't an essential part of Saturday's wedding. Because while both

Lauren and Kate had encouraged Stacy to open up to them about her nuptial jitters, the bride-to-be continued to brush their concerns aside.

"Ryan and I are getting married at 4 p.m. on June 28, so there's nothing to worry about," she'd told Kate over the weekend, then quickly steered the conversation toward what she planned to pack for her honeymoon in Hawaii.

There wasn't anything more Kate felt she could do, especially with the wedding just days away. As for Marie's plight, that didn't look promising, either.

Bev clearly shared that sentiment.

"I've been through the websites of all the area's caterers, noted who the owners and main staffers are. I know you've finished that same list for the venues, and there are no matches for either of them. No one we can say for sure is directly connected to any of the ladies at that luncheon. I had Nancy give all of them a look, and she said the same."

Under the guise of planning a family reunion for the fall, Bev had made a few inquiries about caterers and event centers after Sunday church services, and again yesterday while she walked Aaron's regular west-side route. Those efforts didn't net her any suspicious opinions about regional vendors ... except for Heritage Street and the Prosper community center.

"The gossip is still flowing, when you bring it up. And to think, that luncheon was three weeks ago today! I don't think it's top-of-mind like it used to be, thank goodness. But for those who have a big celebration on their minds, the stigma has yet to fade."

Kate attacked the front doormat with her broom. "Fewer people are talking about the 'burglary,' I've noticed. I'm glad the fear has died down, sure; but that also means folks are less likely to think of Marie and what she's still going through. She needs all the support she can get."

"Well, it's full-on summer now. The Fourth of July is

coming up in a few weeks, there's so much going on. If a situation doesn't impact them directly, people just move on. We all do it."

"I know. It's just that the case seems to have gone cold on every front we can think of." Kate grimaced. "I still have no idea who might have been fooling around with Floyd, or who Marie might have been fooling around with in retaliation."

Bev began to balance the day's receipts. "If he was indeed tomcatting around, it was likely decades ago; and he's not around anymore to fight over, anyway. Besides, Lucille may have gotten her stories wrong; gossip isn't always accurate."

Kate had to admit that was true. "And Heritage Street Grill was fine, you said? No qualms about it, right?"

Auggie had suggested Kate and Bev set up a stakeout at the Prosper community center. Heritage Street was in charge of the dinner for last Saturday's wedding; it was the perfect chance to see the caterers at work. But the ladies hadn't been so sure. Wedding crashers wouldn't be tolerated, and Nancy already had enough helpers for the event.

But the idea had given Bev an opportunity to lure her husband into a dress shirt and tie for an early anniversary dinner. She'd booked a Sunday-night reservation at Heritage Street's Swanton restaurant to do more than just celebrate a personal milestone.

"Our meals were fabulous! The best chicken alfredo I've had in years. Of course, I try not to eat that rich stuff too often these days." Bev patted her waistline. "Clyde was impressed with his steak; the chef cooked it just to his liking. I'd had to badger him to celebrate in style for once, but he later admitted he was glad we did. I might be able to get him back there, even."

The Stewarts made it their mission to evaluate the restaurant's cleanliness. After all, the food served through the catering side of the business got its start at the Swanton location.

"You should have seen him." Bev chuckled at the memory. "Clyde kept peeking under our table when the servers weren't near us, trying to determine if the carpet had been vacuumed recently. He held his silverware up to the light to check for soap-scum spots. I'd drawn the line at bringing a meat thermometer along so he could confirm our dishes were served at the right temperatures."

Kate joined in her friend's laughter. "I would have paid good money to see Clyde turn into a super sleuth. I'm just glad he didn't storm the kitchen and demand a tour."

Bev looked down, then away.

"Oh, no." Kate's broom came to a halt. "You didn't!"

"Well, not exactly." Bev grinned. "That chocolate tart we split for dessert was so good, I'd like to make one. I couldn't decide if it had cocoa powder in it, or melted chocolate, or both. So I decided to take a little detour on my way to the ladies' room."

Bev had managed to chat her way past the bored teenage girl folding fabric napkins just outside the kitchen entrance, but didn't get more than a few seconds' worth of evaluation in the back of the restaurant before a harried assistant chef chased her out.

"He was polite, of course, but made it very clear that the recipe is a secret. 'It's our most-requested dessert for a reason,' he told me as he escorted me back to the dining room." She shrugged. "It may take a little effort, but I'll find some versions online and figure it out. From what I could see, the kitchen was immaculate. I wouldn't have any qualms about it."

Nancy had said the same regarding Heritage Street's efforts at Saturday's wedding. It had gone off without a hitch, at least as far as the food and kitchen prep were concerned.

"The health inspectors seem to feel the same about Susan's business," Kate said. "I didn't turn up anything that raised red flags."

Kate had checked a handful of online databases that catalogued "dirty dining" reports, and was relieved not to find Heritage Street Grill, The Watering Hole, or any of her other favorite local hangouts listed anywhere. But she did encounter a few regional places she might avoid in the future, so her efforts hadn't been totally wasted.

As for this investigation, however, Kate sometimes wondered if it was worth it to keep trying. Bev agreed.

"This is a tough case." She shook her head as she straightened the stacks of forms on the counter. "And it's not just that we don't have any solid leads; we can't even prove that a crime's been committed! Meanwhile, Marie's stuck in that hospital bed, sick as can be, and unable to go home. Where do we look next? Who might be able to help us? I'm running out of ideas."

"Me, too." Kate stared out at Main Street, as if some new clue might suddenly appear on the asphalt baking under the summer sun.

And then, she smiled.

"If we expand our net, maybe we can catch some new leads. Maybe it's time to bust this case wide open, and not worry about the consequences."

✳ ✳ ✳

Dark clouds arrived early Wednesday afternoon, and the skies opened just before Kate finished her route south of town. By the time she reached the post office, the rain was splashing through the gutters and running across the parking lot.

A growl of thunder and a flash of lightning accompanied her on her mad dash to the back door. Although the weekly staff meeting was about to start, Kate took a few moments to shake the water out of her ponytail. She was kicking off her wet shoes when Allison came into the vestibule.

"Mercy!" Allison pulled off her navy ball cap and wrung it

out. "They're not talking about severe weather, thank goodness. At least, not until tonight. But that rain doesn't want to let up!" She eyed the dirty, wet floor, then shook her head. "I'd mop up, but I saw Jack pulling in behind me. Marge isn't back yet, either. We might as well wait until after the meeting."

The carriers' damp clothes made the break room feel like a sauna, despite the old air conditioner wheezing out back. Bev, who settled in next to Kate, grimaced in sympathy. "And here I've been snug and dry this afternoon, working the counter. I guess there are perks to being a part-timer."

"Thanks for the coffee," Randy told Bev as he filled his mug. "It's eighty-nine out there, but a hot cup is just the thing right now."

Roberta soon came in, trailed by Jack, Allison, and Jared. The boss took a quick headcount. "OK, good; everyone who's supposed to be here is back."

The post office's most-recent remodel, which occurred a decade ago, had included a metal-panel roof. As a fresh squall of rain gave way over their heads, Jack laughed. "You'll have to speak up," he called to Roberta over the din.

"I will. And I'll keep this short, if I can."

A loud rumble followed. Roberta shook her head and glanced heavenward.

"Well, that's an endorsement if I've ever heard one. Let's get started. First of all, we're running out of time to sign someone up for the ear-shucking contest at the sweet corn festival." She looked around at her charges. "Does anyone want to volunteer?"

"Sorry, I'm out of the running." Jack's conciliatory tone was that of a man turning down a great honor. "I'm getting too old for that. My hands won't hold up, I'm afraid."

Allison snickered. "It's, what, five minutes or something like that?"

"You sort mail faster than anyone I know," Randy told

Jack while he made a flitting gesture with his fingers. "Are you sure?"

"I'm retired from competition," Jack declared. "It's time for the younger generation to step up."

"We already have." Jared pointed at himself. "I did it last year."

Roberta shrugged. "Well, it won't be me. I'll tell the mayor we'll pass this time."

The postmaster was partway through her list of not-so-essential news when Allison raised a hand.

"I know I'm getting off topic, but has anyone heard anything more about the burglary at the Lindgren house? People are still talking about it."

"I can't tell you how many people are still looking over their shoulders." Randy paused for a sip of coffee. "It's mostly older folks, and some of the other ladies. It's just that the whole situation is so out of character for our town."

"It's still very much on people's minds," Jack confirmed. "I got stopped at the gas station the other day, of all places. I was filling up my mail truck when some woman across the way turned around and said, 'well, did they get that guy yet?' And all I could do was shrug and say I didn't think so."

Kate and Bev exchanged a knowing glance.

"I understand the frustration," Roberta told her team, "out in the community, and in this room. We're public servants, just not the ones handling the case. People see us as approachable, and that's exactly how we should be."

"We're walking billboards, too," Jared said. "Or at least, people assume we are. That we have some special, back-door insight into whatever is going on."

"I wish I did," Randy said. "Because in Marie's neighborhood, people are still uneasy."

The far-east side's proximity to the river and its timber-lined banks seemed to be especially concerning, according to Randy. Between that and the recreational trail, residents were aware of how easy it would be for someone with malicious intent to slip into their neighborhood, then out again.

"That's what happened, I'd say." Jack was confident in his assessment. "The perp probably came in on foot, or even on a bicycle."

Randy crossed his arms. "It had to be some outsider, not from around here."

"It could have been one of those teens hanging out below the trestle." Allison wrinkled her nose. "Some of them are local, but the others aren't, I hear."

"There's a drug problem down there," Jared said. "Was that what they were looking for when they broke into Marie's house? That's the last place you'd go, but who knows what the perp was thinking?"

It was getting harder and harder for Kate to stay silent. The fact that her community, and even some of her co-workers, were pointing fingers in the wrong directions only fueled her resolve to speak.

She had a stack of paper tucked under her notebook. Was this the right time to raise her hand?

"We have to let the investigation play out," Roberta was saying. "I know it's tempting to hypothesize," she added gently. "But there seems to be enough confusion as it is. Let's try not to add to it, if we can avoid it."

Kate looked at Bev, and her friend gave her a slight nod.

"I know something," Kate blurted out. "A few things."

Every face in the room turned her way.

"Quite a bit, actually. Even though it's not enough."

As the rain drummed on the roof, Kate ran through everything she'd uncovered in the past three weeks, with Bev chiming in as needed. When they finished, the break room was silent for several moments.

"So what you're saying is ..." Marge frowned as she tried to piece it together. "Marie conjured all that up? She was hallucinating, or something?"

Jared was as stunned as the rest of the carriers. "What are they ingesting at those club meetings? They're the last people I'd suspect of ..."

"Something that made several of them sick, but not what you're implying," Roberta said. "As for who was behind it, it looks as if there are three possibilities: the caterers, someone affiliated with the center, or a member of the club."

"I'm afraid it's likely to be the last one." Bev's eyes shone with sympathy.

"The members of the Social Society are Marie's friends. Some of them have known her for years, maybe most of her life. They are women she enjoys spending time with, people she relies on. The physical trouble she's in is bad enough. But the betrayal? That's getting to me, too."

Kate held up her handouts. "And that's why we need your help."

She gave the stack to Jack, and motioned for him to pass it around. "This is a list of all the Eagle River Social Society members who were at that luncheon. It's not everyone in the club, but ..."

"How did you get this?" Randy asked.

"Doesn't matter," Bev put in. "But trust us, it's accurate."

"Please look this over," Kate implored her co-workers, "and see if any of the names ring a bell with you. While one of these ladies could be directly responsible, it's also possible that they agreed, or were even forced, to become an accessory to a crime."

Bev explained the various ways someone on the list could be implicated in the case, and why she and Kate were sharing this now. "This staff knows more people, and how those people are connected to each other, than just about any other group of folks around here."

Roberta reached for her reading glasses. "Why do I think Chief Calcott may not have this list, even though he could have obtained it more easily than the two of you did?"

"I'm not sure what he has," Kate said with a smirk, "because I haven't talked to him in over two weeks."

She wasn't about to count the moment she ran into him at the library, and he'd passed her by with nothing more than a nod. "It seemed pretty clear when I picked up the report that unless I come up with something solid, he's not terribly interested in hearing from me."

"As I recall, he asked us to help with this case," Allison mused as she studied the list. "But the last we heard from him, we were supposed to be keeping our eyes and ears open for tips regarding a burglary."

"And one that occurred in Eagle River," Randy reminded the other carriers. "Nothing about someone who tried to poison a bunch of ladies over in Prosper."

"Tried?" Jack let out an exasperated huff. "I'd say they certainly succeeded."

"Wait a second!" Allison gasped. "I think that ... yes, I'm sure I'm right." She reached for her phone. "Carolyn Dahlberg's niece has a catering business. Madison Lantz was a friend of my cousin's way back when. They went to high school together."

Conversation came to a halt while Allison checked online.

"Yep, she's still doing that. 'Fabulous Flavors,' it's called. Madison runs it out of her home, outside of Elm Springs. She accepts clients within a thirty-mile radius, looks like."

Bev raised an eyebrow at Kate. "That's fifteen from Prosper, at the most."

Jared was reading over Allison's shoulder. "She's only been in business for two years. So, new to the game. I'm sure she's eager to get as many clients as she can."

"Let's not get over our skis just yet," Roberta cautioned her crew. "But this is a perfect example of how we can help."

She beamed at Bev and Kate. "Thank you for sharing this with us. Allison, do you think you can ask a few questions without, well, someone questioning what you're up to?"

"I'm certainly going to try. Let me see what I can find out."

Despite the thunderstorm raging outside, Kate felt more energized about the case than she had in days. Bringing it back around to the carriers had been the right thing to do. Except ...

"There's just one other thing," she told the table. "Please don't show this list to anyone, or even let anyone know you have it. The last thing we need, that Marie needs, is for the person behind this to find out we're snooping around. That could backfire, in so many ways."

"Duly noted." Randy nodded in agreement. And then, he thought of something.

"What about the Moores? I wouldn't show this list to them, but what's in that incident report is public record. I could chat with Ed and Dorothy, even if there aren't any packages to drop off. Maybe they've uncovered something new that could be useful."

"Sure!" Kate said. "You know them better than the rest of us do."

As Roberta studied the list, she had an idea. "What if I pass this on to Glenn, broaden our network a bit? He'll keep it quiet if I ask him to."

Glenn Hanson was the postmaster in Prosper; his shop was kitty-corner across the street from the community center. Glenn had his eye on everything, and his finger on the pulse of that little town, in the same way Auggie did.

Kate had considered sharing this list with the proprietor of Prosper's co-op, then decided against it. For all his bluster, Auggie could certainly keep secrets. But his sources seemed most useful for cases that leaned toward a male culprit; ladies who lunched weren't exactly Auggie's cup of tea.

And while Kate hated to make assumptions, it was highly likely the criminal in this case was female. Poisoning, both historically and in modern times, was overwhelmingly committed by women. The more local mail carriers who got a look at this list, the better.

"We need all the help we can get," she told Roberta. "Maybe the Prosper crew will turn up a lead or two."

"I gotta wonder where Calcott stands with all this," Jack mused as he studied the names. "Do you think he might be biding his time? Hoping this person thinks they've gotten away with something, and they'll slip up, somehow?"

"I guess anything's possible." Marge sounded doubtful. "But he did ask for our help. I say, we give it to him in spades."

Roberta checked the clock. "Looks like we need to wrap up. Nothing else I had to share is more important than this list. And everything else can be safely sent in an e-mail."

"Marie Lindgren is as important to Eagle River as that community center is to Prosper," Jared told Bev and Kate as they braced themselves for a mad dash across the rain-soaked parking lot. "Both deserve answers."

✻ **17** ✻

Kate leaned back with a satisfied sigh, and slid off her dressy sandals. While they were surprisingly comfortable, she was ready to take a break.

Come to think of it, her bridesmaid's dress was much better than she'd expected, too. Stacy hadn't quite been willing to let the ladies pick their own styles (symmetry was important for photos), but she had at least asked for, and implemented, the wedding party's input.

Prosper's community center had also benefitted from the bride's keen eye for casual sophistication. Now that it was dark outside, the gleaming hardwood floors reflected the glow of the flickering votive candles and the dimmed overhead lights. The custom-soap guest favors had been a hit, and the pale lavender tablecloths and faux-floral window swags brought a hint of summer into the space.

"What a lovely day this has been." Charlotte's arms were full with Ethan, her infant grandson, while Bryan and Anna enjoyed a much-needed night of fun. Kate's mom had overseen the guest book table, then enjoyed the rest of the celebration as simply a guest. Curtis, Kate's dad, was taking a turn around the dance floor with Grandma Ida.

"You and Lauren put a lot of effort into this day," Charlotte told her daughter. "I know Stacy appreciates it, as do her parents. Even with a few last-minute challenges, everything fell into place."

Charlotte was referring to an eleventh-hour switch in the glass votive holders due to a back-ordered design, and a significant threat of rain that afternoon that had never materialized. She hadn't heard about the drama during the bachelorette party; at least, not from Kate. And it was going to stay that way.

"There's just one more task tonight, but it should be an easy one." Kate tipped her head toward the overflowing gift table. She and Lauren would load up the packages and bags once the reception was over and they'd changed their clothes. "I think it's safe to say we managed to pull this off."

Kate couldn't keep a hint of pleasant surprise out of her voice. "There have been a few times, especially during the past month, that I worried we wouldn't be able to give Stacy the dream wedding she so desperately wanted."

She could have said more; a lot more. But she took a sip of her wine, instead.

The newlyweds were over by the large bank of windows that faced Prosper's Main Street, moving from this group to that couple as they chatted with their guests. Stacy seemed genuinely happy, much to Kate's relief. The stress and strain that had been so apparent on her cousin's face for weeks had evaporated as Stacy walked down the church aisle. Sheer joy had replaced it when she and Ryan recited their vows.

Her cousin's transformation reminded Kate of something she'd come across online, a mindfulness practice called the positive emotion cycle. Happiness was only the start of the process, and it was fleeting. Gratitude and hope were in there somewhere, but the ultimate destination was security and stability. Things that were harder to find, but had more lasting value.

Despite her anxiety about how marriage would change so many aspects of her life, it seemed that Stacy had found stability in Ryan. He complemented her well, and that was what mattered.

"What a transformation this has been!" Charlotte settled Ethan over the shoulder of her dress, which was protected by a towel. It took Kate a second to realize her mom was referring to the former bank, not Stacy's now-content change of heart.

"I know all this architectural beauty had to be here all along," Charlotte went on, "but I don't remember it being this lovely. Removing some of the walls really let the windows and trim stand out."

Kate agreed. "It's so exciting to see this place really shine, especially after all those years of sitting empty. People are gathering here again; this time, to celebrate all of life's milestones."

She took in the peaceful sight of a little baby perched on his grandmother's shoulder; and for just a moment, Kate's heart clenched with a longing that carried both sadness and acceptance. She and Ben had tried to start a family, but were unsuccessful. In the end, their marriage had been the same.

Kate was aware that there was a negative emotion cycle as well, and she was determined not to slip into that loop this evening.

Ethan finally let out a burp, and Charlotte smiled. "He's getting sleepy. He's completely content, even though he didn't get a taste of that wonderful dinner the rest of us enjoyed. Do you think Jessie would part with her recipe for the potato casserole, if I asked her for it?"

"It's become one of her specialty dishes, so she might want to keep it under wraps. But we might be able to recreate it. Or get close enough. Lots of cheese, of course; I think the green chiles and poblano peppers are what make it stand out."

The Watering Hole certainly hadn't disappointed tonight. Kate knew its burgers and hot-plate dinners were tasty, but she'd been impressed by how the casual bar across the street pulled together a menu for such a special occasion. Doug had returned to the restaurant while Jessie remained at the center, hovering over the wait staff as they poured drinks, gathered used plates and utensils, and prepped the hot dog bar that would give guests a tasty way to wrap up the evening.

"I don't even remember what we served at our wedding dinner." Charlotte shook her head. "Some sort of chicken, I'm sure." Then she laughed.

"I was so nervous, I hadn't been able to eat hardly anything all day. Your grandma was worried I was going to pass out, right there at the altar. My sister made sure I stayed hydrated, at least, and said she wasn't going to let me have even a sip of champagne at the reception until I ate something."

Once the ceremony was over, Charlotte told her daughter, she had been fine. And ravenous.

"I was stuffing a sandwich in my face in the church kitchen, a dish towel draped over the front of my gown, while the rest of the wedding party was gathering on the lawn for photos. My dress stayed clean, I reapplied my lipstick before I went out to join them, and no one had been the wiser."

This wedding reception was dissolving into more of a straight-up party, as all the good ones eventually did. As the playlist switched to a pop tune, several more revelers merged onto the already-crowded dance floor.

With their greeting duties finished, Stacy and Ryan were now hanging out with some members of their wedding party. Many of them had reunited with their plus-ones, and several more of the couple's friends were gathered around a table close to the bar.

It was just as well that Alex hadn't come. The entire day had been a blur of busyness; Kate wouldn't have had a moment to spend with him. More than once during the dinner she'd noticed that while the wedding party's dates were trying to enjoy themselves at their corner table, some of them looked as if they felt rather left out.

When the upbeat music switched to a slow song, those who had been dancing in groups either paired off into couples or took a break. Before Kate could decide if she should rescue her dad, who seemed caught in a drawn-out conversation by the cake table, Corey appeared.

"Hey, cuz." Like the rest of the men in the wedding party and many of the male guests, Stacy's brother had long since lost his tie and rolled up his sleeves. "Want to take a twirl?"

"You two go on." Charlotte swayed from side to side in her folding chair, Ethan still in her arms. "I have my own dance partner, right here."

Kate slipped on her sandals and followed Corey to a nearby spot on the dance floor.

"I've known you all my life," she told him, "but you are a man of hidden talents. Along with accounting and firefighting and emergency medicine, I had no idea you moonlighted as a disc jockey and emcee."

Corey laughed as they settled into the slow tempo of the music.

"Yeah, those last two are a special gift to the bride and groom. You know my sister; she knew exactly which songs she wanted. By the time Ryan added his picks, the playlist was good to go. I have a string of several slow songs queued up next. We wanted to give the older folks an incentive to enjoy a few more dances before the party is over."

As they moved in a small circle to the music, Kate stifled a yawn. She soon felt as tired as Ethan, who was now zonked out in Grandma's lap.

"It's been quite the week," Corey said, "and not just because my sister got married today. How are those goats working out at your place?"

"They are champion chewers, I'll say that for them. In two days, they've already cleared a quarter of the pasture."

Adam had arrived Thursday afternoon with a dozen munching machines inside his livestock trailer. All the goats were some version of brown and white, curious and friendly, and very cute.

Kate had been impressed by how quickly they'd settled in at her little farm. They were in an unfamiliar place, with a strange woman and a strange dog clocking their every move. But once they figured out where their water buckets were, and toured the old chicken house, they'd tucked into their buffet of weeds with barely a flick of a tail.

Their impish personalities were often on display. The goats loved to hop on, and over, the upside-down metal wash tubs Adam had left for them. And when they weren't butting around their brought-from-home beach balls, the old tires Kate had dragged out of the machine shed were put to good use.

It was fun having the goats around, but Kate knew better than to get too attached. Because next Thursday, Adam would take them home for the Fourth of July weekend before they went out on their next assignment. He was going to take Hamlet and Juliet, too. The meet and greet with the rest of the Fairlanes had left no doubt in Kate's mind that it was meant to be.

In only five more days, two of the kittens would be gone. Tears were about to spring into Kate's eyes; she needed to stay in the present.

"Lauren and I hope to pack up all the gifts tonight," she told Corey. "Nancy said they'd be safe here until tomorrow, when we take down the decorations, but it'll be one less thing to do later."

"I can help. Ryan and Stacy want to say a few parting words to everyone, but it won't take but a few minutes to ..."

Corey grinned as his attention was pulled away by something over Kate's shoulder. Or more like, someone.

"Hey, man! I thought you weren't going to make it."

Kate turned her head, and saw Alex. His hair was slightly damp, and he was freshly shaved. His button-down shirt and trousers were a far cry from the jeans and tee shirt that made up his bartending gear.

"Neither did I." The appreciative way Alex eyed Kate's loose bun and lovely dress warmed her to her toes. "But I was told to get over here, and show up for my girl. Can I cut in?"

"Absolutely."

Corey slapped Alex on the back before edging away across the crowded dance floor. Kate let out a deep breath she hadn't realized she'd been holding as Alex's arms slipped around her.

"What are you doing here? Who's watching the bar?"

"Nick says he can pour drinks while he minds the kitchen the rest of the night. It's been slow, anyway. The Fourth isn't for a week yet, but there seems to be a lot of people out of town."

Alex gave a sheepish smile. "The regulars said they would help close if it came to that. Bob was particularly insistent. I told him you were fine with me passing on tonight, but he said I'd better store up some points for the next time I mess up."

"Are you planning to?" Kate raised an eyebrow. "Is there something you need to tell me?"

"No." Alex pulled her closer. He smelled nice; his aftershave was a far cry from the beer-and-grease aroma that always seeped into his work clothes.

"I mean, other than that I'm sorry I'm always working. I enjoy running the bar, but, well, owning my own business is a lot of work. You look beautiful, by the way. I really like your hair."

"Thanks. But it's not that different from how I sometimes wear it. Did Bob put you up to that, too?"

"Yeah. But he's been married for, oh, over forty years. Linda keeps him around; so I figured, the guy must know what he's doing."

"I don't think you have to worry." Kate gave Alex a quick kiss, then settled her head on his shoulder.

"Neither do you," he whispered as the music slid into another slow song. Corey had stacked the playlist to perfection. "I may not be around as much as I'd like to be. But I'm not going anywhere."

"Neither am I."

Even so, a twinge of guilt pierced Kate as she leaned into Alex's embrace. She still hadn't told him about her involvement in the Marie Lindgren case, even after she and Bev had drawn all the Eagle River mail carriers back into their active investigation.

Her co-workers would keep things quiet, Kate knew, given what was at stake. But as the days and weeks flew by, it grew more and more likely Alex would hear something, find out something, that would reveal what Kate was keeping from him.

Would he understand? Or would he resent her for shutting him out? Kate wasn't sure. But as they clung to each other on the dance floor, she knew she had to tell him the truth.

Not tonight, though. Tonight was too special.

Happiness bloomed in her heart. And then, gratitude and hope. There was security with Alex, too; at least, as much as she needed right now.

Kate took a few moments to savor the love she felt for him, and feel the love he offered her in return. And then, she pulled back just enough to look him in the eye. His answer to the question that had just popped into her mind wouldn't set the course for her future. But given her exhaustion, it was still an important one.

"Do you have a tarp in the back of your truck? Because we could use your help once the party is over."

* 18 *

Hazel gave the weeds along the gravel road a thorough sniff while Kate waited.

"Take your time." Kate's sarcastic tone was wasted on the dog, who was so focused on her investigation that she didn't even look up. "We have two-thirds of our afternoon route still to go. And you'll be able to stretch all the way across Bertha's back seat once we drop off the rest of those parcels."

Kate swatted at the brazen mosquito that tried to land on her arm. The creek Bertha had just crossed, with its low and stagnant water, was surely to blame. They should have stopped elsewhere, perhaps on a nice rise in the road where there wasn't a puddle in sight. But Hazel had made it clear, through her whimpers and whines, that this rest stop was a priority.

Kate scuffed the gravel dust with the toe of one of her dirty work shoes, then adjusted her ball cap with the hand that wasn't holding Hazel's lead. Goodness gracious, it was hot out here. Hot, and humid.

"I thought you had to go. Or were you just bored?"

She stared at the cornfield on the other side of this ditch, and then at the mirror-image one behind her. The sweltering air fairly shimmered in the sun. It was filled with the endless drone of lazy insects, and punctuated by the chirps of birds concealed within the branches of the volunteer shrubs rooted along both field fences.

"The birds know enough to stay in the shade," she informed Hazel. "I'd like to do the same."

Finally, Hazel squatted. "Good, we're making progress."

Out here, Kate didn't have to pick up after her dog. Even so, it was hard for her to leave things behind. She felt a responsibility to the rural neighborhoods in general, and to the critters that owned these gravel-road shoulders. But Randy had talked her out of it the first day she'd brought Hazel along for the ride.

"The rabbits and squirrels aren't cleaning up after themselves," he'd said, and Kate had to agree. "If someone's cows get out, they'll make a bigger mess than what Hazel can. I say, leave it alone, and leave it to nature."

A sharp tug on the leash brought Kate back to the present. With her duty done, Hazel was on her way into the ditch.

"Hey, don't go there." Kate was quick to pull her dog back. "I don't want you roaming around, it's not safe."

It probably was; and until a few weeks ago, Kate had never given a quick ramble through overgrown vegetation much of a thought. At worst, she might have to comb weed seeds out of Hazel's thick coat when they got home.

But after Adam's visit to her pasture, and a few hours spent perusing the vintage reference book Melinda had loaned her, Kate's eyes had been opened in a way that showed her more than a harmless patch of unruly weeds in a ditch.

The county crews didn't spray the roadsides, so Mother Nature always had the upper hand. That clump not a foot from Hazel's curious snout might be phlox, which was as friendly as it could be; over there, a few native coneflowers waved their pink-purple petals in what little breeze could be found this afternoon. But to Kate, the rest of these plants now looked like nothing but trouble.

Hazel reluctantly followed Kate back to the car. Kate got

them both a drink of water, and the dog settled on the back seat with a contented sigh as Kate put Bertha in gear and got back on the road.

Kate wished she felt the same. But now that Stacy's wedding had come and gone, she was back to mulling over Marie's case like a dog worrying a bone.

Today was the first of July, already. And while the carriers were wracking their brains to uncover any questionable connections to the ladies who had been at that luncheon, they had yet to turn up another lead. Allison's had been promising, but she'd been able to disprove it over the weekend.

Madison Lantz was still running her catering business, but she had a great deal on her mind these days. Because along with two children under the age of five, she was halfway through another pregnancy, according to Allison's sources. While her client list was still small, Madison was struggling to keep up with requests. Rather than trying to steal work from other caterers, she was searching for a business partner to help her manage the events she'd already agreed to serve.

When Kate's cell phone rang, her eyes slid toward the passenger seat. "Prosper post office" appeared on the screen.

"I wonder what this is about?"

It was rare to meet another vehicle on this remote road. With her left hand on the wheel, Kate snatched up the phone with her right.

"Kate here."

"Where are you? Are you driving right now?"

It was a male voice, and it took Kate a moment to recall who it belonged to. "Hey, Glenn. What's going on?"

"I swear, I can hear the gravel rumbling under that car! I think you should pull over."

Prosper's postmaster was right. Not only that, but he was a close friend of Grandpa Wayne's. Glenn wasn't likely to rat Kate out to Roberta, but she couldn't be sure about Grandpa.

She hit the brakes, perhaps with a little more force than

was necessary. Hazel, who'd been nearly asleep, sat up in the back and began to bark.

"Is that a dog?" Glenn was stunned. "You have Hazel with you?"

"Yep, that's her."

Hazel was an excellent postal assistant on the random days she rode along with Kate. She elicited smiles from the customers along the routes, and spread cheer through the post office and among the carriers whenever she trotted in the back door.

"Does Roberta know about this? She must, if you girls started out from the P.O."

The car came to a stop in a cloud of gravel dust. Hazel barked again.

"Roberta's on board, it's not a problem. You know how she feels about the federal handbook, Glenn."

He chuckled. "Yeah, I sure do."

There must be a reason why Glenn was calling; Kate tried again. "What's going on?"

"I've got a lead!" Glenn nearly shouted with excitement. "It's about Marie. Or, more like, about someone who might have it in for her."

Kate sat up straighter. Had Glenn uncovered a connection to one of the ladies at the meeting?

"Pete was just in here, on a late lunch. He got some dirt today, and I put a few things together and, well, this can't wait. Especially since the lobby's empty right now."

As the senior Prosper carrier under Glenn, Pete MacLeod was an expert on the families that lived along the gravel roads farther west in the county. While chatting up a customer this morning, Glenn reported, Pete mentioned how sad it was that Marie had yet to return home.

"You're not the only one who thinks something smells rotten," Glenn told Kate. "This woman has her own theory, and you won't believe what it is."

He lowered his voice in a dramatic way that had Kate on the edge of her seat yet rolling her eyes. "She swears that Judith Prescott is the woman Floyd was having an affair with, all those years ago."

"Interesting! I guess there was more than one. Or at least, that's what I heard."

"Sure, yeah, I bet. But see, Judith was the one he was going to run away with. The deal was, Judith was going to leave her husband, and Floyd was going to leave Marie. But, nope! Marie said she wouldn't hear of it. She wasn't going to have everyone gossiping behind her back because she was divorced."

Kate frowned. "How long ago was this? I mean, divorce isn't the social shame that it used to be."

"Oh, maybe forty years, at least," Glenn said mildly. "But it doesn't matter. The point is, you know Judith has to have it in for Marie. And ... she's on that list! Not only that, but I can confirm she was there!"

He had Kate's full attention now. "You saw her come out of the community center that day?"

"Oh, better than that! She came into the post office after the meeting to drop off a package and buy stamps. She was all dressed up special, which stood out to me. She told me the club had just had their annual luncheon and that she had leftovers out in the car."

Kate gripped the steering wheel in anticipation.

"A fruit salad, it was. With coconut, and some sort of berries. Strawberries, maybe? And that weird green stuff, too; and I don't mean avocados. Does that make sense? I'm a meat-and-potatoes guy."

"Yes, it does; I bet you're thinking of kiwi. That would be the sort of salad you'd take to a special event."

Kate tried to recall where she'd encountered Judith's name before, other than Nancy's list.

It seemed some Prescotts had attended Eagle River

schools while Kate was young; maybe this woman's grandchildren? But Judith herself was a mystery to Kate.

"Judith told me she had the salad leftovers in a cooler, but she was going to toss them when she got home," Glenn recalled.

"'Not worth getting sick over,' she said. Those were her exact words! Was she trying to throw me off the trail, or something? I mean, if she was responsible ..."

Glenn was so pleased with his recollection of his conversation with Judith, as well as the salacious rumor Pete had picked up on his route, that Kate hated to take the wind out of his sails.

"I know who Judith is," he said breathlessly, "but until Pete got this hot tip, I had no idea *who* she is, if you know what I mean. Is that what you needed? Does that solve it?"

It was as if Glenn expected Kate to snap her fingers, proclaim the case closed, and immediately reach out to law enforcement. Did he think a battalion of sheriff deputies would march Judith out of her home this afternoon while the neighbors watched from their porches and whispered behind their hands?

Cases are only solved that quickly in movies and television shows, Kate wanted to tell Glenn. In reality, they take an awful lot of patience and time.

She turned to check on Hazel, who had sensed all the fuss and was getting rather active in the back of the mail car. They needed to keep moving, and not just because Kate's mail case was still packed full. Kate thought the dog might start barking again, and she didn't care to rehash federal protocol with the Prosper postmaster.

"I'm glad you called." Kate hoped she sounded sincere, because she meant it. "It's a good tip, really it is. I'll see if I can make heads or tails out of it."

But she had to wonder: How exactly did Pete get this woman to share such personal, targeted gossip about Marie?

She was certain Roberta had cautioned Glenn and his crew to not mention the possibility of poison.

"Oh, no, it was nothing like that," Glenn promised after Kate asked. "Pete knows the deal. He just mentioned how wonderful Marie is, how she and Floyd always did so much for the community."

The postmaster gave a rueful laugh. "People like nothing more than to knock someone off their pedestal, you know? Especially if they're dead, and Floyd's not exactly around these days to defend himself."

Kate heard a faint chime in the background, then a murmur of voices as customers entered the Prosper post office.

"Oh, hey, I gotta go." Glenn chuckled. "This is so much fun! No wonder you and Bev love to stick your noses into things around here. I'll call right away if we dig up anything else."

* * *

The skies had clouded over by the time Kate and Hazel turned up their own lane. Hazel couldn't wait to jump out of the mail car and run around the yard with Scout and Maggie, but Kate only wanted a shower and a nap.

All that had to wait, though. Because in addition to four barn cats who would soon be demanding their supper, twelve goats were watching her expectantly from the other side of the pasture fence.

"Did you get enough to eat today?" Kate inquired as she handed out nose scratches and ear rubs. "You've made quite a dent in my weeds, and I'll be forever grateful."

The pasture was transformed; there was no other way to describe it. Clumps of tall vegetation still pockmarked the ground here and there; but in the last five days, most of the greenery had been chewed down into short, manageable leftovers. Bare earth was visible in several places.

"It's going to rain tonight," Kate informed the goats while she moved the garden hose from one water bucket to the next. Scout and Jerry supervised from around her feet, while Patches kept watch from atop a nearby fence post. "I hope you all have enough sense to go into the chicken house if it starts to storm."

By the time the barn cats were fed, the afternoon's stagnant air had given away to a stiff breeze. As Kate began her evening routine inside the house, her mind turned to the gossip Glenn had shared that afternoon.

There was a well-known saying, "Hell hath no fury like a woman scorned." Even so, Kate found it hard to believe Judith Prescott would have waited forty-some years to retaliate against Marie. Especially since the object of both of their affections, if the story Pete heard was even true, had been gone for a few years already. It wasn't as if Judith could still harbor any hope Floyd might leave Marie, that he could convince his wife to agree to a divorce.

As for the fruit salad, Kate used her phone to investigate that possibility while she reheated leftovers in the microwave for dinner.

There were countless variations for the colorful dish, including options based on seasonal produce. Some indeed featured kiwi, which made Kate pause for a few peals of laughter at Glenn's expense. A little crunch was sometimes added through sunflower seeds or nuts. The dressing tended to be sweet and creamy.

While the main ingredients were too obvious to be at fault, it would be easy to blend something toxic into the dressing. Those components were pulsed into a liquid; it would be difficult to confirm exactly what was in it.

"And that makes this nearly impossible to prove," Kate told Charlie as she sat down with her dinner. He and the kittens and Hazel had already been served.

"The ladies were there to have a good time, dress up a bit,

enjoy a special lunch. I can't believe anyone would have given more than a passing glance at anything on their plate, especially with so many dishes from accomplished cooks to choose from."

As Kate washed up and wiped down the kitchen counters, she pondered how just one phone call, one tip, had expanded the case.

Engaging the "hive mind" of the Prosper post office crew, along with the Eagle River team, had been a good way to generate leads for a case that was going cold. But while Kate believed Glenn's explanation of how Pete handled today's inquiry, there was always the possibility someone might accidentally reveal more than they should while trying to help. It was the reason why she and Bev had always been careful to keep their past investigations close to the vest.

"There's another saying; one about having too many cooks in the kitchen. I think the mail carriers can be trusted, but ..."

Kate shook her head as she draped the damp towel over the oven handlebar to dry. "Enough about that for tonight. I have at least one cat, and maybe five, who are going to want a brushing before we settle in to watch a show."

Charlie vaulted into Kate's lap as soon as she landed on the couch. Juliet and Romeo, despite their coats being a fraction of Charlie's thick mane, wanted a turn, too. Hamlet was busy chasing his own tail on the rug, and Ophelia had already settled into Kate's reading chair with Hazel.

A severe thunderstorm watch was issued just before Kate collapsed into bed, but she wasn't concerned. There was no expectation for tornadoes, according to the bulletin; the advisory was only for the possible threat of small hail and strong wind, along with rain.

But at some point overnight, Kate's phone sounded a series of warning tones.

"I know, I know; it's loud." Kate fumbled for her device as

Hazel barked and Charlie's eyes widened in surprise. "But it's better that we know what's happening. Especially since it's the middle of the night."

Romeo, who had snuggled behind Kate's knees since she often slept on her side, barely looked up from his nest. Juliet, as usual, was wedged between Kate's hair and the top of the pillow.

"Hmm, let's see. A thunderstorm warning until four a.m. for us. The hail chances don't look too bad, though. Mostly just wind."

A trip to the basement wasn't going to be needed, thank goodness. Just before she drifted off, her phone chirped news of a text from Alex.

Just got home. The wind is starting to pick up. Moose has crawled under the bed, so I think we're going to get some of this. Hearing of power outages west of Prosper.

And then, a second text arrived.

Where are the goats?

Kate gasped. She needed to herd all the goats into the chicken house, then close their pasture door. And she had to hurry.

If the power went out, the electric fence's zapping abilities would disappear with it. Service along this gravel road might not be restored for several hours. As soon as the sun was up, if not before, the goats would be feasting on Kate's garden as well as the prairie plants along the creek.

She tried to get out of bed, but her first attempt was a failure. Through the top sheet and a blanket, Hazel still had Kate's toes tucked underneath her. Charlie was out of the way, even though he was grumbling at Kate from his side of her pillow; Hamlet and Ophelia were camped out on the other.

Romeo refused to move from where he was blocking Kate's knees, and Juliet unsheathed her tiny claws in a flash when Kate tried to disentangle her hair from the kitten's grasp.

"This is how cat ladies die." Kate groaned as she tried to free herself from her furry friends and the bedding. "They have medical emergencies, and the pets don't move enough to let them reach their phones and call for help. Hazel, get down!"

Finally, Kate was free.

I'm on my way out there, she texted Alex. *I'll let you know when I'm back.*

Kate pulled on long chore pants and heavy socks. Downstairs, she reached for boots and a rain jacket, a headlamp, and a flashlight.

Hazel had followed her into the kitchen, but Kate didn't let the dog's curious whimpers wear down her resolve. "No, you have to stay here. I don't want you running around in that pasture, even if you are capable of herding goats."

Could they be herded? Kate wasn't sure. Or, like sheep, was it better to lure them with a snack? The goats followed Adam around, but he was the leader of their pack. Could she get lucky enough that they'd do the same for her?

It was starting to rain by the time she hurried down the back porch steps. The wind had picked up, and she could feel what Moose had sensed minutes ago from inside Alex's house. A storm was certainly on the way.

Movement at the front corner of the machine shed caught her eye. Then a small, dark figure with a few splashes of white. Kate aimed both of her lights in that direction, and was relieved to find Scout instead of a roaming skunk. "We have to get the goats. Let's go!"

Kate heard goats bleating inside the oversized coop, which was a good sign. She was about to open the garden-side door, but decided against it. The last thing she wanted to do was startle them, send them tumbling out the back door.

She hurried to the propped-open pasture gate, climbed up and over its rain-slicked rungs, then slowed her steps as she followed the electric fence-lined pathway to the coop.

Ten goats were already inside. They were surprised by her arrival, but seemed unfazed by the approaching storm. "Where are the other two?"

She spotted the stragglers just beyond the pasture entrance. The goats were impressively calm when Kate started in their direction. Even when she circled behind the pair, they were more curious than alarmed. Kate clapped her hands, and motioned toward the chicken house.

"Off you go! Head in!" When she crowded their personal space, one of the goats trotted ahead. Miraculously, the other followed. "Let's go, goats!"

It was with great relief that she closed the door behind them and checked the latch was secure. Crisis averted.

Another gust of wind-driven rain rolled in, along with the first rumble of thunder. Kate made sure Scout had slipped through the cats' opening into the machine shed before she hurried to the house, peeled off her damp and dirty clothes, washed her face in the kitchen, and climbed the stairs.

Mission accomplished, she texted Alex. *All goats are in custody.*

An hour later, Kate was awakened for a different reason. The nightlight in the hallway was dark; the floor fan in her bedroom, as well as the air conditioner outside, had gone silent.

She hated it when the power went out. The profound quiet always felt strange, and her room would be humid and stuffy before morning arrived. She heaved a deep sigh, rolled over as best as she could given the animals crowded around her, and pushed down the top sheet.

Maybe she wasn't much of a farmer, Kate decided as she waited to fall asleep. But for one night, maybe she was a halfway-decent goat herder. And that was good enough.

* 19 *

Alex gestured at the hexagon floor tiles with his screwdriver. "White with a little black, you can't go wrong there. Classic!"

Kate beamed with pride; she'd installed the powder room floor herself before Richard put in the fixtures. The space was so small, it had only required a few cartons of tile. Richard gave her some pointers, and promised to get her back on track if she ran into trouble.

But Kate had accomplished it all on her own. Bathroom floor tile? Check. Kitchen backsplash, someday when she had the money to gut the adjoining space? Now a possibility.

"The mosaic pattern fit the Craftsman style of the house," she reminded Alex as she ensured the baby gate stretched across the doorway was secure. While fresh air needed to enter this small space during painting, Kate's furry friends had to stay out. "The tiles you installed in your bathroom gave me the idea."

"I hadn't thought of it until now, but our Craftsmans couldn't be more different. Mine's a small bungalow, yours is a big brick farmhouse. But yeah, they are from the same era."

Alex made sure the plastic sheeting was securely taped over the floor before he reached for the gallon of paint.

Although he'd asked about the color, Kate had kept it a secret. Until now.

He whistled as the lid popped open. "Lavender, huh? This will look nice in here."

"I was thinking light blue, at first." Kate reached for the two plastic trays waiting nearby while Alex stirred the paint. "Or maybe some sort of beige."

Alex wrinkled his nose.

"Exactly. Too boring, I decided. At the same time, this house is a classy lady; I didn't want anything too bold."

Kate had found so many ideas online; rich, moody colors were coming back in style after years of gray-based tones. She'd considered a shade of olive green the influencers were raving about, and even a few plum purples that were popular choices for those who dared to go darker. All of them had natural undertones that echoed the Craftsman style.

But in the end, Kate had decided she wanted a color that was light and fresh. Something the opposite of the former pantry, which had always been full of shadows. This soft lavender had some warmth to it, and would pair nicely with the white beadboard wainscotting. Once Kate and Alex painted the walls, rehung the mirror, and touched up the baseboards and trim, this compact bathroom would be complete.

Kate could have handled the painting on her own. In fact, there was hardly room for two people to be inside the bathroom at the same time. But Alex had been a part of this project from the start, offering ideas and energy. Even though Kate had taken on some of the work herself, she wanted him to share in its completion just as he had at its beginning.

As she climbed the lone ladder to cut in the lavender paint where the north wall met the ceiling, Kate felt blessed to have what was, in some ways, the best of both worlds: Alex had added a welcome dimension to her life, but he wasn't at the center of it.

By contrast, Kate and Ben had done everything together. They'd met in college through overlapping circles of friends, moved to Chicago after graduation, and shared an apartment before buying a bungalow just before their wedding. But ultimately, all that togetherness had come at a cost.

There'd been so many arguments while they put their personal touches on their house in Chicago. But most of the fights, in hindsight, had been about more than curtains and paint colors, and if the shrubs along the front porch needed to be replaced. Those disagreements had revealed deep cracks within the relationship that Kate hadn't been able to see, or willing to acknowledge, until it was too late and everything had ended.

Before she'd moved back to Eagle River, Kate had never had her own place. And now, she could paint this bathroom whatever color she wanted.

"I think this is going to take two coats." Alex smoothed the last of the painting tape along the top of the chair rail. "I may need to come back tomorrow night."

Kate turned on the ladder and smiled at him. "Two nights in a row? You'll spoil me, Alex Walsh."

"This bathroom reno has been a good gig," he said with a smirk as he filled his own paint tray. "I hope you'll decide to keep me around when my handyman skills are no longer needed."

"I most certainly will. Besides, you found a woman with a hundred-year-old house; what makes you think that you could get away from me that easily? Just this morning, the knob on the front closet door fell off, right into my hand. This place is going to require constant projects for years to come."

"Some of which, I know you can handle on your own." Alex gave her a proud smile. "You already fixed the knob, I bet."

"Yep." Kate turned back to her painting. "But it's fun to work on this house with you."

Hazel paused on her way to her food and water bowls to lift her snout over the baby gate and take a curious sniff.

Charlie was right behind her, his nose raised for the same reason. The kittens were upstairs, tucked safely inside what had become their nursery during the past two months. Because while the gate was enough to deter Charlie and Hazel from entering the bathroom, Kate knew the kittens would have climbed right over it.

Having her home overrun by four rambunctious kittens had made for some challenging moments. But the bond she'd forged with them, and the pride she felt as they learned to navigate their world, had made it all worthwhile.

Juliet and Hamlet were going home with the Fairlaines tomorrow evening when they came to collect the goats, and Kate blinked back a few tears as she focused on holding her paintbrush steady. And then, Minnie Trowbridge's granddaughter, Nicole, and her family were coming Saturday to meet Romeo and Ophelia.

Kate's house would feel markedly different within a few weeks. Whatever happened, she reminded herself as she moved the ladder, *she* wasn't going anywhere anytime soon. This house, and the security and stability it offered along with its tired decor and historical charm, was one thing Kate could count on.

If only Marie Lindgren could do the same. But given the gossip Bev had collected at the post office counter that afternoon, any hope there'd been about Marie going home was gone.

It had become clear in the last week or so that her health had been permanently compromised by her ordeal. Rehabilitation efforts hadn't been able to restore her strength and vitality, and she was moving to a long-term care facility.

Marie had suffered greatly, and that was bad enough. But to find out she was going to lose her home over this, too? That made Kate's simmering frustration boil over into a determination to keep looking for answers.

It had taken Randy a few tries to catch the Moores at

home, but he'd been successful yesterday afternoon. They were able to shed light on two pieces of the puzzle.

Dorothy and Ed were fairly certain no one had visited Marie's home between the time she'd returned from the Social Society luncheon and when her son asked them to check on his mom. Ed had mowed the lawn that afternoon, and Dorothy was weeding their garden before and after supper; they would have seen anyone coming and going next door.

So, just as Bev and Kate had always suspected, it was highly unlikely someone had poisoned Marie at her home.

Second, further reflection on the chaotic scene at the Lindgren house that night had helped the Moores nail down explanations for most of Marie's hallucinations.

While they couldn't come up with a reason for why the imaginary perpetrator's skin was purple, they had an idea who the image was loosely based on. Floyd had loved to fish, and he'd always worn a canvas, bucket-style hat decorated with dangling lures.

One of Marie's favorite hobbies was feeding the birds, which meant she fed the squirrels, too. She never forgot to set out peanuts for the pesky critters.

And the monstrous-sized spiders she'd claimed were crawling across the ceiling? Marie, who was afraid of arachnids, had recently found some in her basement. She'd paid extra to get a pest company out to her home that same day.

It all made sense to Kate. And it all spoke to how our pasts, our experiences, lived on in our memories. Marie's home, and the things that happened inside and outside its walls, were such a large part of her life that her mind had reached for them in an attempt to explain what was happening that night.

Thirty-some years in the same house. And nearly all of those lived with the same person, the person you loved the most. As Kate and her paintbrush turned a corner, she wondered what that would be like.

If even half of what Kate had heard was true, the Lindgrens' relationship hadn't been perfect. Some of the years Marie and Floyd spent together were rocky, at best. But they'd stuck it out, even as more and more people had decided they were unwilling to be miserable to keep a ring on their finger.

Kate and Ben had done the opposite. And while she was sorry their relationship hadn't worked out, Kate wasn't sorry they'd gone their separate ways in the end. Life with Ben, even a second decade with him, would have felt like how this bathroom did right now: confining, crowded, with not enough fresh air.

Kate reached for her paint roller, and a wave of excitement enveloped her as the wall in front of her was suddenly transformed. The lavender color she'd chosen was even better than she'd expected.

The original plaster had been saved, a bonus for both the home's historic character and Kate's bank account, even though it had taken several hours to fill the holes and smooth the cracks. And now, the past was being erased with a few turns of her wrist.

This little room was coming to life. It was being transformed into what Kate had imagined it could be, what she'd seen in her mind's eye that first night as she'd ripped down the old pantry shelves.

"I'm going to get that fan." Alex's voice broke into her swirling thoughts. He put down his paintbrush and stepped over the baby gate. "The exhaust vent can't keep up. I'll put the pizza in, while I'm at it."

His steps echoed away toward the living room, and Kate had a few moments to herself.

Could she see herself here in this house, for decades even, with someone else by her side? With Alex?

While their relationship seemed to be on solid ground,

she couldn't say for sure where it might lead. The way he'd surprised her last weekend at Stacy's reception was thoughtful and, if she had to admit it, terribly romantic. It had been like something straight out of a swoon-worthy movie.

But there would be many more times when Alex wouldn't be able to get away, when he couldn't be where Kate might want him to be. She understood; she was fine with that. Because Alex showed up for her emotionally, in so many ways; and that was far more important to Kate than any date on a calendar. And she tried to do the same for him.

As she dipped her roller into its tray, her involvement in the Lindgren case weighed on her yet again. She might paint herself into a corner with Alex by telling him what she had been up to, but wasn't it better to be honest?

At first, she'd assumed she'd fill him in once Marie's situation was figured out. There would be answers, and justice, to help sugarcoat news of her secrecy and smooth over any awkwardness that might emerge between Alex and Ray. But now, this case was starting to seem unsolvable for so many reasons.

Pete's lead from yesterday was intriguing, of course; but Kate and Bev had agreed it was quite a leap to implicate Judith in Marie's suffering given the decades that had gone by. And while Randy's conversation with the Moores had tied up those loose ends, nothing within it offered any hope for bringing the case to a close.

At some point, Kate was going to have to let this one go. Quit snooping around, stop asking questions. But even admitting defeat wouldn't solve her dilemma regarding Alex.

His cousin was going to be the town's police chief for the foreseeable future. Ray Calcott and his family were already established in this community, so much so that he'd encouraged Alex to move here, too. Ray was going to ride out this assignment until his pension kicked in; Kate was sure of that.

And she also felt certain that she and Alex would remain in each other's lives. The idea made her grin like a fool as she rolled more paint on the wall.

Alex was back with the fan. As usual, he noticed everything. "What?"

"It just looks so good." That was true, at least. "I can't wait to see how amazing it is when we're done. Even just this first coat."

Alex agreed, then turned back to the wall he'd been working on. Kate took a deep breath as the fan pushed fresh air in from the kitchen.

When she'd thought about how to tell Alex the truth, she had always envisioned them face to face. Together on a couch, for instance; or across a table.

But having this conversation while painting the powder room might be to her advantage. Standing on a ladder, with her back to him, might make it easier. And he would have a little room to process her news before he reacted to it. Besides, they were working with fast-drying paint; brush and roller marks were a possibility if they paused for too long.

Kate decided to seize this opportunity. Not just because she needed to clear the air with Alex.

But because she wasn't quite ready to give up on this case. Even if she should.

"I need to tell you something."

"What is it?" Alex's tone was suspiciously neutral, but Kate glanced his way in time to see tension settle into his shoulders.

"It's about Marie Lindgren."

"What about Marie?"

Kate ran through everything she knew; which wasn't much, especially one month into an investigation. Then she told him everything she suspected, and why. That took much longer.

"But I can't make the pieces fit. Neither can Bev. We don't

have a motive, we don't have a suspect. We aren't even certain something criminal occurred."

The top of her wall was finished, and she started down the ladder. The words were coming out in a rush now, and it felt so good to say them.

"And I didn't want you to know. I didn't want you caught in the middle, between me and your cousin. It complicates things. But it's always going to be complicated. I'd like to think nothing bad's ever going to happen again, but ..."

Alex's knowing laugh made her turn around.

"Oh, I'm sure it will. It always does, everywhere." He finished his section with a few more flicks of his wrist, then set his roller in its tray. He was silent for a few moments, and Kate waited.

"Thank you, I guess," he finally said. "And I don't just mean for ... keeping me out of the loop."

"I lied about it." Kate shook her head. "You can call it what it was. I'm sorry."

He shrugged. "Well, you had your reasons for doing that. But thank you for thinking of me, for how it might affect me if I knew what you were up to."

"Well," Kate said with a sigh, "I'm not sure it's going to matter for much longer, anyway."

In two very short steps, Alex was at her side. "What? You and Bev aren't giving up, are you?"

"We need to talk it over first, but ... I don't see how we can keep going."

"No." He put a gentle hand on her arm. "No, don't do that."

It was Kate's turn to laugh. "I never pegged you as being an eternal optimist. Your level-headed approach to life is one of the things I like about you."

She had almost said "love," but caught herself just in time.

"Same here." The look in Alex's eyes told her he was in agreement with her on more than one front. "But another of your admirable qualities is your intuition, and your determination to follow where it leads you."

"Maybe. But I think this case is approaching a dead end. It's time to bail out of the car before we run into that tree up ahead."

"There's no tree," he insisted. "A bump in the road, sure; and it sounds like there have been many of those. But your intuition is telling you to keep going, right? If you're honest with yourself?"

Kate nodded slowly.

"Then keep going." The conviction in his voice was unmistakable. "Sure, it's only just a hunch, but I can't tell you how many times a case has been solved because those investigating refused to give up. You never know what you might come across, what you might hear, when someone thinks no one is paying attention."

Alex put his arm around her. Kate leaned into his embrace, mindful of the splash of wet paint on the shoulder of his tee shirt.

"If anyone can stop this person, it's you." His words in her ear warmed Kate to her toes. "I believe you can do it. Marie deserves answers, and the community needs answers." He chuckled. "Hell, my cousin needs answers."

Kate wanted to find out what Alex had heard, but decided to let that go. While what she'd just told him had put her mind at ease, Alex was still caught in the middle. It would always be this way.

"I don't know all the details." Kate heard the ring of truth in Alex's words. "But I know Ray's at a loss on this one, for sure."

"OK," she finally said. "OK, then. Bev and I won't stop looking. At least, not yet."

"That's good enough for me." Alex gave her a lingering kiss before he picked up his roller. "Let's tackle this smaller wall next. Maybe we can finish it before the pizza is ready."

✳ 20 ✳

"I can't believe we're a week into July already." Roberta shook her head in awe as the carriers wrapped up their tasks for the day. Then she crouched down to where Hazel lounged on the cool concrete floor.

"Thank you for spending time with us today, Miss Hazel." The dog gave a happy whimper as the postmaster petted her plush fur. "You'll be going home to see Charlie soon. I bet he misses you when you're gone."

Kate wasn't so sure. "He still has Ophelia and Romeo to look after. They keep him busy. For now."

"When is Minnie's granddaughter picking them up?" Marge asked. "I'm so glad the kittens were adopted in pairs!"

"Nicole's coming back later this week. And you're right; this is the happiest ending I could have hoped for."

Kate tried to put a positive spin on the situation, one that was a bit more than what she actually felt. She was excited for the babies to have permanent homes, hopeful about their futures ... and also very sad to see them go.

"It'll be one more thing off my summer to-do list." She started to clean her mail case. "The powder room is done. Stacy's wedding is in the books. The goats came and went. I could spend the next two months lounging in the porch swing, and that'd be just fine with me."

"Now that we're past the Fourth of July, things always slow down," Jack proclaimed as he reached into his locker. "There's a reason they call it the lazy, hazy days of summer. Of course, that ends when the sweet corn festival rolls around. And school starts the week after that."

"Don't remind me." Mae rubbed Hazel's ears, then fed the post office mascot a scrap of leftover roast beef from her lunch tote. "I'm just trying to make the most out of summer. How is my oldest going to be in seventh grade in the fall? But I guess they can't stay small forever. I need to get to the sitter's and pick up the littles, by the way."

As Mae hurried out, Kate readied Hazel's leash. "We have a stop to make on the way home, too. I promised Hazel a walk on the bike trail after she wrapped up her shift."

As soon as Kate said "bike trail," Hazel's fluffy tail began to wave back and forth.

"She knows exactly where you are going." Roberta held the door for Hazel and Kate and all their gear. "You girls have fun!"

Kate dropped her stuff on Bertha's passenger seat while Hazel settled on her blanket in the back. Out to Main Street they went, then turned south and over the river bridge. A block past the stoplight, Kate took a left and parked along a side street near the former rail line.

"We won't go too far in this heat," she promised as they got out of the car. "Maybe we'll make it to the trestle, then double back." The entire jaunt wouldn't be more than ten blocks, but it was enough to give them a little extra exercise after a long day on the road. And some fresh scenery, too.

While Hazel enjoyed their walks down the gravel roads, a trot on the trail had become one of the dog's favorite activities. There were so many houses to look at in town, different birds to study. And those bold, bossy "urban" squirrels were another fun distraction.

Hazel had been especially in need of distractions ever

since Juliet and Hamlet left Thursday evening. The dog had spent the long Fourth of July weekend searching high and low for her two tiny friends, and seemed increasingly protective of Romeo and Ophelia.

While Charlie had been a bit unmoored by Hamlet and Juliet's departure, Kate sensed he now accepted their absence. But when the last of the kittens left in a few days, Kate knew Charlie would turn unsettled again. And Hazel might become downright despondent. This Monday post office shift had lifted the dog's spirits; several more might be needed in the coming weeks until Hazel adjusted to her old, and quieter, routine at home.

The trees were thick along the asphalt trail, and provided some privacy for the backyards along the way. Some of the older specimens almost met overhead, giving the recreational path welcome patches of shade. It was still a bit early for most people to be off work but, given it was summer, Kate and Hazel might meet a few runners, walkers, or cyclists before they reached the east edge of Eagle River.

That was another reason Kate liked to bring Hazel out on the trail. Her social skills were solid, but she didn't get many chances to give them a workout since she spent most of her time in the country.

"Maybe we need to take in the farmers market some afternoon," Kate mused as they meandered along. "There'd be lots of new people there for you to meet. Dogs, too."

The rush of flowing water soon came to them on the breeze, then grew louder as they reached the river's banks. Or rather, found themselves high above them. The trestle-turned-pedestrian bridge was the crown jewel of this section of county-owned trail, and Kate admired the patina of its weathered iron beams while Hazel spied on three men fishing along the water's edge below.

Kate and Hazel were on their way back through town when Kate spotted movement off the path. Hazel noticed it, too; her ears pricked up as she pulled on the lead.

Someone was zigzagging around on a property up ahead and to the right. Through one of the gaps in the shrubs and trees, Kate thought she saw the flash of a white shirt and arms moving up and down. Was someone washing windows? Or, even in this modern age, hanging laundry on a clothesline?

Hazel was impatient now, and picked up her speed. Kate had no choice but to do the same. As they drew closer, Kate realized the man wasn't on a homeowner's lawn; he was at the old depot property.

"What's going on?" Kate and Hazel were still too far away for the man to hear her, but she kept her voice low. "The depot's vacant, has been for years. Fred said that ..."

Hazel began to bark; that guy was somewhere he wasn't supposed to be! The other folks they'd met, one on two wheels and the other on foot, had stayed on the asphalt. They'd respected the "no trespassing" signs posted on many back fences along the trail.

"Hazel, stop it!"

But the dog pretended she couldn't hear the command. There was a buffer strip of mowed grass between the trail and the back property lines, and Hazel lunged toward it. With Kate still holding tight to her lead, the dog ran through a break in the trees and charged at the young man.

His shirt was indeed white; a polo paired with sharply creased khakis. Not exactly the uniform of someone intent on vandalism, or mischief of any sort, but Kate couldn't be too careful. Something was definitely not right here.

"Hazel!" she hissed again. "No!"

The guy turned away from the dusty depot windows long enough to give them a wide smile. But it wasn't clear what kind. Disarming, perhaps? Just friendly, or suspiciously so?

He calmly went back to whatever he was doing, which seemed questionable to Kate. The young man was trying to look inside the building, but the glass was beyond dirty and the sun bouncing off the walls made that even harder. Then he crouched in the weeds, and brazenly tried to wrench open the bottom pane even though Kate and Hazel weren't ten feet away. When it didn't budge, he moved to the next window.

Kate braced herself for whatever the guy might do next. His hands were empty, but what about his pockets?

She was in a bind. She had ahold of Hazel's lead with both hands, as it was the only way to keep her dog from charging the intruder. She'd have to give up half of her control of Hazel to even attempt to pull out her phone and call dispatch.

It had been apparent to Kate for several weeks now that no one had tried to break into Marie Lindgren's home. But this? It looked like attempted burglary to her, with the potential to turn into vandalism, too.

The young man turned around again as Hazel continued to bark. This time, he raised a hand in greeting.

"Hello, there! Hey, doggie," he sang to Hazel, who wasn't quite ready to stand down but seemed a few degrees calmer. "Are you on patrol today?"

"What are you doing here?" Kate didn't know what else to say. "This place is ..."

"Empty, I know." He reached for his phone, and calmly tapped at its screen for several seconds. Texting someone or taking notes; Kate wasn't sure which.

"It's pretty rough, right? I was just checking the windows, making sure they're tightly closed." He rubbed one dirty window with his palm, and tried again to see inside. "I would hope whoever was in there last turned the latches on all the sashes, but I can't be sure. I mean, I don't have a key."

Well, obviously. Kate stared at him in disbelief as he moved on to the next bank of windows. There were over a dozen of them on this side of the depot alone; this could take a while. Hazel, for whatever reason, had decided he was nice enough; and had gone into a "sit" on the broken concrete slab that jutted out from the back entrance.

"We need to be sure the property is secure," the guy explained as he waded back into the weeds. "It wouldn't do to have anyone trying to get in."

Kate and Hazel followed behind, but at a safe distance and away from the volunteer vegetation. Kate's now-experienced eyes checked for signs of poison ivy and stinging nettle, but didn't find any. Which was good, because the young man seemed oblivious to such dangers.

She searched for conversation while she waited for a plausible explanation of what was going on. "I doubt anyone's going to be skulking around here. This depot hasn't been used in decades; I can't imagine there's anything of value inside."

"That's what I'm thinking." He nodded in agreement. "It's a dump, to put it kindly." He almost wiped his hands on his chinos, then thought better of it. "Not worth much. But the land? Now, that's something else, entirely."

He gave the lot an appraising glance, and nodded with satisfaction. "It's worth a pretty penny! Location is everything in this business. Over half an acre, right here in town. Quick access to the shops along Main Street, and both highways."

Kate was stunned by the admiration in his voice.

"But the best feature of all is that rec trail! Just step out your back door, hop on your bike, and ride all the way across the county if you want to. You couldn't find a better parcel, if you ask me. There's absolutely nothing in Eagle River that can hold a candle to this."

Kate's mind tried to keep up with his musings, while Hazel turned her attention to sniffing for signs of wildlife. "Are you telling me," she said slowly, "that this piece of land is being considered for redevelopment? Is it for sale?"

The guy stared at her for a moment, as if weighing his words carefully.

"Well," he finally said. "Not really. Or, sort of."

He gestured toward the street side of the building, which was out of sight. "I have the signs in the car," he said, more to himself than to Kate. "Word's going to get out as it is." When he turned back toward her, she saw excitement in his eyes.

"There's an offer coming in on this property, maybe as soon as tomorrow. My boss says he'll cut me a third of the commission if I handle most of the paperwork. It'll be my first deal, you see."

And then, the young real estate agent shook his head in a show of disbelief.

"But the seller wants to play it all by the book, I guess. He wants to give others a chance, if they want in the game." Then he shrugged. "If there's a bidding war before this is all over, that's fine with me."

"You'll get more money, of course."

"I sure will!" He grinned. "Hey, do you know anyone who might be interested?"

Me, Kate thought. *Because I want to know what the hell is going on here.*

"I think I know who the owner is," she said evenly. "Let's just say, I'm surprised he's considering selling it." She gave the young man an engaging smile. "Who's the buyer?"

He laughed.

"Now, that I can't talk about. It's confidential. Besides, we don't have a formal offer yet." He rubbed his hands in anticipation as he headed for the corner of the building. Kate and Hazel followed him around to the front.

"I already checked this side; everything's locked," the young man said as he ambled toward a freshly washed black SUV, and pulled a key fob from his pocket. Two chirps, and the back hatch opened.

"It was nice to meet you," he told Kate as he hauled out a sign and planted it in the weed-choked lawn, close to the sidewalk. "What's your name again?"

"I didn't say." Kate returned his shallow smile. "But it's Kate. And this is Hazel."

"Such a pretty dog! I thought she might take my arm off,

for a few seconds there. I'm Dylan." He gave Kate a quick wave, one that felt more like dismissal than friendliness. "If you hear of anyone else who might be interested, our number's right there on the sign. Have a good evening!"

Kate only nodded, too surprised to do anything else, as Dylan shut the hatch and got behind the wheel. In a house across the street, she caught the subtle motion of window blinds being adjusted.

Dylan was right: word was going to get out fast.

Kate didn't know exactly what was going on, or how she could find out as quickly as possible. But she did know one thing.

"We need to get home, Hazel. Let's go."

*　*　*

Kate hardly noticed Scout by the back steps as she hurried toward the house, Bertha left parked in the driveway. There wasn't time to put the mail car in the garage.

"Something's happened." She gave Scout only a quick pet before reaching for her house keys. Hazel had already dashed off across the yard. "And I need to find out what it is."

She dumped her purse on the kitchen counter as Charlie, trailed by Romeo and Ophelia, stared at her with a curious expression. Kate snatched her phone from her purse, and brought up Bev in its contact list.

"What happened?" Bev was alarmed by the tone of Kate's voice. "Are you OK?"

"Yes, sorry." She paused for a deep breath. "But something's going on with the case, something big. The depot is for sale!"

Bev was stunned. "Wait a sec. Marie is selling the depot? She and Floyd have that handshake agreement with the historical group! Why would she ever ..."

"I don't think Marie is in charge of that anymore, given her health these days. I'm sure her son in Cedar Rapids is still the trustee; he was listed as such in the online assessor records a few weeks ago."

Kate quickly filled Bev in on everything that just happened.

"You and Hazel were in the right spot at the right time! So, someone approached the Lindgrens, and now the land's for sale. What are the odds that the people behind the offer had something to do with what happened to Marie?"

"It's the biggest lead we've found so far!" Kate was trying not to hope this development was the key to unlocking the whole mess, but she had a feeling it might do just that. "The kid wouldn't tell me more, but ..."

"Do you have Fred Winthrop's number? I might have it here somewhere. I wonder what he's heard?"

"I think I do, from when we were in the community chorus for the holiday festival. I'm going to call him right now!"

Kate heard movement in the background on Bev's end of the call, and Clyde asking her why she was "so riled up."

"I'm going out to feed and water the horses," Bev told Kate, "but call me the second you have anything. Thank goodness I have a good signal out behind the barn."

Kate did indeed have Fred's number. He must have had hers in his phone, as he picked it up right away. She didn't waste any time.

"I just heard the depot is for sale. What is going on? Is there even a chance the historical society is buying it?"

"Not one damn bit!" Fred's anger was unmistakable. "We're poor as church mice, for goodness' sake. There's no way we can compete with those developer folks and their deep pockets!"

"Who exactly is trying to buy it? Do you know?" Kate gripped the edge of the kitchen counter for support. Charlie had jumped up on it and was wandering about, but she didn't even notice.

"Powell Construction is what I was told. They want to tear down the depot, then slap a couple of duplexes on the property and rent them out. Can you imagine?"

That company's title sounded like it was based on a surname. But whose?

And then, Kate realized where she'd heard it before.

Stacy's friend Kelsey was married to Chad Powell. This company had to be owned by someone in their extended family. Kelsey worked in an insurance office, but what did her husband do? Kate wasn't sure.

But she knew Kelsey was a member of the Eagle River Social Society. And she'd been at that luncheon.

"Scott Lindgren called me last night," Fred went on while Kate leaned against the counter, her mind running a mile a minute.

"He sounded sorry, I'll give him that. Swore up and down that this company came to him, not the other way around. Marie's in bad shape, as you know; and assisted living costs a fortune. Between being trustee and Marie's son, he feels like it's an offer he can't refuse. He wanted me to know about it before anyone else."

Fred suspected the Lindgrens didn't have long-term care insurance, which surprised him since Floyd always seemed like a smart fellow, and his real estate business had a reputation for being profitable. "But then, you never really know about people."

Kate couldn't have agreed more with that statement, especially given the shocking events of the past hour.

Fred believed Scott was being honest when he insisted he wished things were different.

"His parents wanted the society to have the depot, and he knows that. But now that he's been approached by someone else, he says he has to look after his mom, first and foremost. I can't fault him there."

The historical group should have gotten something in

writing years ago, Fred said. "When I first joined the board, I'd pushed folks to do that very thing, set up a formal deal that couldn't be challenged. But no one wanted to ruffle feathers, you see; and there would have been attorney fees to pay. They never got it done."

What Fred had heard from the Lindgrens' son matched what the real estate agent had just told Kate: The depot parcel was perfectly positioned for redevelopment, making it highly valuable to the right buyer.

Marie and Floyd's home would eventually be sold, Fred told Kate, but it would be several months before that transaction could generate a profit. The house required upgrading to maximize its potential, Scott had told Fred, and its contents needed to be sorted and divided among the Lindgrens' descendants. Fred didn't know what the family planned to do with the farmland held within the trust.

Kate wanted so badly to tell Fred what she suspected, but didn't. She needed more information, something solid; and then, she and Bev needed to go straight to law enforcement with everything they'd uncovered.

Kelsey had taken a carrot cake to the Social Society luncheon. Kate needed to confirm what its ingredients had likely been, and then figure out how Kelsey might have altered the cake to make people so sick.

Kate's laptop waited on the dining room table, and she started in that direction while Fred continued to vent his frustration.

"When exactly is Scott getting this offer?" she asked as she powered up her computer. "That agent told me it would probably be tomorrow."

"That sounds right. Scott called one of Floyd's old real estate buddies, who rushed to get the parcel officially listed. It's not likely anyone has the interest, or the cash, to force those developers into a bidding war. But you never know."

Fred gave a bitter laugh. "I'd love to see someone give the

Powells a run for their money. If they want to undermine us like this, then they can pay top dollar to do it."

Shocked gossip and unkind whispers were sure to surface as word got out about the depot offer, and Kate knew that could prove helpful to the case. End-running someone's long-held agreement with a local nonprofit wasn't going to win the Powells any points in the court of public opinion. But they either cared too much about money, or simply didn't care at all.

Kate let Fred ramble while she searched online for carrot cake recipes. She recalled Kelsey claiming she'd made her grandmother's version, but that didn't matter. Because at this point, Kate couldn't put stock in a single thing Kelsey had said.

Fred's boiling fury eventually lowered to a simmer. "Well, I should let you go. I'm glad you called, though. This has been beyond disappointing for me and the other officers in the historical society. And I think it's going to be the same for the rest of the town."

Kate was typing as fast as she could, pulling up recipe variations and copying them into a blank document, but her hands suddenly paused over the laptop keyboard.

Hadn't Mayor Benson mentioned something about a developer wanting to build duplexes in Eagle River? Maybe that morning at Peabody's when Kate was trying to track down goats to rent?

If she remembered right, the project hadn't been anything more than an idea when it was pitched to city leaders.

"If those developers want to put up duplexes," she told Fred, "the depot property has to be rezoned. And I don't think I've heard of the city council voting on such a change. That would've been huge news."

"You're right. They haven't yet." Even so, Fred already sounded defeated. "And that's the other reason I know we're never going to get that depot turned into a museum. The whole thing's already been settled off the record."

One of Eagle River's five council members, Jim Abernathy, was part of the Powell family by marriage. Jim had been quietly asking the panel's other members for support, Fred had been told by someone he wouldn't name.

The rest of the governing board was so eager for new housing in the community, especially rentals, that they were willing to set aside hopes for a museum in the name of progress. Because if the parcel was redeveloped into a for-profit project, it would generate property-tax cash for decades to come.

While the land was currently zoned for industrial use, it was surrounded by single-family homes. Those residents were sure to protest against a higher-density residential development being built in their neighborhood, but it was too late.

"It won't matter one bit," Fred told Kate before he hung up. "The council already has the votes to get this done, even if Jim abstains as he should. There is nothing we can do to stop them."

* * *

Alex had warned Kate she'd need more than a suspect to hope to close this case. Now, after all these weeks, she finally had one. And a motive, as well.

But because it was unlikely that Kelsey would confess to what she'd done, even that wasn't going to be enough. Kate had to keep looking.

As she reviewed some of the carrot cake recipes she'd pulled from online, Kate realized there were many different variations. Some had raisins, others featured nuts. Pineapple was sometimes added. Several spices were usually included: cinnamon, nutmeg, cloves, ginger; but nothing out of the ordinary.

"Some of these use coconut, some don't. But they all have

several ingredients that affect the taste and give the cake texture. It would be easy to add something suspicious, and no one would notice. Especially if it was finely ground."

A hefty overdose of pulverized nuts, if the rest of the dry ingredients were reduced to make up for their volume, would have been difficult to detect. Even so, Kate wasn't convinced that was the answer. A quick search confirmed her hunch.

Nuts could make people who were allergic to them very sick, and some of the symptoms overlapped with what all the women experienced. But that didn't explain Marie's hallucinations.

Kate put her head in her hands, tried to come up with a better answer.

"It might have been a poisonous liquid," she told Charlie, who'd hopped up on a nearby chair to supervise her search. "If not, I bet Kelsey used a finely ground toxic plant. Either way, it could be just about anything. There's no way to know what it was."

Bev was waiting for her call, but there was one more thing Kate wanted to try. It would only take a few minutes to run each common ingredient through an online search, just to make sure she wasn't missing something.

She started with the dry ingredients. Flour wasn't poisonous, as long as the dish it was added to had been baked or cooked. Sugar, salt ... the usual health warnings came up, but nothing else. Baking powder, however, raised a red flag. Kate discovered that extremely high concentrations made a person's blood very alkaline, which could lead to confusion and seizures. Baking soda carried some of the same warnings.

"Who knew such common ingredients could be so dangerous? But confusion and hallucinations aren't quite the same thing."

And too much of either baking soda or baking powder would have ruined the carrot cake. The dessert would have risen too quickly, then collapsed into a sorry-looking lump that no one would dare serve at a party.

Kate moved on to the spices. Cinnamon had some worrisome issues, if it wasn't processed properly or was consumed in excessive amounts, but ...

She gasped, then leaned forward. Read the last sentence again.

Nutmeg?!

Another example of having too much of a good thing. But this time, the symptoms were noticeably more varied and unusual. And dangerous.

"Look at these neurological conditions! Dizziness, anxiety, *hallucinations.* 'In severe instances, seizures can occur.' Death is possible? Those are very rare cases, sure; but ...”

Every carrot cake recipe Kate had found contained nutmeg. The amounts were very small: half a teaspoon at most, often less. But it would have been easy for Kelsey to overload her cake batter with the spice, which was sold in the baking aisle at every grocery store.

"Did she set out to kill Marie, and didn't quite accomplish her goal?" Kate stared at the wall, trying to process what she'd just uncovered. "In the end, she didn't even need to take it that far. Given Marie's age and a few health issues, Kelsey had Marie right where she wanted her to be."

Suffering with declining health, then shipped off to a care facility. Her adult children grappling with a list of sudden, staggering expenses ... and holding the deed to the perfect parcel for a multi-family housing development.

Kate saw it all unfolding in her mind. And then, she saw nothing but red.

White-hot anger, truth be told.

She was furious about what had happened to Marie, of course; but it was so much more than that. A great wrong had been done to the community as well.

All those nights Eagle River residents checked their locks multiple times, had been afraid to walk their dogs at dusk.

The moments they feared some evil person was waiting in the shadows to attack them, or break into their homes.

It was the opposite of what small-town life should be, of what people in and around Eagle River usually enjoyed and even took for granted.

Just like trust, support, friendship ... the same things that had drawn local women to join the Social Society for over a hundred and fifty years. The same sort of camaraderie that had so quickly developed among the women invited to Stacy's bachelorette party.

Kelsey had been a part of that, too. Or at least, she'd done a fine job of pretending.

Even with a stack of new clues, Kate still couldn't say how Kelsey had sickened Marie so terribly while the other women affected had only one night of misery, and most club members had no symptoms at all.

There was only one way to find out. Kate and Bev needed to circle back with the ladies in the Social Society, find one woman who could dissect that luncheon in greater detail. Someone would have to point the finger at Kelsey in whatever way they could. And not say a word to anyone else about what they revealed to Bev and Kate.

Because if Kelsey had been willing to permanently harm, or perhaps even murder, Marie Lindgren so the Powells could seize a piece of property for a song, what might she do if she discovered someone was closing in on her scheme?

Kate reached for her phone. Bev picked up on the second ring.

"Well? Did you find anything?"

"You bet I did. And while I tell you, I need you to think about who within the Social Society you trust the most to do the right thing."

✳ 21 ✳

"This is going to be quite the tea party," Kate muttered as she turned up the Stewarts' lane the following afternoon.

"What exactly are we going to say? 'Why hello, Sonja! It's so good to see you. Would you like something to drink? Oh, by the way, do you think Kelsey Powell tried to murder Marie Lindgren?'"

It was the perfect summer day: blue skies; warm, but not hot; a refreshing breeze. Bev's beloved horses were in the side pasture, feasting on the thick grass. Her rosebushes were in full bloom, their pink blossoms lining the white picket fence that separated the front yard from the driveway.

Two well-fed cats lounged on the steps of the farmhouse's generous front porch, where Kate spotted Bev and Sonja Carlson sitting at a small table covered with a blue-and-white-striped tablecloth.

Kate had brought something for this gathering, but it wasn't food.

Along with serving as a witness to Sonja and Bev's conversation, Kate's role was to drop off one of her lunch totes and pass it off as belonging to Bev. It was the first idea that had come to mind as the sleuths pondered how to explain Kate showing up at the Stewarts' farm on a late Tuesday afternoon.

Kate rehearsed her lines in a whisper before she got out of the car.

"Oh, Bev left this in the breakroom yesterday. I'm on my way over to my parents' place, they live only a few miles from here. I just thought I'd drop it off ..."

At some point, she would have to drop the charade. So would Bev. They'd decided to figure it out as they went along, take their cues from Sonja and what she had to share.

Sonja and Bev had known each other nearly all their lives. And since they were both in their fifties, it was a friendship they'd enjoyed for several decades. In addition to attending school together, they'd been in the same confirmation class at their church. When their now-grown children were still at home, the Stewart and Carlson families had grown closer at sporting events, weekend sleepovers, and 4-H meetings.

When Bev first reached out to Sonja about the Social Society's luncheon, she hadn't pried too deeply into the situation. Sonja had been sick following the meeting; and it had seemed too violating, too calculating, to press her too hard.

And at the time, Bev and Kate had no idea which direction this case was going. Or if there was even a case, at all. But now, armed with the information they had in hand? It was time to dig into every tiny detail.

Kate heard a radio playing in the kitchen as she came through the back door. Clyde, his shirt sleeves rolled up to reveal his farmer tan, gave her a nod of greeting and solidarity as she passed by the table.

"I was told the television in the living room would be too loud on the porch." He tipped his head toward the radio, which was broadcasting a baseball game. "The Twins are up by two already; I don't want to miss even one inning." He paused for a sip of his iced tea. "By the way, I hope you girls hit a home run."

"Me, too. Thanks."

It was one of those rare July days when the air conditioning was off and the windows were open. As Kate made her way toward the porch's screen door, she heard Bev and Sonja laughing and chatting.

"Hey, Kate! Thanks for stopping by!" Bev's smile was genuine, even though Kate caught a hint of nervousness in her friend's tone. Could they pull this off? And, more importantly, get the answers they needed?

"Here's your lunch tote." Kate handed it over. "I'm glad you called when you did, I was just about to leave. Now you have it for tomorrow."

Sonja motioned toward one of the empty chairs, then scooted her own to the side. "You're such a good friend to bring it by. Why don't you join us, if you have a few minutes? This iced tea is delicious!"

"I always add fresh mint from the garden," Bev said. "And Sonja brought her famous chocolate-chip cookies."

Sonja leaned in as Kate sat down. "They stay soft thanks to a box of vanilla pudding mix. It's my secret ingredient."

Bev raised her eyebrows at Kate.

"I was so glad when you called last night." Sonja's blonde curls were streaked with gray, and they caught the breeze blowing up from the road. "We haven't seen each other in ages! I told Joe, we can still go into Swanton for groceries when I get home."

She passed the cookies to Kate. "It's so important to maintain friendships, especially as we age. I hope you younger ladies always remember that."

The conversation went in several expected directions for a few minutes. Kate and Bev had agreed to give Sonja a chance to settle in before they approached her with their request. Finally, Bev spoke up.

"And how is Marie Lindgren doing? I heard she's moved to assisted living. Have you had a chance to visit her?"

Sonja gave a rueful sigh as she shook her head. "Here I

am, going on about how important it is to keep up with your friends, and I haven't gotten over to see her yet. I hope to do that yet this week, or next. I called her, once, and she sounded … tired, I guess. It's just so sad how quickly she's declined."

"She's been through a lot," Kate said. "It sounds like she's not likely to get back to her old self."

Bev leaned across the table to pat Sonja on the arm. "My dear, I have to confess: I lured you here today under a bit of false pretense. There's something I want to talk to you about." She cut her eyes at Kate. "That we both need to talk to you about."

Sonja seemed more curious than offended. Kate was relieved.

"Well, by all means, Bev Stewart, don't keep me in suspense! Let me guess: Do the post office folks have an idea for a fundraiser? I might be able to get the Social Society ladies on board. I'm not an officer these days, but …"

"It's not about a charitable project," Kate said gently. "But it does concern the women's club."

"And Marie." Bev blinked back a few sudden tears. "Oh, poor Marie! Kate, why don't you share what you discovered yesterday?"

As Kate ran through everything she and Bev now knew, Sonja's eyes went wide with interest, then shock, and then terror. She started at Kate, and then Bev, and then back again, as her mind tried to take it all in.

"You think …" It was hard for Sonja to say it out loud. "You think Kelsey tried to murder Marie to get that property? Or at least, make her so sick she'd have to sell it?"

Sonja stared out at the freshly mowed front lawn, and the pasture beyond it that went all the way down to the gravel road. "Good Lord, it's …"

"Terrible," Bev said. "Evil. Monstrous. Every bad word you can think of? It fits."

"And that's why we wanted to talk to you," Kate told

Sonja. "Especially about that carrot cake Kelsey brought. I heard it was her grandmother's recipe, but I don't know ..."

"It wasn't a cake," Sonja interjected. "I mean, it was a 'carrot cake,' yes. But she brought cupcakes to the luncheon." Sonja's expression darkened with fury. "They were cupcakes! Separate servings, for all of us."

Kate and Bev stared at each other for a second. This changed everything. This was exactly what they needed to know.

The Eagle River Social Society acknowledged members' birthdays every month, Sonja reported. Because of the club's summer break, the early-June meeting was when they celebrated several of those milestones. Three women, including Sonja, were honored at the last luncheon.

"Kelsey used that as an excuse!" Sonja hissed. "She said she wanted to bring cupcakes because of the birthdays! She had them in one of those carry-along potluck totes, you know what I mean. All lined up, row after row, and three of them had candles on top." She frowned. "Mine was green."

The junior club member had made quite a fuss about using a family recipe for the birthday cupcakes. Kelsey's grandmother had been a longtime member before she'd passed away, and Sonja now believed Kelsey knew the ladies would have a built-in layer of trust in what she served that day.

Kelsey passed out the cupcakes herself, Sonja recalled. They never made it as far as the buffet table.

"And that makes sense, doesn't it?" Bev crossed her arms. "Because of the birthdays. It gave her an excuse to control who got which cupcake."

But Kelsey had been careful to make everything appear random. Robin Granath, one of the members who'd fallen ill, was not one of the "birthday girls." Nor was Marie.

Kate had to hand it to Kelsey; the younger woman had given this a great deal of thought. "She marked the cupcakes somehow, then. Either on the bottom of the liners, or the order in which they were placed in the container. And of course, a few of them had candles of different colors. She knew beyond a doubt which was which."

Sonja groaned and covered her face with her hands. "And none of the rest of us were the wiser! Everyone was exclaiming over the cupcakes and the candles. It felt so special. Normally we serve ourselves from the desserts that are brought, then sing 'Happy Birthday' once everyone is settled."

Kate had one more very important question for Sonja. "What did your cupcake taste like?"

Sonja looked down for a moment. When she looked up, there were tears in her eyes. Anger, humiliation, and embarrassment were visible, as well.

"It was awful! It tasted like, I don't know ... sawdust, or something. No, that's not it. It was ... spicier than what I expected." She shook her head in frustration. "It's hard to describe it, but something was definitely off about it."

Sonja slapped one palm on the table in frustration. "But I ate it, anyway! And I didn't say a word! If I had known, if I'd had any idea ..."

"But you didn't," Bev said gently. "Who would ever think someone would do something like this?"

"I guess it's how we were raised." Sonja looked at Bev, and Bev nodded in understanding.

"Girls of our generation, and older, had that drilled into us when we were children," Sonja explained to Kate. "You never, ever, criticize someone's cooking. Women were proud of what came out of their kitchens. Especially since cooking and baking was such a chore; far worse than today, with all our boxed mixes and shortcuts."

"If you went to someone's house," Bev added, "and they served you something, you cleaned your plate and thanked them for it. Or, at the very least, you had to eat enough to be polite; then push it around with your fork, slip some into your napkin, or whatever. But you never complained about what was put in front of you."

Kate was so angry, her heartbeat was pounding in her ears.

"And Kelsey knows that. She knew the older ladies wouldn't question any of it, not even to each other! Is it safe to say that none of the club's younger members were sickened?"

Sonja thought for a moment, then nodded.

Kate was still furious, but now she felt a small dash of hope. It all added up; as crazy as it was, it made a great deal of sense.

And that's what would be needed to have any chance of Kelsey being charged with a crime.

"How much nutmeg did she put in Marie's cupcake, then?" Sonja shook her head in disbelief. "It had to taste terrible, even worse than mine. So ... what do we do now? I want to help, whatever that requires."

"I knew you would." Bev smiled at her old friend. "I think you and I need to have a chat with Sheriff Preston. The poisoning occurred in Prosper; as you know, they contract with the county for law enforcement. It's under his jurisdiction."

"When?"

"Today," Kate said, even though it was already late afternoon. "That offer's coming in on the depot property; Scott Lindgren may already have it in hand. Word's going to get out about that, people will be talking."

"We can't risk anyone putting two and two together," Bev explained, "and blabbing that around, too. If Kelsey thinks her cover's been blown, who knows what she might do? The sheriff needs to sort this out and, hopefully, arrest her before she has any clue what's coming her way."

Sonja agreed. "But I'm scared. That girl ... what she did ..."

Bev reached for her phone. "And that's why we need to take action right now."

Despite her worries, Sonja allowed herself a small chuckle. "Well, now," she told Kate in a teasing tone, "I guess there are advantages to being the sheriff's high-school sweetheart, hmm?"

"I'm calling the non-emergency number." Bev gave her friend a playful swat. "We're going to do this by the book. They'll reach out to Jeff, and he'll get back to us right away."

"I know you're nervous," Kate told Sonja, "but think of what Marie has been through."

Sonja nodded. "Marie deserves justice. We all do. If I can make that happen, I will."

Tuesday evening, Sonja did much more than tell Sheriff Preston what she knew about the Social Society's luncheon. She also rallied four other members of the club to make their own statements regarding what they observed that day at the Prosper community center.

None of the women had ever witnessed a crime before, and all of them were unsure about how to proceed. But when it mattered, every single one of the ladies set their nervousness aside to do the right thing.

Wendy Teague recalled that not only had Kelsey passed out the cupcakes herself, but she'd lifted them high when she removed them from their container. It had seemed odd to Wendy at the time; but she now understood that Kelsey had marked the liners and wanted to ensure the toxic treats were passed out according to her plan.

Kelsey had taken an especially fond interest in Marie in the months leading up to the incident, club president Carolyn Dahlberg told the sheriff. Judith Prescott, who may or may not have been Marie's former romantic rival, reinforced that idea by saying the same.

Judith had initially assumed Kelsey's motive was mere friendliness; or, at most, an attempt to network through Marie's real-estate connections to benefit the insurance agency she worked for, the Powells' construction business, or both.

And Alyssa Livingston remembered how Kelsey, despite not being on the committee for the annual luncheon, had been all-too eager to clear plates and dispose of trash the moment any of the ladies finished their meals.

Mere minutes after eight on Wednesday morning, Sheriff Preston and one of his deputies walked into an insurance office in Swanton and asked to speak with Kelsey Powell. Determined to keep a low profile and not cause a scandal for the young woman's employer, they'd arrived in an unmarked vehicle.

Based on his Tuesday-night consultation with the Hartland County attorney, the sheriff then arrested Kelsey on one count of attempted murder.

At first, she loudly protested her innocence. But she broke down in tears as Jeff Preston put her in handcuffs and guided her out the door while her co-workers looked on in shock and disbelief.

* * *

"Jeff doesn't know if the charges are going to stick," Bev told the mail carriers Wednesday afternoon as they wrapped up their post-route tasks. "But he and the county attorney decided to aim high at the start."

"So Kelsey could plead that down, cut a deal?" Mae frowned. "Or her attorney might be able to get the charges reduced? That's ridiculous! Look at poor Marie! Her whole life has been turned upside down. She's never going to be the same again."

One of Randy's friends had a daughter who worked with Kelsey.

"Now, that tells you how third-hand this is," Randy told the other carriers, "but you won't believe how Kelsey reacted when Preston read the charge to her."

Roberta raised her eyebrows in mock surprise. "Let me guess: She was defiant?"

"Even better than that. She apparently said, 'It's not like I killed her or anything!' To which Preston replied, 'Whatever you did, you sure did a damn fine job of it.'"

"I heard she blamed her husband," Allison said. "She claims Chad put her up to it, pushed her into doing this. Or at least, that his family did. His dad and uncle run Powell Construction these days. They took over from Chad's grandpa about fifteen years ago."

Kelsey was obviously smart; too smart for her own good. And she might be greedy, as well. But no one knew what sort of power dynamics played out behind closed doors. What if she had been bullied or threatened into taking such desperate action? Sadly, Kelsey wouldn't be the first woman who'd found herself trapped in a toxic relationship.

The ladies in the post office back room gave each other knowing looks, but none of them said a word.

"Well, it'll be interesting to see what happens," Jack added mildly, as if that wasn't the understatement of the year. "It'll all come out at the trial, if things even get that far. Maybe she'll confess. Or maybe Preston will uncover some details that point toward Kelsey being coerced."

"'More charges may be filed,'" Marge quoted from the press release that had been circulating since just before noon. "That could mean just about anything."

"I can tell you what I'd like to see happen," Roberta said, "regardless of how things turn out for Kelsey. And that's for Jim Abernathy to step down from the city council."

That proclamation was met with murmurs of agreement from the rest of the carriers.

"I don't care if he knew exactly what Kelsey was planning, or not," Jack said. "This sort of back-door nonsense makes all of Eagle River look bad. I know the council talks amongst themselves outside of open session, but this? This is a new low, especially given the agreement the Lindgrens had with the historical society."

"Scott Lindgren has already turned down the Powells' offer for the depot property," Marge reported. "Apparently, he told them if they try to contact him again, his attorney will come after them for attempting to tamper with a murder investigation."

Aaron nodded his approval. "I'm glad to hear it. Sure, he could have just put the deal on hold until the case is settled. Innocent until proven guilty, right? But I say, it's highly likely Kelsey did exactly what she's been accused of."

The conversation around the tables then turned toward the specifics of the case, which had started to spread through the community as soon as Kelsey was arrested. Because while Sheriff Preston's press release had been relatively brief, the ladies of the Eagle River Social Society had found their collective voice.

The women's outrage at being played for fools, along with their affection and admiration for Marie, had fueled a firestorm of truth that threatened to scorch Kelsey and her family's business to the point of ruin. Several of those ladies, including the three other women who'd been sickened at the luncheon, had filed formal statements with the sheriff in the past few hours.

"How is Sonja holding up?" Kate asked Bev. "This has been a lot for her to process."

"Strength in numbers, I think, is helping her immensely. They're all going to be called as witnesses at the trial, if it comes to that. And I'm sure it will." Bev sighed. "Because as much as I hope that Kelsey's going to confess, I doubt that's going to happen."

Kate was no attorney; but even she understood that, despite the bravery shown by the members of the Social Society, the case against Kelsey Powell had as many holes in it as a block of Swiss cheese.

The county prosecutor now had a motive in hand, along with several witnesses to the incident. But the doctored cupcakes were long gone. Neither Marie, nor any of the other ladies who'd been sickened at that luncheon, had bloodwork on file that would show any traces of nutmeg in their systems that day, much less the excessive amounts of the spice that could prove anything.

Sheriff Preston had visited Marie before the charges were finalized. Word was, she'd been more confused than coherent about what happened five weeks ago. She'd be asked to testify, of course; but whether her recollections would offer many details, much less hold up under cross examination, seemed doubtful.

The one bright light in this mess was that the sterling reputation of Prosper's community center had been restored.

Mayor Jerry and the venue's steering committee were beyond relieved that an arrest had been made in the case. One client who'd canceled an event was already on the books for a rescheduled date, Nancy had reported with glee, and her inbox was filling up with more requests for weddings and reunions in the fall and beyond.

Kate soon turned back to the tasks at hand. While today's developments were certainly encouraging, she had to get home. A few guests would arrive at her little farm within the hour, and she wanted to be ready.

Just as she was about to head to her locker, her phone beeped with a text. A local number was attached to the message, but no name; it wasn't from anyone in Kate's contacts.

Thank you. Please share my gratitude with Bev and the other carriers. - Ray

Grinning from ear to ear, Kate passed the phone to her friend.

"Well, will you look at that!" Bev crowed. "The police chief, himself. My, my, do I feel special."

She waved Roberta over, and the postmaster nodded her approval. "I always say, I have the best crew west of the Mississippi."

Roberta clapped her hands to get the rest of the carriers' attention. "Everyone, gather around for a second before you go. I have some feedback from a happy customer to share with you."

Kate was smiling as she headed out to the parking lot. Whoops and cheers echoed in her ears before the back door closed behind her.

"A 'happy customer,' indeed. Roberta loves to remind Ray where he fits in the governmental pecking order around here."

* * *

The clean breakfast dishes, which had been waiting in the kitchen sink since that morning, were put away. The faded laminate counters were now clear, and had been wiped until not a crumb remained. Or any hint of cat hair. Kate had changed out of her work clothes, and into a wrinkle-free tee shirt and clean shorts.

"I want everyone looking their best for our guests," she told Charlie as she brushed his thick coat. "Hazel is next, if I have time."

Romeo and Ophelia scampered across the freshly mopped kitchen floor, oblivious to how little time they had left at this farmhouse. Or the fact that another home, holding the promise of a lifetime of love with a forever family, waited for them not ten miles away.

"I'm not going to cry," Kate promised Charlie as she slid the brush through his fluffy brown tail. "This is the best outcome I could have hoped for. Hamlet and Juliet have settled in with the Fairlanes, and now it's time for the other two to move on."

Hazel started to bark in the living room; Kate knew the

dog was stationed at the bank of windows that looked over the front porch and out to the road.

"They're here. Places, everyone."

As she checked the powder room one last time, Kate admired the soft lavender paint and gleaming tile floor. All those hours spent dreaming, planning, and measuring; the scrubbing, and the plaster dust, and the holes cut in the walls and floor. It had all been worth it.

And Alex had been at her side, every step of the way.

He'd offered to go into work late this afternoon, have an employee open the bar so he could be here for emotional support. Kate had thanked him for his offer, but declined it. She could do this on her own, like so many other things she'd faced in the past few years.

But in the coming days, when the house felt a little too empty and not even Hazel and Charlie could provide enough comfort, Kate would lean on Alex as much as he'd let her.

She hurried toward the back door, as she wanted to witness the moment Minnie Trowbridge and her granddaughter stepped out of their vehicle. Because just as Kate had suspected they would, all four of her barn cats had gotten the memo about incoming guests. How would Patches react when she saw Minnie again for the first time in almost a year?

The elderly woman carefully stepping down from the SUV had short white hair and a sparkle in her blue eyes. Her floral-print blouse was a spot-on match to her pink capris. While her tennis shoes looked brand new, they were as sensible and comfortable as they could be. Kate loved Minnie already.

"Here, Grandma," Nicole hurried around from the driver's side. "Do you need help?"

"No, honey, I can get out just fine."

Patches, who'd been lounging halfway inside the Hosta bed with Scout, raised her head at the sound of Minnie's voice. Her nose twitching with curiosity, the calico sprang to her feet and nearly tumbled over a bewildered Jerry as she ran straight toward Minnie.

"Oh, there you are!" Minnie put one hand on the side of the SUV to steady herself, but was rather agile for someone in her mid-eighties as she crouched on the gravel. "Come here, my girl!"

Patches was already there, meowing and pacing with her tail held high, trying to sniff Minnie and rub against her all at the same time.

Nicole put one hand over her heart. "Are we crying?" she asked Kate.

"You bet." Kate wiped her eyes with the back of one hand.

"I wanted you to have a good barn home," Minnie was telling Patches. "You and Smokey. I knew you wouldn't want to be town kitties. Why didn't you stay? You walked so far! How did you know how to get back here?"

"Because this is her home." Nicole looked at Kate, and at the Three Mouseketeers now crowded around Kate's feet, and nodded. "No matter who else is here, *this* is home."

Nicole stepped close enough to Kate that Minnie couldn't hear what she said next. "I brought a second carrier, just in case. I'm sure the kittens will share, but ..."

"Thanks. We need to try, at least. But I want Patches, and Minnie, to make that choice on their own."

Nicole, her husband, and their children had met Romeo and Ophelia over the weekend. Just as it had been with Hamlet and Juliet, the last two kittens had somehow recognized their new family the moment all of them walked in the back door.

The cat distribution system worked in wondrous, sometimes mysterious, ways. Who else might choose a new life on this lovely summer afternoon?

Kate was still torn about the second part of her and Nicole's plan. But it had been her idea, and they were going to see this through.

Minnie finally turned her attention away from Patches, who didn't seem willing to leave her old friend's side.

"Kate, it is so wonderful to meet you!" The older woman's hands were veined and wrinkled, but her grip was surprisingly firm. All those years of being a farm girl, and then a farm wife, had kept Minnie in relatively good health.

"You, too! We can take a little tour, if you like."

"I want to see the pasture." Minnie started for the back of the yard, Patches matching her step for step. While Jerry and Maggie seemed content to stay by the house, Scout insisted Kate carry him along.

"She's going to be so pleased," Nicole told Kate as they followed a short distance behind, letting Minnie explore on her own. "She was so worried about all those weeds, how bad it looked when she put the place on the market. There hadn't been any livestock here in years."

"The pasture didn't faze me one bit," Kate insisted. "The market was so tough; those weeds could have been ten times worse, and I still would've had to fight fifteen people to get this place."

"That letter you wrote? It made her smile. She said, 'this is the person who is supposed to have our farm.'"

Minnie was delighted with the reclaimed pasture. She exclaimed over the neat, lush rows of Kate's garden, then paused for a peek inside the cleaned-out chicken house.

"My, this brings back memories." Minnie adjusted her glasses and leaned further through the doorway, although she didn't go inside. "All those chickens! They saved our farm more than once over the years, when times were hard."

"Farming can be a tough life." Kate nodded in understanding. "You must have so many stories to share."

"Oh, I do." Minnie's eyes sparkled with excitement. "But I can't wait to see that new bathroom!"

Patches was still attached to Minnie's side, and Kate wondered if the calico would want to go indoors with the visitors. But the cat hesitated for only a moment before settling down on the back steps to await her friend's return.

Minnie clapped her hands with joy when she saw the powder room. She and Will had wanted a bathroom on the first floor, especially as they'd aged, but had never gotten around to finding the time and money.

"It's just how it should be." Minnie admired the small space's vintage style. "You'd never know it was new, it blends right in!"

"We were careful to keep the layout of the house the same. I didn't want to mess with all this lovely oak trim, and this paneled door."

While the old home's woodwork was original and in excellent condition, the rest of the house was a haphazard jumble of eras and colors. Only a fraction of it was historic, and none of it was exactly modern.

Other than adding the powder room, Kate had only managed to paint a few rooms over the past year and cover the old wallpaper in the dining room with an updated, peel-and-stick design. She had so many ideas, so many things she wanted to change; but she'd decided not to share any of those hopes with Minnie today.

After all, the older woman had picked out the sculpted carpet, and added the apple-basket wallpaper border in the kitchen. Kate wanted Minnie to enjoy her trip down memory lane, to revel in the fact that so much of her former home was just as she'd left it last summer.

They wandered slowly from room to room, then toward the open staircase in the front hall. With Kate and Nicole shadowing her, Minnie was determined to see the second floor one more time.

"This was my room when I was a girl," she whispered as they paused in the smallest bedroom and admired the built-in bench under the main window.

"I was the tag-along baby by several years, you see. Both

of my siblings were out of the house around the time I started school."

Charlie had claimed this cozy room as his special space after he and Kate moved in last fall. More recently, it had served as a kitten nursery. With guests present to admire their agility, Romeo and Ophelia were determined to show off their pouncing skills. They raced through the fabric tunnel on the floor, and batted at the plastic tower whose colorful balls spun around in endless fun.

"I want you to take those," Kate told Nicole. "Charlie has his own toys. If he seems to miss these, I'll replace them."

Kate had planned for iced tea and chocolate cake if her guests were interested, but it was soon clear Minnie had tired from all the excitement.

It was just as well, Kate decided as they slowly made their way back downstairs. Minnie had already been invited to visit again, and had heartily accepted. Kate still had to put Ophelia and Romeo in Nicole's loving arms and let them all drive away; the sooner that was done, the better.

The kittens were easily rounded up after they were given one more gentle sniff by Hazel. Both the dog and Charlie seemed to understand what was happening; after all, Juliet and Hamlet had departed in the same way just a week ago. Charlie touched noses with both of the babies, then calmly sat back on his haunches while Kate and Nicole settled Romeo and Ophelia on the fleece blanket in the carrier.

Patches was still out on the steps. She gave her kittens a sniff through the grid of the carrier's front door, and both returned her greeting. There was more curiosity in the exchange than heartbreak, and Kate was relieved. Patches had reacted the same when the first two kittens left. She had raised them until they could be independent, with Kate's help; and then, her work had been done.

Minnie and Patches enjoyed a few more minutes together while Nicole turned on the SUV's air conditioning and settled the kittens in the back. Kate fetched a tote bag overflowing with the kittens' toys and their favorite blankets. It was almost time to go.

"Minnie, I want to ask you something."

The older woman barely looked up from playing with Patches. "Sure, my dear."

"Do you want to take her with you? Try it, at least? She walked all that way to get back home. I'm sure she thought you'd be here, waiting for her."

Minnie seemed to carefully consider Kate's proposal. "Well, I don't know. She never wanted to come into the house. Oh, once in a great while, for a snack or something. I tried several times to get her to stay inside with me, and she wouldn't."

Some cats didn't want an indoor life, Kate knew. And she understood the dangers awaiting a former farm feline who insisted on roaming outside in town. It meant facing off with unfamiliar dogs, possible fights with feral kitties who'd already claimed their territory, and run-ins with vehicles.

Patches' life in Eagle River would be a precarious one if she refused to stay inside with Minnie. But there was no way to know what was going on in the crafty feline's mind.

Had she changed it, during all those months and miles as she made her way home?

"I miss her," Minnie admitted sadly. "And Smokey, too. But I want what is best for them. It gives me peace to know he loves his new barn home, so much so that he refused to leave with Patches when she set out for here."

"Grandma, why don't you get in the car?" Nicole suggested. "And then, well ... let's just see what happens."

Minnie climbed in, but left her door open. Patches looked on as her old friend settled on the passenger seat. And then, the cat looked up at Kate and meowed.

"Yes, Minnie is leaving. But she's promised to visit us again, sometime soon. Do you want to go with her, Patches?

Do you even understand what I'm saying?"

Patches looked at Minnie again. The older woman smiled at her former pet, but didn't wave to the cat or make any emotional plea that might sway her one way or another.

"I will let you go," Kate said through sudden tears, "if that is what you want. If you want to live with Minnie, it's OK."

Patches was now staring off into the distance. She seemed to be studying the yard, the sheds, the garden; and then her gaze landed on Scout, who sat by the garage, watching this scene unfold. Soon, the calico looked back up at Kate.

And then, she rubbed against Kate's bare legs. Once, twice, a third time. The cat touched Kate's hand with her nose when Kate reached down toward her.

Kate had been chosen. Or at least, this little farm had.

But Kate was no fool; she knew better than to try to pick up Patches. That was a lesson for another day, and it would only happen if this sassy cat wanted it to.

Kate shook her head at Minnie, who nodded and smiled.

"This is how it should be," Minnie told Kate before she closed her door. "This is her home. You, Kate, are her home."

Nicole shrugged and waved to Kate. "I had no idea how that was going to go, but I'm glad we tried. Now we know! I'll tell you tomorrow how the kittens are settling in."

"Will you send me pictures?" Kate knew she'd be haunting her inbox first thing in the morning.

"Absolutely!"

Kate and Patches lingered in the driveway as Nicole's vehicle went down the lane, then turned north toward the blacktop.

"Well, it looks like you're stuck with me, Miss Patches." Then Kate laughed.

"You know, it's a strange thing. I've seen the way you look at me sometimes; don't think I haven't noticed. Like you wondered if I did something terrible to Minnie, got rid of her somehow, so I could take over this little farm and this house.

Well, now you have proof that Minnie is alive and well, and I'm innocent. I hope that counts for something."

Kate leaned down to rub the calico's back, but her hand suddenly stopped halfway.

What she'd just told Patches had so many similarities to the case she and Bev had just helped solve. Despite the sweltering air, a chill rolled down Kate's spine.

No piece of land, no matter its potential, was worth the cost of someone's life. Would Kelsey ever understand that?

Kate didn't know. And she couldn't expect to ever get a straight answer to that question. She'd taken that case as far as she could.

But Kate still had plenty of work to do.

"Let's get back to the house," she told Patches as Scout hurried to meet up with them in the lane. "I need to water the flower baskets and pick some green beans, and then it'll be time for supper."

WHAT'S NEXT

More crimes for Kate: Book 6 in this riveting series is on the way!
"The Trail That Leads to Trouble" follows Kate and her friends as they untangle a situation in a remote corner of Hartland County. Look for it in fall 2026. Sign up at **fremontcreekpress.com/contact** to get notifications about this title ... and future books, too.

While you wait: Don't miss this hidden gem! "Tales from Eagle River" digs deep into the town's past as seen through the eyes of the ladies who lived it. Ten women, one hundred-and-fifty years of secrets; how many connections can you find between these stories and the "Mailbox Mysteries" books? None of the tales contain clues to the series' crimes, so they are "safe" to read if you have yet to catch up on all of Kate's adventures.

More heartwarming stories: If you haven't already, be sure to explore Melinda Foster's return to Prosper through the "Growing Season" series. And there's more! Discover recipes featured in the "Growing Season" books online at **fremontcreekpress.com/extras**.

Thanks for reading!
Melanie

ABOUT THE BOOKS

Don't miss any of the titles
in these heartwarming rural fiction series

THE GROWING SEASON SERIES

Melinda is at a crossroads when the "for rent" sign beckons her down a dusty gravel lane. Facing forty, single and downsized from her stellar career at a big-city ad agency, she's struggling to start over when a phone call brings her home to Iowa.

She moves to the country, takes on a rundown farm and its headstrong animals, and lands behind the counter of her family's hardware store in the community of Prosper, whose motto is "The Great Little Town That Didn't." And just like the sprawling garden she tends under the summer sun, Melinda begins to thrive. But when storm clouds arrive on her horizon, can she hold on to the new life she's worked so hard to create?

Filled with memorable characters, from a big-hearted farm dog to the weather-obsessed owner of the local co-op, "Growing Season" celebrates the twists and turns of small-town life. Discover the heartwarming series that's filled with new friends, fresh starts and second chances.

FOR DETAILS ON ALL THE TITLES
VISIT FREMONTCREEKPRESS.COM

THE MAILBOX MYSTERIES SERIES

It's been a rough year for Kate Duncan, both on and off the job. Being a mail carrier puts her in close proximity to her customers, with consequences that can't always be foreseen. So when a position opens at her hometown post office, she decides to leave Chicago in her rearview mirror.

Kate and her cat settle into a charming apartment above Eagle River's historic Main Street, but she dreams of a different home to call her own. And as she drives the back roads around Eagle River, Kate begins to take a personal interest in the people on her route.

So when an elderly resident goes missing, she feels compelled to help track him down. It's a quest marked not by miles of gravel, but matters of the heart: friendship, family, and the small connections that add up to a well-lived life.

A TIN TRAIN CHRISTMAS

The toy train was everything two boys could want: colorful, shiny, and the perfect vehicle for their imaginations. But was it meant to be theirs? Revisit Horace's childhood for this special holiday short story inspired by the "Growing Season" series!

www.ingramcontent.com/pod-product-compliance
Lightning Source LLC
Chambersburg PA
CBHW061619190726
48288CB00007B/2385